What readers are saying about . . .

THE MURDER OF SUSAN REED

and

The Val & Kit Mystery Series

FIVE STARS! "Even better than the first! Another page-turner! Take it to the beach or pool. You'll love it!!! I did!!!"

FIVE STARS! "I couldn't wait to get this Val & Kit adventure after reading the authors' first book, and I was not disappointed. As a fan of this genre . . . I just have to write a few words praising the incredible talent of Roz and Patty. One thing I specifically want to point out is the character development. You can completely visualize the supporting actors (suspects?) so precisely that you do not waste time trying to recall details about the character. . . . Roz and Patty practically create an imprint in your mind of each character's looks/voice/mannerisms, etc."

FIVE STARS! "Val and Kit are hilarious! I love a good girlfriend silly caper. . . . I see a big fan base growing here."

FIVE STARS! "This second book in the series was as great as the first. It's a well-written, fun story about longtime friends who can't help but stumble into trouble. I enjoyed getting to know Val and Kit better and look forward to the next book!"

FIVE STARS! "Having thoroughly enjoyed Val and Kit's adventures in *The Disappearance of Mavis Woodstock*, I was both looking forward to and a bit nervous about reading its sequel. No need to worry. This is a terrific follow-up with the two ladies back with a bang together with some characters we already know and a batch of new ones. I had a great time going along with Val and Kit as they put the pieces together to solve the murder of a young woman known to them. The book is superbly plotted and very well written, with a little romance thrown in. A good whodunit should keep the reader guessing right to the very end, and this one really did the job for me."

FIVE STARS! "Once again Val & Kit star in a page-turner mystery! It's always fun to see where a book series story picks up and where it will take you! Getting to know the characters is half the fun."

FIVE STARS! "I love these stories . . . I was reading in the car and laughing out loud. My husband looked over and just shook his head. Thanks again for another good one."

FIVE STARS! "I enjoy reading about Larry and Tom as much as I enjoy reading about Kit and Val's relationship. The stories are always very exciting."

FIVE STARS! "Val and Kit's interactions and Val's thoughts about life in general were probably the best part of the book. I was given enough info to 'suspect' just about every character mentioned."

The Murder
of
Susan Reed
A Val & Kit Mystery

Rosalind Burgess
and
Patricia Obermeier Neuman

Cover by

Sheila Bradley
Laura Eshelman Neuman

Copyright © 2012
Rosalind Burgess and Patricia Obermeier Neuman
All rights reserved.
ISBN-13: 978-0692283400
ISBN-10: 0692283404
www.roz-patty.com

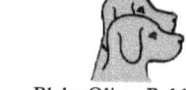

Blake Oliver Publishing
BlakeOliverPublishing@gmail.com
This is a work of fiction.

Acknowledgments

Thanks to our beta readers for their eagle eyes, suggestions, and support: Kerri Neuman Hunt, Jack Neuman, John Neuman, Laura Eshelman Neuman, Betty Phelps Obermeier, Sarah Paschall, and Melissa Neuman Tracy. And huge thanks to Al for his contribution!

To Auntie Joan,
who made me laugh every time we
were together
and always made me feel brilliant.
Love, Roz

To my kids' Auntie Roz,
who makes us all laugh every time
we are together.
Love, Patty

The Murder
of
Susan Reed
A Val & Kit Mystery

The Val & Kit Mystery Series

CHAPTER ONE

Susan Reed's body was discovered at nine thirty on Saturday night, April 5, by her mother. Marjorie Reed had used her own key to get into her daughter's apartment and found Susan lying dead on the kitchen floor. There were two bullets lodged in Susan's chest.

At least that's what the newspaper said. When I read the article the next day, I felt as if I had two bullets lodged in my own chest.

***

During the twenty-five years I was married to David Pankowski, I suspected he was unfaithful many times, but I was always reluctant to admit it. At least out loud. I didn't want to upset our applecart. The fabulous house, our outwardly perfect life, and most of all, our daughter, Emily. Looking back, I realize what an idiot I was. That applecart was more than upset: it was broken, squashed, ground into applesauce.

When my best friend, Kit, approached me with her own wobbly applecart, it was even harder for me to accept. Unlike my ex-husband, her Larry's a good guy. I'd trust him with my life. There's no way he would cheat.

"Wear these, Val." Kit handed me a pair of Versace sunglasses.

We decided a decade ago, when we entered our forties, that sunglasses improve our looks more than any makeup or beauty cream. Sunglasses shave years off our faces, we only half joke.

But they didn't seem appropriate right now. So I asked, "Why?"

"Disguise."

"Kit, it's raining, and it will be dark out. Don't you think the sunglasses are overkill? We might look suspicious." I fixated on the form our disguise would take, rather than why we needed a disguise in the first place.

"Not in the least. Bono wears sunglasses 24/7."

I shook my head like a dog that has just come in from the rain. "Wait a minute; what have you got planned? And what does an Irish pop singer out to save the world have to do with it?"

"Bono has nothing to do with it. These glasses are for you to wear when we spy on Larry. Oh, and let's find you a hat. A hat would be good."

"Ah," I said, as if the brilliance of her plan were starting to sink in. "But just one question. What will *you* be wearing? Groucho glasses and a false nose?"

"I'll be crouching down in the front seat, so no need for me to wear any disguise." She'd clearly thought it through and was pleased with herself.

"Front seat of what?"

"We're borrowing a car."

"Well, why don't we just steal one instead? Wouldn't that be better? Then we can switch out the plates and—"

Kit put a firm hand on my shoulder, her face close to mine. "This isn't a game, Val; this is serious."

I was about to disagree, laugh even, but her tone and the tiny little quiver of her lower lip stopped me. "Okay," I said. "It's not a game. But you haven't really told me what this is all about. If it's not a game, just what is it?"

"I still think Larry's having an affair," she said.

"You haven't convinced *me* of that yet. So tell me why I should wear this getup and spy on him."

"Susan Reed, from his office. She's been there almost a year. You met her at the office Christmas party. Dyed black hair. Bad teeth. No boobs."

"I remember." I sat on a stool facing her.

"What else can I say?" Kit waved a hand in the air, as if a bad dye job proved her husband's infidelity.

"Give me the details."

"Ah, the details. Oh, it's all so cliché. Late nights at the office. The answering machine kicks in after hours when he's supposed to be there, and apparently he's forgotten how to turn on his cell phone, so I can never reach him. Unexplained charges on his credit card. Lipstick on his collar."

"Wait." I held up a hand to stop her. "Lipstick on his collar?"

"Okay, no lipstick; I just added that. But something is going on, Val. He's different. Distant. We hardly ever talk anymore. The few hours he is home, he's locked away in his den doing who knows what."

"Kit, it's April."

"So what?"

"Well, isn't April for accountants like December for Santa Claus?"

"Oh, please. Larry's got ten thousand drudges down at that office of his. He should be no busier in April than any other time of the year."

"And you've asked him what's going on?"

"Yes. No answer. Just mumbling and bullshit."

"Okay, so let's assume Larry is consumed by another woman. Why do you think it's Susan? Because honestly, if I were going to have an affair with someone in his office, it would be that redheaded chick who wears the slit skirts. Or wait; what about Daphne? Talk about a blond bombshell. What about her? Why Susan?"

"That's the point entirely. Why would Big Red or Blondie be interested in Larry? Susan's got desperate written all over her."

"Well, that still doesn't explain why Larry would find *her* so fascinating."

Kit did a little jump off the stool. I thought I saw her lip quivering again. But she crossed to the Sub-Zero fridge and took two Diet Cokes from the door. "He said her name, Val. In his sleep. He said her frigging name. Sooooosan, Sooooosan." She sounded like the Ghost of Christmas Past calling to Ebenezer Scrooge. She stopped her moaning long enough to open and sip from one of the soda cans.

"Is that all you have to go on? He said her name in his sleep?"

"I have this." She rummaged in her purse that lay on the granite counter and retrieved a telephone bill. She handed it to me, and I was indeed struck dumb by the number highlighted at least twenty times. "This is Susan's number. Larry called her eleven times when he was in Las Vegas at that golf thing three weeks ago. He called me once. And that was only to remind me to record some stupid golf match."

"Okay. He called her eleven times. Could have been work-related calls."

"Work-related calls, my ass."

I could have kept trying to explain away the eleven phone calls, but by now my stomach was starting to churn a little. I had been through all this before. Only I had been so dumb that eleven phone calls wouldn't have sounded any alarms. In those days a dozen fire trucks racing through my kitchen wouldn't have alerted me to any danger. I suddenly felt determined to help my pal in her quest. And I was cashing in my membership to Larry's fan club.

"Okay," I said. "You better tell me what you have in mind."

***

An hour later we were parked in the lot across from Larry's one-story building, with a perfect view of his office. Reluctantly, I had agreed to tuck my freshly bobbed and highlighted blond hair under a Yankees baseball cap. My blue eyes were hidden behind the Versace sunglasses.

Kit, who for some reason felt it was safe to sit up in the passenger seat when we weren't in motion, had a Chanel scarf wrapped around her head, the way Queen Elizabeth did when she walked her corgis. We had borrowed a 1994 Lincoln Continental from Kit's neighbor on the pretense that neither of our cars was working. Since the neighbor, an eighty-year-old widower, just handed over the keys, requiring no further explanation, I assumed he was either senile or in love with Kit.

After an hour of watching Larry's back as he sat at his desk, we finally saw him stand, put on his jacket, and turn off his computer. Then he glanced at his watch, took his trench coat from the rack, and left the room.

I glanced at my own watch, where I learned it was five minutes after six on April 5.

"Son of a bitch," Queen Liz said.

"What? What do you see?"

"That son of a bitch leaving the office at six. He hasn't been home this early for months. Now we'll catch him in the act."

We watched in silence as Larry came through the glass front doors of the building. His white Suburban was parked in his reserved spot. We watched him get in and make a phone call. A few minutes later he backed out of his parking spot.

As I put the Lincoln in gear, another figure emerged from the building and headed in our direction, toward the parking lot.

"It's her," Kit whispered, as if Susan could hear us.

"Are you sure? She looks taller."

"Wearing fancy five-inch heels, no doubt, for her little date with Larry."

We watched the figure enter the parking lot and then disappear. I swung our car out through the exit, trying not to lose sight of Larry's Suburban. Wearing dark glasses made it difficult (I assume Bono has his own driver), but by the end of the road, where Larry's brake lights came on at a stop sign, I was right behind him in the mammoth Lincoln. So far, so good. Except for my poor vision and Kit yanking at the leg of my pants from where she was crouched down on the floor.

"What's going on?" Kit asked. "What do you see?"

I flung the glasses onto the back seat. "That's better," I said.

"What? Do you see her? Where is her car? Is she in the car with Larry?"

"Kit, Larry is alone; you know that. Unless he had Susan stashed in the back seat all afternoon."

"Huh." Disgust. "That wouldn't surprise me."

"Well, if that were the case, who did we see leaving the building?"

My friend and partner in crime didn't answer. Seemed she had more questions than answers.

Five minutes later Larry's Suburban turned onto Ogden Avenue, and I lost him in the traffic. We drove up and down the busy road for another ten minutes. But at six twenty we decided to call it a day. Or night.

Next time we'd do better.

CHAPTER TWO

I wasn't born yesterday, ya know." Kit's voice blared through the receiver as I wedged the phone between my shoulder and ear and snuggled beneath my duvet. "Does Larry think I'm stupid?"

"Kit, Larry would be even stupider than you if he thought that. What are you talking about?" I didn't add *now*, because I didn't want my irritation to show. Kit had been too good to me throughout my breakup with David.

But we'd seen Larry leave the office at a reasonable time (even if it was a Saturday, it was also tax season, and I didn't care what Kit said: accountants are busy in April, drudges or no drudges). And he'd left the office alone, no less, so I just could not encourage her suspicions.

"Did you and Larry talk when he got home?" I asked. I muted *Law & Order* and squished the duvet down a little more, settling in for a talk with my friend and feeling cozy as I heard the rain patter against my window.

Obviously, she'd waited for Larry to go to bed before calling me, and miraculously, she'd found me still awake even though it was almost eleven o'clock. "That's what I'm trying to tell you," she said. "Larry's still not home. That asshole."

I sat up straight. "Well, maybe he went back to the office, after getting a bite to eat?"

"Yeah, that's the sort of bullshit you believed from David for all those years, remember?"

Like I'd forget. "Did you call the office again?"

"Yes, I called the office. I called it six times. And I called his cell six more times. That's why I'm going back there," she said. "I'll cram that cell phone up his ass. If he's there, that is."

"You can't go back there in the middle of the night, Kitty Kat. It's not safe to go gallivantin' around town by yourself at this hour, even if it is Downers Grove." Not that I really believed our little corner of the world was guaranteed safe. It was, as my mother liked to warn me, a Chicago suburb, not some burg in the southern part of the Land of Lincoln. But I wouldn't consider living anywhere else in the world. I love everything about Chicago, including its suburbs. Chicagoland, as my boss Tom loves to call it, making it sound homey and cosmopolitan at the same time.

"Who said anything about going alone? I'll pick you up in ten minutes, Valley Girl."

I groaned, but my drama was wasted on Kit. She'd already hung up, no doubt dashing out to her BMW to come fetch me.

***

I was waiting out front under my umbrella when Kit pulled up. "Ooh, I thought it was so dangerous to be outside alone," she said, as soon as I opened the car door. But she didn't wait for me to defend myself. Before I was even done buckling my seat belt, she lambasted Larry. "Ya know, it's like I told you about David: if a guy wants to date, why doesn't he get a divorce first? Isn't that the least he can do for a wife of decades, the mother of his only child?"

I felt a sudden urge to argue the resilience of children of divorced parents. My own daughter seems to have fared well. Emily remains happily married and still passionate about pursuing an acting career—all while living in crazy Los Angeles.

Kit and Larry's son, Sam, is also married, and the last time I saw him, when he was home from Texas for Christmas, he'd proudly if drunkenly boasted about his newly acquired ranch. On the off chance there was a family upheaval headed his way, I doubted he'd need the services of a child psychologist.

"Well, let's make sure Larry *has* been dating, okay?" I refused to give up hope that this was a huge mistake.

I knew I'd said the wrong thing even before Kit responded. "Whose side are you on, anyway?" She sounded as accusatory as if I had fixed Susan and Larry up.

I realized my role was not to try to talk sense into Kit or to defend Larry. He would have to defend himself. I'd just have to help her carry out her plans until she managed to prove Larry guilty or, I hoped, innocent. "Kit, I'm on your side, of course. And that's why I'd like to think Larry is as good as I've always thought he was. But you're right. Something seems off."

We drove in silence for a few minutes. Then Kit said, "I don't even know what the hell Susan does down there."

"Down where?"

"Down at the office. Where did you think I meant?"

"That's what I thought you meant. Down at the office."

I pulled the collar of my trench coat up around my neck. I was staring straight ahead at the road before us, but out of the corner of my eye I could see Kit begin to grin. And then she laughed. When it seemed safe to join her, I did so.

"Some friend you are," she said. Her laughter had subsided. "My husband with Miss Nice'n Easy is amusing to you?"

I put a hand on her arm. "Honey, none of this is amusing. But let's be sure Larry's guilty before we get too worked up."

The bright lights of an oncoming car suddenly lit up Kit's auburn hair and porcelain features. I was struck by her beauty in that burst of artificial light. But I was aware that men cheat on beautiful women. Look at Tiger Woods.

I knew Susan Reed was no oil painting, so if Kit was right, maybe Larry's affair wasn't about looks. Maybe Larry found Susan's *demeanor* more desirable than his wife's tough-girl act. And an act I know it to be. But did he?

When we turned the corner and Larry's office came into view, it was clear no one was there. No one was parked by the dark building, and no one was parked across the street.

I felt a stab of disappointment, although I wasn't sure what I'd expected to see: Larry burning the midnight oil studying *Accounting for Dummies,* or Larry spread-eagle on his desk with Susan Reed on top of him, dressed as a French maid.

With a sigh, Kit pulled out of Larry's reserved parking spot, and we headed for home.

As she turned the corner at the end of the street, I spoke. "He's probably with a client or something."

"Or something."

Twenty minutes later I returned to my bed with a splitting headache.

It set the stage for the whole-body ache I felt the next morning when I read in the paper about Susan Reed's murder.

***

"She's dead," I whispered into the phone.

"Are you on your way over here?"

"Kit, did you hear me? Have you read the paper? She's dead, murdered, last night. Can you believe it?" I was still whispering, as though one of my neighbors would burst in and ask me how I knew the victim.

"What are you talking about? Who's dead?" Kit was whispering too. "Did you hear *me*? That asshole still wasn't home when I got back last night. He came in about a half hour later and said he'd been at the office. *Now* try to tell me how innocent your friend Larry is."

"Stop. Do you understand what I'm saying? Susan Reed was murdered last night. I just read it in the paper."

She was silent for a few seconds. Then, "Oh."

"I'm on my way over."

***

We've had a standing date for our weekly Sunday brunch ever since I divorced David and moved into my apartment. Larry makes omelets and pancakes and fresh-squeezed juice, accompanied by strong coffee. While he spoils us, Kit and I trade sections of the newspaper. It's a delicious start to my work week at Haskins Realty.

Kit answered the door with her reading glasses perched on the end of her nose and the newspaper tucked under her arm. I hugged her as if she'd just lost a close relative, but she pushed me away.

"Can you believe it?" I followed her as she headed toward the kitchen. "It's unbelievable."

She stopped and turned to look at me. "It happens."

"Kit!"

"Look, don't go getting all Pollyanna on me. This kind of thing happens all the time. It's a dangerous world we live in."

She proceeded into her spacious kitchen, and I followed once again. As I climbed onto one of the stools at the counter, I asked, "What does Larry say?"

11

"We haven't spoken, so he hasn't said anything. You did hear me say he wasn't home when I got back last night, right?"

"Yes, I heard you."

It was the last thing I wanted to hear right now. I wanted her to tell me Larry was already home when she got back after dropping me off. That he'd somehow proved to her he was at his office all evening and we'd simply driven by right after he left.

As unnecessary as I hoped it would be, I realized I wanted Larry to have an *alibi*. I wanted to feel the peace that would come with that certainty.

I watched Kit mechanically pour two mugs of coffee and place them on the counter. She wore a puzzled expression, indicating she was thinking hard about what to do next. "I'm not sure what we have to eat." She gazed around her kitchen as if she'd never seen it before. "You want eggs? I could make a cheese omelet."

I leaned across the counter and whispered to her. "Kit, you've got to talk to Larry. You've got to find out where the hell he was last night."

She looked at me and smiled. "That would be nice, wouldn't it?"

We both looked up toward the door when we heard Larry enter. He's a tall man with a pleasant face, an honest face, and thinning brown hair. His body, in spite of a little extra padding, still shows signs of the athlete he was in high school, where we cheered him on at basketball and baseball games.

"Hey, Val." Larry's monotone set off an alarm, although I knew it might just be that Kit was rubbing off on me. But normally, he's cheerful and always acts tickled to see me.

He poured himself a cup of coffee and turned to face us across the wide counter. He didn't dig through the cupboard for pans as he usually does, and I noticed how dressed up he was for a Sunday morning. Not for the office, exactly, but maybe church or a meeting somewhere. I was used to his Sunday-morning sweats and bed-head hair.

"Have you read the paper, Larry?" I asked.

He nodded, and I don't think I'd ever seen him look so sad. "Yep, I read it."

"I'm so sorry," I said. "You must feel terrible."

He nodded again, his lips pulled into a tight line, as if his face would crumble if he loosened his expression.

"It's incredible," I said, just for something to say, and I heard Kit's frustrated sigh.

"Yeah, it's incredible," she repeated, although her tone indicated it really wasn't *so* incredible and she was ready to move on. "Larry, Val was just telling me she was over by your office last night. About eleven o'clock, wasn't it, Val?"

She grasped her coffee cup with both hands and appeared to be studying her manicure. I wondered if she'd maybe gone insane due to stress.

Larry turned to add sugar to his cup. I felt like an actress thrust into a scene from a play without knowing the script. Were we really not going to discuss Susan Reed? I began digging in my oversize purse for some imaginary important thing, all the while trying to think of something to say to bring these two zombies back to Planet Earth.

"Larry, did you hear me? I said Val was at your office last night."

"Really?" Larry turned to face us again from the other side of the granite counter. "Why?"

I still had my head burrowed in my purse, and when I looked up, I saw them both staring at me, waiting for some response. This was classic Kit. Ever since we were children, she's hatched plans that need my participation. Only one problem: I am rarely privy to my role in the plot.

She looked amused. Larry looked panic-stricken.

I finally found my voice. "Well, I don't think that's really important right now, Larry—"

"Tell him, Val." Pure evil lurked behind Kit's nonchalant expression.

"Well, er, I was looking for an address. Over there by your office, Larry. Realtor stuff."

"Did you find it?"

"No, I was completely lost. I just drove around for five minutes, then left."

I went back to my purse, moving all the junk around as if sifting sand in hopes of finding a gold nugget.

"Excuse me, ladies; I think I should make some calls." Larry turned and left the room.

"This is going to be one hell of a Sunday," Kit said.

"Are you kidding me? Susan Reed was *murdered*."

"What do you want me to do, Val?"

I shrugged. I didn't really know what I wanted her to do. Show some compassion, maybe. Perhaps feel bad. But as I watched her take a carton of eggs from the refrigerator and crack three of them into a glass bowl, I could see her hands were shaking a little.

And that, at least, made me feel better.

CHAPTER THREE

No matter how many TV crime shows you watch, you are never prepared for a police squad bursting into your home in the middle of the night to shake you down.

Okay, so it wasn't the middle of the night, and it wasn't even my home. But when Kit escorted Detective Dennis Culotta into her sunny kitchen, two minutes after she'd finished whipping the eggs into a yellowy froth, I wasn't prepared.

First of all, this guy should have had his own TV show. He wasn't handsome in the traditional pretty-boy way. He was tough-looking, almost craggy, the kind of guy you'd want beside you when you were meeting a suspect at an abandoned warehouse down at the docks. At midnight. More than six feet tall with thick white hair and blue, blue eyes, he looked as though he hadn't cracked a smile since the Reagan Administration.

"Valerie, this is Detective Culotta. Detective, this is my dear friend Valerie Pankowski."

I noticed she'd memorized his name during the short walk from her front door to the kitchen. Obviously, he'd given her some sort of business card, which she waved under her chin as if she were in the Deep South and having an attack of the vapors.

"Ma'am." Detective Culotta nodded without looking at me. Then he took a small leather-bound notebook out of his inside jacket pocket. "I'm here to see Lawrence James. Is he home?"

"Why, yes," Scarlett/Kit said, "let me just get him for you." I could see she was reluctant to leave the room, and I avoided her gaze, hoping she wouldn't ask me to follow her.

"So," I said, as soon as the detective and I were alone. "I think the weather is starting to warm up."

He looked at me for the first time, blue, blue eyes clearly puzzled. "Ma'am?"

"The weather." I waved a hand toward the French doors as proof that I would never lie to a police officer.

His blue eyes returned to his notebook. "Hmm." He shook his head slightly, making me feel like I'd just blown my alibi and would soon be confessing to a crime. Any crime.

"This is Detective Culotta," Kit said, flouncing back into the kitchen with an agitated Larry in tow. "This is my husband, Lawrence James, Detective. I believe you wanted to see him."

I knew I had to get Kit out of there before she started fixin' us all mint juleps and pushing us toward the front porch to sit a spell. "Kit, perhaps we should leave these guys alone," I said.

"That would be fine," Detective Dishy said, and Kit reluctantly followed me out to the living room.

"Wow." Kit's hand hit her forehead.

"No kidding." I peeked around the doorway to get another look at Blue Eyes.

"Can you believe it? That skank is dead less than twenty-four hours, and already they're questioning Larry."

"Huh?"

She grabbed my elbow and led me farther into the living room.

"Do you think they think he did it?"

I shook myself free of her grasp. "Are you nuts?" Okay, I might have been starting to buy into the possibility of Larry's infidelity, but murder? That was laughable. Larry is the guy who catches spiders in his hands and transports them outside.

"He could have, ya know." Kit is the woman who grinds the spider into the kitchen tile with her stiletto heel and then waits for the maid to clean it up.

"Oh, for crying out loud. Larry was her employer—"

"And her lover—"

"Okay, maybe her lover. We're not sure of that. But definitely her employer. Of course the police will interview him. They interview everyone who knows the victim, trying to establish who was the last person to see her, if she had any enemies—"

"Yeah, yeah, we all know you watch a lot of television, Val."

"Like you don't?"

"Cooking shows and the History Channel."

"Okay, so you know what year John Kennedy was born. Big whoop. I'm telling you, this is normal police procedure."

Just then my cell phone rang. The theme song to *Law & Order*. I thought it was so clever when Emily programmed it for me as my ringer.

But now, with a real live policeman in the next room and Kit accusing me of watching too much TV, it seemed so juvenile. Luckily, when I crept back into the kitchen, I saw both men had moved to another room. I snatched my phone and silenced the offending ringtone by answering it.

"Where the hell are you, Valerie?"

It was Tom Haskins, my boss, who calls me every Sunday with more or less the same rant. Even though he knows I have brunch with Larry and Kit, he feels compelled to remind me that Sunday is Monday for Realtors.

"I'm having brunch with—"

"I don't want to hear it. Just tell me this, Valerie. What does the term *open house* mean to you?"

"It means—"

"It means *open*. It means I should have my best Realtor actually *opening* the house in question. It means you should have been on Briarwood fifteen minutes ago."

"Calm down, butch. I'll be there in plenty of time. We are just having a little, er, situation here."

"Susan Reed?"

That shut me up. How the hell did Tom know about Susan Reed? Okay, it was in the paper, and public knowledge, but as far as I could remember, Tom read only the *Wall Street Journal* and *Playboy*.

"How—"

"I hear things, Val. Didn't she work for Larry?"

"Yes." I moved slowly around the room, whispering. "And the police are here now, talking to him."

"Dennis Culotta?"

"Good grief. How do you know *that*?"

"I know Dennis. He's a good man."

"Okay, we'll discuss that later. But Tom, it's merely routine, right? I mean questioning Larry?"

"Why? Did that dingbat wife of his turn him in?" Tom, who has known Kit and Larry James for almost as long as I have, isn't impressed with Kit. Like my own mother, he thinks she is a bad influence on me.

"I'm leaving now," I said. "I'll call you later."

***

The open house was slow. I always suspect that visitors to open houses are really having open houses of their own

18

somewhere else in town. But I used the time to catch up on some e-mails, especially a long one to Emily. Touching base with my daughter via my new laptop—thanks to someone in the neighborhood who didn't lock the access to his wireless service—was not as satisfying as the good old-fashioned telephone, but it was better than nothing. She had several auditions lined up, but I was long since conditioned not to get my hopes up. I celebrate each job she gets as it comes, and not before.

I also called my widowed mother, who lives up in Door County, Wisconsin, and doesn't do e-mail. She cautioned me not to be fooled by the warmer weather and reminded me that the flu could strike me dead at any moment.

Having caught up with the women in my family, I turned my thoughts to Larry, wondering how his interview with the police was going. The paper said Susan's body was discovered at nine thirty, but gave no actual time of death. We knew that Larry was in his car around six, but not where he was going. I had to urge Kit to find out. And quickly, if for no other reason than to settle the sickening feeling in my stomach.

At four o'clock, a half hour before I was due to close up shop, a Mercedes pulled into the driveway. It was Tom, probably coming to check up on me. Occasionally, he calls me his best Realtor, which isn't as flattering as it sounds because I am his only Realtor. Unless you count his nephew Perry, whose desk is next to mine in the small office we share. Even with Perry on the payroll, I still consider myself the only Realtor in the office.

As always, when Tom Haskins entered the room, he filled it. He is a large man, not so much overweight as husky. Impeccably dressed as always, he removed his camel-hair coat and revealed a custom-made suit.

Tom is a few years older than me, a high school friend of my brother's. A million years ago, when I was a comfortable housewife looking for a little part-time work, he gave me a job at Haskins Realty. The comfortable housewife has long since disappeared, and the job has become full-time.

"So, how's it going, Kiddo?" He plunked down on one of the leather couches in the living room. "This place ain't half-bad."

"I've had exactly two couples, one looking for decorating ideas, the other probably just casing the joint. I'm telling you, open houses are a waste of time."

Tom gave me a little grin and patted the aluminum case of the cigar in his top pocket. "Trust your old Uncle Tom." He then cracked up at his own joke. He's said this, or some other pun involving his name, a thousand times, and it always amuses him.

"So." I joined him on the couch. "Tell me about Dennis Culotta. How on earth do you know him? What's he like? Is he married? He seems humorless. Although I guess there is nothing funny about his line of work. Is he from Chicago?"

"Wait." Tom stopped me by holding his hands up in surrender. "Too much babbling. What do you care what he's like? He's doing his job."

"How do you even know Susan Reed?"

"Ah . . ." Tom patted his cigar again, and I knew he was dying to light it. "I heard stuff, that's all."

"What stuff? Were she and Larry having an affair?"

This caused Tom to roll back his head in hearty laughter. "Larry having an affair? With that wife of his? She makes Lorena Bobbitt look like Mary Poppins."

I'm never pleased when Tom is mean about Kit, but I knew that could have just been his way of avoiding the question.

"Okay." I said. "Then Dennis Culotta." I made a mental note to grill Tom later about Larry and Susan.

"What about him?"

"Well, first, is he married?"

"Is he married, she asks."

"Well, is he?"

"You crack me up; you really do. Okay, gotta go. Close up early if you think this open house sucks. I got a feeling this house will sell without it."

He rose, put his coat back on, and headed out of the house. I watched him through the glass panel of the front door. As he backed his sleek car down the driveway, he had a slight grin on his face that was maddening. And he knew it.

I waited until five and then locked up the house and threw my open-house sign in the back of my Lexus. I hadn't spoken to Kit all afternoon, so once I was in the car, I hit her speed-dial number on my phone.

"Oh, Val. We have to talk. Where are you?"

"Actually, I'm just headed home. Why don't you meet me there? I'll order a pizza."

***

Thirty minutes later the pizza was on its way, and Kit arrived at my apartment looking like an older sister of Audrey Hepburn in her heyday. A black silk blouse and narrow black pants that stopped just above her ankles accentuated her slim frame. Black ballet flats completed her ensemble. She threw her Burberry on the couch and then dropped onto the cushions.

"So." I handed her a glass of pinot grigio. "What happened after I left?"

She took a long sip before answering. "Do you think we should get a lawyer?"

"*What?*" It was almost a screech. I plopped down next to her, spilling a little wine on my lap.

"They wanted Larry to go down to the police station to give them a statement. Merely routine, they say. Hah! Merely routine, my ass."

"It could be," I said. But even to me, my reassurance sounded lame.

"He got all manly and I-know-my-rights, but in the end agreed to go down in the morning. Apparently, they asked

Brad Parkinson the same thing. He, of course, went with no problem."

"Makes sense. Brad is Larry's partner and technically was Susan's employer too. And you know the police asked Brad Parkinson to go to the station because . . . ?"

"Because I called Ellen Parkinson. Remember, Brad's wife? In fact, I told Ellen you and I would meet her tonight. I think I need to have a long talk with her. She might know something—"

"Wait a minute. You want me to go with—"

"Of course, Val. I can't do this alone." She ran a hand through her auburn hair.

"Do what alone?"

"Find out what the hell is going on."

I sighed deeply. Through our forty-plus years of friendship, it has been this way: Kit charging off, me following closely behind. She looked at me, her eyes open wide, as if there were some chance I wouldn't do her bidding.

I smiled and patted her knee. "Of course I'll go with you. I'm just gonna take a quick shower. Let the pizza guy in; the money's on the kitchen counter."

She nodded, and I felt sorry for her, although I wasn't sure it was warranted.

Fifteen minutes later, when I emerged from the bathroom showered and with a change of clothes, she had her coat on, ready to go. "I put the pizza in the freezer. You can eat it later. I don't do pizza unless I make it myself, ya know."

"Right." I sighed and put on my coat. "Well, let's go."

CHAPTER FOUR

Don't the Parkinsons live in Naperville?" I asked, when I saw Kit turn in the opposite direction.

"Yeah. But Ellen didn't want me—us—coming to their house. For some reason, she doesn't want Brad to know we're talking."

"Hmm . . . doesn't that strike you as strange?"

"It doesn't strike me as anything. I got my own issues, with my own husband, in case you haven't noticed."

"Well, that's my point. If she's suspecting *her* husband, maybe that's proof enough—if we need it, which we shouldn't—that your husband is innocent."

"Innocent? I don't think he *killed* anyone, Val."

"I know," I said. But I didn't know. I didn't know that Kit thought him innocent of murder, and I didn't know that I did. Though I desperately wanted to. It was bad enough that I'd been disillusioned by David. I didn't want to lose

Larry to deceit too. "I meant innocent as in not having an affair with Susan."

"Yeah, right." Kit pulled into the parking lot of a mom-and-pop burger joint in Westmont.

Famished as I was, I hoped they had the secret to a good burger as well as the apparent secret to surviving in a world of chain eateries.

We followed the aroma of fried food into the restaurant and found the place packed with people of all ages. After glancing around, Kit led me to a table in the back corner, where I saw Ellen hunched over a menu. Like there was going to be a big choice of what to order.

But it was enough for me. I was already promising my grumbling stomach a large vanilla shake to go with an even larger cheeseburger with everything. And don't hold the fries.

"Thanks for coming, Ellen." Kit removed her trench coat, which was too expensive to trust to one of several coatracks lining the room, and hung it on the back of her chair.

"No problem." Ellen looked up from the menu, as if she hadn't been aware of our presence until just that moment. She looked at me, her eyes saying what her mouth was apparently too polite to: *I don't see why you are here.*

Ever one to head things off at the pass, if not shove them right off the pass, my cowgirl friend Kit said, "You remember Val, don't you? You guys met—"

"Yes, I remember. At Christmas parties. Nice to see you, Val." Again, her eyes said differently.

Her cool reception didn't spoil my appetite, and I felt gluttonous if not guilty when I placed my order following the delicate requests of Ellen and Kit. They both ordered just a glass of wine, but I remembered how husband woes could suck the appetite right out of a person. No diet or diet pill could compete.

Contentedly divorced by now, I dug into my burger and listened to Ellen and Kit compare notes.

"So, Kit, what did you want to see me about? I don't know a thing about Susan or her death. Why would you think I would?"

Ellen was as plain as Kit was pretty. If either of these women had to worry about a husband straying, my money was on Ellen.

Years before, when I'd first met Larry's business partner and his wife, I thought anyone not knowing the four of them would match Larry with Ellen, and Brad with Kit. Brad was no stereotypical accountant, with his thatch of dark-blond hair and his boyish good looks—all atop a six-foot athletic frame.

"I didn't think you knew anything about Susan's death, of course," Kit answered. "I just wondered what you knew about Susan at all."

"Why?"

"Why? Why *not*?" A look of anger began to mar my friend's face, but she quickly forced it off. "Did you trust her, Ellen? That's what I really want to know. Did you trust her?" The anger having been shut out, Kit's vulnerability took over. I'd gone from never having felt sorry for my friend in our lifelong friendship—never having any reason to—to having sympathized with her deeply and often in the previous forty-eight hours.

Ellen put her wineglass to her thin lips and avoided Kit's eyes. After taking a sip, eyes still averted, she said, "What would I have to trust her—or not trust her—about? She worked for Brad, not me. And Larry." Ellen looked up then, as if saying Larry's name erased any need for self-consciousness on her own part. "Why are you asking me this, Kit? Did you have some reason to . . . do you know about the . . ."

The three of us sat quietly for a few moments, me stuffing myself with the last of my fries while they sipped their wine, no doubt hoping to take the edge off.

"About *what*?" Kit asked at last.

"I think you know."

Well, I was done eating, and with nothing else to do, I silently cursed Kit for making me tag along. I was of no use, and my discomfort was becoming unbearable. I squirmed in my seat and finally decided to speak into the silence. Someone had to just dig in, and Kit was not being her normally aggressive self. But I hadn't watched her all these years for nothing. The least I could do, having been trained by her so well, was to step in where she apparently feared to tread.

"I think what Kit wants to know, Ellen, is whether you ever had reason to suspect Susan of having an affair . . . with anyone." I was soon sorry I asked.

Totally prepared for her continued denial of any reason to give Susan a second thought, I was *not* prepared for her response. "Yes," Ellen said, "I did. I think Larry and Susan were having an affair. And I assumed you knew, Kit."

I saw my friend appear to shrink by half, crumpling in on herself as if she'd just been given proof that she was indeed no longer whole, that she wasn't the beloved wife of decades she thought she was. I knew the feeling all too well.

But I refused to believe my friend had a real reason to feel that way. "What makes you think that?" I asked.

"I thought Kit knew everything," Ellen answered, sounding like the unpopular geek revealing bitter jealousy of the homecoming queen.

"I meant, what makes you think Larry and Susan were having an affair?" I sounded like the school principal who thought he could stop a childish rivalry with the mere use of a stern voice.

"Because I saw them."

"You saw them having sex?" Kit rose back to her full sitting height, as if she wanted to be fully present for Ellen's answer.

"Of course not."

"Well, then how do you know they were having an affair?" I asked. I wanted to do this for Kit. I didn't want her to have to ask the questions that must be killing her. Besides,

I'd already been down this road with David and figured I knew best what questions to ask.

Ellen sighed and picked at her paper napkin. "I saw them having dinner together, and they looked awfully darn cozy."

"That doesn't mean they were having an affair." I reached one arm around Kit's shoulders and gave her a squeeze, all the while glaring at Ellen. I knew I should feel at least a little sorry for her. We asked her for this very information, if she could give it; but when she gave it, I treated her like the guilty party.

"Don't kill the messenger," Ellen said, looking at me squarely with her close-set blue eyes.

"Ellen's right, Val." Kit took a sip of wine and chased it with a deep breath. After an equally deep exhale, as if she were preparing to run a marathon, she said, "Where there's smoke, there's fire and all that. And besides, Val, haven't we often said an affair of the heart or a mental affair would be worse than a purely physical one?" She reminded me of a chocolate Lab, as she looked over at me with a doleful expression in her brown eyes.

But my thoughts turned quickly to what a dog David was, with the series of physical affairs he'd had. And I'd actually comforted myself with the fact that they were "merely" physical, before I found the courage to leave. As long as I was the one he really loved, yada yada yada. I was yanked out of my self-centered thoughts when I realized Kit was crying—and *Ellen*, not I, was comforting her.

"I'm so sorry, Kit." Ellen actually had tears in her own eyes. It didn't make her any more attractive, but it did soften my attitude toward her. "I really did think you knew. I'm sorry."

"Where were they having dinner?" Kit asked, as if it mattered.

"Rosebud in Naperville. It was lunch, actually."

"Well, then it could have been business," I said, but they both ignored me.

"Lunch, dinner, breakfast—what difference does it make what time of day they were fucking, mentally *or* physically?" The old Kit was back.

I wondered what she wanted to do next.

CHAPTER FIVE

So, what do we think?" I asked. We were buckling our seat belts in Kit's BMW. I watched her raise her chin to peer into the rearview mirror, ready to back out of the restaurant's parking space.

"I think she's a malicious cow." Kit turned to her driver's window to give a small wave and a strained smile to Ellen, who was pulling out two spots over.

"Not exactly a cow. She's actually gotten a lot thinner since I saw her last," I said.

"Okay, then she's a skinny malicious cow. That suit you better?"

"Well, she didn't tell you anything that proves Larry is having an affair. *Was* having an affair."

"Ya think?"

"Yeah, I think. Larry and Susan were seen having lunch. Big whoop. By the way, I loved your line about not actually seeing them have sex. That was great."

Kit gave me a little sideways smile. "What pisses me off is that she thought I already knew."

"She made it all up. She doesn't have a clue."

"No kidding. We really should speak to Brad. At least he'd tell the truth. Ya know, I think he has a little thing for me."

I dismissed Kit's immodest insight into Brad. He might indeed have had a little thing for her, but Kit believes most men she comes across have the same inclination. And she's probably right. "What has Larry said about where he was last night?"

"I haven't asked him."

"Still? Why not?" I was shocked. But only for a second. I quickly recalled my own avoidance of questioning David when I was pretty certain I knew the answer. Then again, Kit wasn't me. She has, or so I thought, tougher skin. Not to mention that ego of hers.

"I will, but after that damn detective left, Larry had ten thousand phone calls to make. I couldn't find a good time."

"But you will, right?"

"Val, of course I will." She glanced at the clock on the dashboard. "It's early. Why don't you come over and let me fix us something to eat."

"Er, did you notice how much food I just put in my stomach?"

"Oh, that?" Kit waved a dismissive hand in the air. "That wasn't food, for crying out loud."

It always surprises me how Kit, who is a gourmet cook, can remain so slim. She should be the size of Paula Deen at the celebrity chef's heaviest, since she always seems to have tasty leftovers in her fridge and something equally mouth-watering in the oven. Since my divorce, I've discovered that cereal makes the perfect dinner: quick, easy to prepare, and never any pesky leftovers to decide what to do with.

"Okay, I guess I could manage something sweet," I said. "I didn't really have dessert." I conveniently counted my vanilla shake as a beverage, not a dessert.

"That's my girl," she said. I thought I heard relief in her voice, and I wondered if she just didn't want to face Larry alone.

Once again, I knew that feeling all too well.

***

Larry was in his den when we arrived, but he came out to greet us, even giving us each a cool kiss on the cheek. I was impressed by how well he was coping because the last time I'd seen him, he was being interrogated by the police.

"Val, sit here." Kit pointed to one of the stools at the counter.

I'd sat on this stool in her spacious kitchen at least ten million times since they'd moved into their house. Did she think I didn't know its purpose, or that I was going to stand?

"Larry," I heard my friend address her husband. "Wine."

Larry seemed relieved to be given a chore, and he set about opening a bottle of pinot that he took from the refrigerated wine cabinet under the counter. Kit, meanwhile, took a dish of manicotti out of the fridge and threw it in the microwave as if it were garbage she was tossing down a chute.

"Nothing to eat for me," I said, wishing I had let her take me home instead of coming back here. "Unless you do have something sweet."

"Do I have something sweet for my Valley Girl?" She opened the fridge door and perused the inside, like a store clerk trying to find just the right shoes for a difficult customer. "I have half a pineapple upside-down cake and a walnut cheesecake."

"Give me a small slice of the cheesecake." I watched Larry place a glass of wine in front of me. Even though he avoided any eye contact, I noticed how tired he looked. It was the exhaustion that comes when everyone is trying not to discuss the proverbial elephant in the room.

"Voilà," Kit said a few minutes later. She put a generous slice of her delicious walnut cheesecake in front of me, and suddenly I was hungry again.

But for the first time ever, we dined in silence. Well, *they* did, at least.

I tried to make conversation, but Larry kept his eyes focused on his manicotti, never looking up, just nodding his head at my inane chatter. Kit didn't eat at all, but sat across from me, twisting the stem of her wineglass as if she were trying to work it loose. I felt like a child whose parents had just had a big fight and neither one of them wanted to upset me.

"So, Larry." I pushed my empty dessert plate away. I was fortified and ready to tackle the elephant head-on. "Kit says you're going down to the police station tomorrow to make a statement."

I thought that sounded as innocuous as if I were asking him where he bought his ties. But for the first time since I'd arrived, his eyes met mine, and I was taken aback by how frightened he looked. He nodded vigorously, making me want to pat him on the head and tell him it would all be okay.

Kit bolted upright from her sitting position. "Look at the time. Val, you're wanting to get home, I'm sure. Larry, drive Val home."

I couldn't quite believe she'd said that, but as she gathered up the empty plates from the counter, she gave me a little wink. There was meaning in the wink, I was sure, but I didn't know what the hell it was.

***

"Thanks for the ride, Larry," I said. "You don't have to pull in—"

"Look, Val, I know Kit is mad at me. And I'm really sorry about that. This . . . this thing with Susan, it's killing us both."

Spurred on by Kit's secret wink in the kitchen, I took a deep breath. "Larry, were you having an affair with Susan Reed?"

I thought he might look shocked or even order me out of his car. But instead, he stopped by the curb in front of my building and put the car in park. He smiled a little and then slowly shook his head. "No," he said softly. "No, I wasn't."

"Kit thinks—"

"Kit's wrong. I wasn't having an affair." His voice rose, maybe in defense. "I've never had an affair. It's laughable."

I leaned back in my seat and took a deep breath. "Not as laughable as you think."

"Oh, I'm sorry, Val. You mean David and his affairs. You're right; it's not laughable. But I, at least, was not having an affair."

Okay, so now we had both said *affair* too many times. It was starting to sound like a foreign word that had no meaning for us.

"Do you know who killed her?" I switched from an uncomfortable topic to a downright dangerous one.

"Of course not," he said, and this time he did sound angry at the question.

"Where were you last night, Larry?"

"I can't believe you would ask me that."

Why not? I wondered. The police most certainly would, if all my episodes of *Law & Order* were accurate. "It's just that Susan was your assistant—"

"She was Brad Parkinson's assistant too."

"Yes. And the police will ask him the same question."

He shrugged, as if he didn't care what the police asked his partner.

We sat in silence for a few minutes more, until I gathered my purse from the floor of the car. "I gotta go." I reached for the door handle.

"I wasn't having an affair, Val." Enough time had passed that the dreaded word had reestablished itself into the English language.

"Well, I'm glad to hear it, Lar." I hated the way that sounded. Like my mother telling the ten-year-old me she was glad I hadn't had a cookie before dinner. *I'm glad to hear it, Valerie,* she would say. And I would sigh with relief that my lie had worked.

***

I'd just taken off my coat when the phone rang.

"Val, it's me."

I walked to the window and looked down at the street where Larry's Suburban was still parked right where I had left him.

"Larry," I said. "Are you okay?"

"I was in church last night."

"Okay," I said slowly. "Church. I didn't realize you went to church."

"I don't, normally. But I . . . I just needed a little private space. Somewhere I could think."

"Okay." I kept my tone neutral to indicate that if there was more to come, I could take it or leave it. At last, all those years of listening quietly while my teenager filled me in on the latest school gossip were paying off. I had a vision of the teenage Emily sitting at our kitchen table spilling the beans while I pretended to be more interested in cooking them. The more absorbed at the stove I became, the more she blabbed.

"St. Ignatius," Larry said. "When I left my office, I drove over there and just sat for an hour or so. It was good. I'm not Catholic. I'm not really anything. I just needed a quiet place to be by myself."

"Okay. You went to church. That's nice, Larry."

"And then, when I felt better, I went to a bar."

"So you went first to a church and then to a bar?" So much for nonchalance.

"Yes." He sounded irritated. "Don't you believe me, Val?"

"Of course; why wouldn't I believe you? I'm just wondering . . . well, why?"

A memory suddenly flooded my head. One night after David and I had had a vicious fight, I'd gone to a movie alone for the first time in my life. I couldn't remember any of the plot, only that Demi Moore had blond hair, which really didn't suit her.

"Look, Larry," I said, "I do believe you. I can even understand it a little if things were just too much for you. But why don't you go home and tell Kit all of this?"

"Yeah, right. Tell Kit. She'd be sooooo understanding."

"She might surprise you. She loves you, Larry. She feels shut out and alone."

"Me too," he said. "Me too."

And suddenly silence filled my ear.

CHAPTER SIX

Everyone warned me that leaving a four-bedroom house with a study and atrium and moving into a nine-hundred-square-foot apartment would make me feel cramped. But I relish the compactness of it. That nothing is ever more than a few steps away. I love that I can do laundry, eat a tuna fish sandwich, and rearrange my meager pantry all at the same time, without taking more than a few steps.

I was having my second cup of coffee, leaning over the counter of my tiny galley kitchen while watching *Good Morning America* on my new living room TV. But I wasn't really focusing on the show. I was thinking of Kit and Larry, hoping he had gone home the night before and had a long talk with his wife. Rather than feel manipulated by Kit into questioning her husband, I felt pleased with her trust in me. But exactly how much Kit would believe of the church/bar story, I wasn't sure.

When the phone beside me rang, I expected it to be Emily calling from California. Apparently, no one in the Golden State sleeps for more than twenty minutes at a time, so I was used to early morning calls (which were even earlier, by two hours, for her).

"Do you buy it?"

It was Kit. And her tone clearly indicated she was far from pacified by Larry's explanation of his whereabouts.

"Well, yes. Yes, I do."

"And is the Easter Bunny having coffee with you this morning?"

"Look, your little plan worked, okay? I asked Larry the burning question, and he answered. Kit, he seemed sincere. How did he sound to you?"

"The way any bullshit artist sounds."

"Well, I have to go to work. Do you want to meet for lunch?"

"No. Houdini has to give his statement, remember? I said I'd go with him."

I took that to mean she *told* him she'd go with him, but I let it pass. "Okay, well, call me after. And say hello to Detective Culotta for me."

"Who?"

I couldn't believe she'd forgotten Detective Culotta so soon. How do you forget six-foot-something of pure gorgeous? "The police guy, the one at your house."

"Oh, him. Yeah, I'll kiss him for you."

***

When I got to the office, Perry was shopping on the Internet for designer shoes.

"Hey," I said. I dropped my briefcase on the floor beside my desk and switched on my computer.

"Hey, Val. How was the open house yesterday?"

I was impressed that he remembered there had been one. Perry is a sweet, although simple, thirty-year-old.

Blessed with the looks of a handsome movie star, his main mission in life seems to be improving what God has already given him.

"It was dead," I said, which immediately made me think of Susan Reed. I shuddered a little. "What's going on here?"

"Big sale on Jimmy Choos, Val. You should take a look."

"Ha," I said. "I'll stick to DSW. And you should be careful. If Tom comes in and catches you shopping . . ."

Just as I said it, the man himself appeared. He always enters with a flourish, like the lead actor in a play making his first appearance on the stage. You can almost hear the audience applaud.

"What's shaking, kids?" For once his mood seemed jovial, and Perry and I exchanged *what's that about* looks.

"Nothing, Uncle Tom." Perry hit the *escape* key. "Just lining up the day."

"Yeah, you better not be lining up shoes, or you'll feel one of mine on your ass." Chuckling at his own humor, Tom breezed past us into his office. The only room with a door. "Where's Billie? Why don't I smell coffee?" he called back at us.

Billie Ludlow, the fourth person in our little office clique, and the only person on the planet who can make coffee that is satisfactory to Tom, appeared at the entrance of the tiny kitchen. "It's coming, Tom. Chill."

I took a seat at my desk as Windows did its thing on my screen. Within a few minutes, Billie stopped by my desk and placed a steaming cup of her excellent brew next to my keyboard.

"That was really something about Susan Reed," she said.

"You knew her?" I took the cup in both hands.

Billie Ludlow is twenty-two years old, cute as a baby rabbit but as tough as a Navy SEAL. Her position at Haskins Realty is not clearly defined, but we all know that if she ever left, we'd have to close up shop. I'd like to say that the difference in our ages makes me more of a mentor than friend. But the sad truth is that if anyone is mentoring anyone, she is mentoring me most of the time.

Billie is a whiz at the computer, can handle complicated contracts and purchase agreements in her sleep, and then there is that coffee of hers. She also seems to have some kind of sixth sense and knows just about everything that goes on, reducing our Chicago suburb to the size of a small New England village.

"Yes, I met her once," she said.

"No kidding?"

"Kit and Larry must be devastated." Billie opened a file and absently looked over some papers.

"Yes, they really are."

"Hmm, how terrible for them."

"*Billie.*" We both heard Tom's voice boom from his office. "Why am I not drinking coffee?"

I raised my eyebrows, and Billie looked at her watch. "So much for the good mood," she said. "I guess it's time to go into the lion's cage. Wish me luck."

The busy Monday morning progressed normally. I took several calls, one of which resulted in a meeting for a potential listing. I placed even more calls than I took. Business was slow, and everyone in the industry was hustling more than usual.

During a quick sandwich at my desk for lunch, I called to check on my mother. "How was church, Mom?" I removed a slice of tart pickle that rested on the chicken between two slices of wheat bread.

"Minnie Ebert was wearing way too much perfume, as usual. I must have sneezed thirty times. Did you go to church down there?" She was referring to the First Presbyterian Church, where we'd gone together every Sunday before she moved up to Door County.

"Mom, I meant to, but yesterday was so busy for me." The truth was, I hadn't been since she'd moved away years ago, except when she was visiting.

"Her lipstick alone could have stopped traffic, it was so red." I smiled to myself, picturing Minnie, the Marilyn Monroe of Door County's St. Luke Presbyterian Church. She was close to ninety and had a charming, childlike way of speaking. When I occasionally accompanied my mother to church, Minnie was always glad to see me and pronounced my name Valawee.

"I had brunch with Kit and Larry and then had an open house." I was trying to change the subject, but that was a big mistake.

"Ugh," she said, at the mention of Kit's name. In my mother's eyes, Kit is one lipstick shade away from Minnie, the harlot of Northeast Wisconsin.

After promising I'd at least crack open the Bible during the week, I hung up and drove over to a new condominium complex in Lisle that was begging for tenants. The contractor was desperate to move people in and gave me a tour of the model unit. I tried to appear as unimpressed as most of my clients do when I am pushing to sell a place. And the truth was, his price had not come down nearly enough to make it the quick sale he wanted.

At the end of the day, I still hadn't heard from Kit. With Tom and Perry both gone, and Billie engrossed at her desk doing some accounting work, I gave Kit a call.

"How did it go at the station?" I asked, as soon as I heard her say hello.

"As you would expect. They took Larry into a room, he gave them a statement, and that was that."

"What did they ask him?"

"How well he knew Susan. What kind of person she was. If he knew anyone who might harm her. Did he kill her. Ya know, the usual stuff."

"Oh boy. Really, they asked him if he killed her?"

"I guess they ask everyone that."

"Did they ask you?"

"Of course not. I mean everyone who knew her."

"Well, you knew her."

"And so did you, if you think about it." She sounded irritated and tired. I figured accompanying your husband down to the police station would cause that.

"Do they have any clues? Any idea who murdered her?"

"Val, they would hardly share that with me, would they? Oh, by the way, your Detective Columbo was there. And he's a real ass."

"It's Culotta, and he's only doing his job." I doubted that Dennis Culotta needed me defending him, and I wondered why I was.

"He's a dick, and I'm not referring to his profession."

I decided to change the subject. "So how are things with you and Larry?"

"Oh, just peachy, Val. We're going samba dancing tonight, and later we thought we'd renew our wedding vows."

"Kit, Larry is upset. You two will work it out. I'm absolutely positive Larry did not have an affair with that chick."

"I'm glad to hear you say it. But just to be sure, I have a little plan for the two of us." Her tone brightened, as if she were about to announce the winner of the Publishers Clearing House Sweepstakes.

Oh boy. I took in a deep breath. Whatever Lucy-and-Ethel scheme she had cooked up could only be bad news. Well, bad news for me, delightful for her. But good friend that I am, I forged ahead.

"Let's hear it," I said, already convinced it would be far too ridiculous for me to swallow.

I could almost see the glee on her face as she spoke, and I was instantly transported back to our teenage years and the time Kit unveiled her brilliant plan to kidnap our opposing high school's quarterback and stash him in her parents' basement until game time.

"The deceased lived at those apartments on Lamont," she said. "The really old, trashy ones, which were perfect for her, ya know. I think we should go over and take a look at her place, see what we can find."

"You mean break in?" I was being facetious, of course, and it did nothing to dissuade Kit.

She was serious. "If we have to. I'd just like to take a look around. See if any of Larry's things are there. Ya know, case the joint, so to speak."

"Okay, hold it right there, Lucy," I said, lowering my voice to be sure Billie couldn't hear my half of this insane conversation. "First of all, her apartment is a crime scene. *Crime scene.* That means yellow tape or whatever wrapped around the building with the words *do not cross.* Second, she was murdered two days ago, so don't you think there might still be a policeman or two working at the scene? And third—" I stopped. It seemed ludicrous to even continue.

"Go on. Third?"

"Kit, it's the worst idea you've ever had."

"But it's such an opportunity to see if Larry ever visited her there."

"What the hell do you expect to find? Larry's boxers stashed in her nightstand?"

"I just want to do something, Val. Larry might be denying anything ever went on between the two of them, but I can't trust him. I want to, but I can't."

I felt a sudden pang of empathy, but my assignment, which I had apparently chosen to accept when we were ten years old, was to steer her off this disastrous course. "Look, Kit, your plan is out of the question. Don't you see? You're looking for evidence of infidelity. The police are looking for a murderer. You have to stay the hell away from there. Promise me you won't do anything dumb."

There was silence at the other end, and I started to panic. "Kit, promise me. Please."

"Okay," she said, but it was reluctant at best. "Okay, nothing for now."

"Good girl," I said, able to breathe again. "Just let it rest. Let the police do their job. Meanwhile, you work on

42

that husband of yours. Maybe the two of you *should* go dancing tonight."

"Ha," she said. "That's a laugh. You've seen Larry dance. It's like Big Bird trying to lay an egg."

***

I felt satisfied Kit would stay put, at least for the night. So I turned off my computer and said good-bye to Billie. (I sometimes wonder if she ever leaves the office. She's almost always there when I arrive *and* when I leave for the day.)

As I started my car, I planned my evening. I would stop at Dominick's to get a few groceries and then go home and make some macaroni and cheese and snuggle in bed to watch TV.

But when I found myself only one block away from Lamont Street, I told myself there was no harm in just driving down it. I didn't have Kit in pit-bull mode beside me, so there was no danger that I'd do anything rash. What harm would it do to just drive by the building? Obviously, the police hadn't closed down the street, and I wasn't the only person in Downers Grove on the road.

I'd just finished convincing myself when suddenly there it was. A three-story building. Old, worn, neglected. Maybe fifteen apartments in total. There was even a For Lease sign on the weedy patch in front that passed for a lawn. Surely it wasn't Susan's apartment already.

I parked across the street, where I had a good view. But a good view of what? Contrary to my lecture to Kit, there was no evidence of a police presence. Not even the police tape that I seemed to be so familiar with. The car was still running, in case I needed to make a quick getaway, and I stared hard, trying to discern which apartment might have been Susan's. A few of the windows were lit, but overall, the place seemed deserted and unlived in.

I was about to put the car in drive and leave when a tap on my window made me jump.

Detective Culotta.

He was conveniently standing under a streetlight, and his eyes were so blue he could have given Ol' Blue Eyes himself a run for his money. He tapped again and then motioned for me to roll down my window.

"Detective," I said. A wave of guilt washed over me. He would surely ask what the hell I was doing here, as if I were some lunatic murderer returning to the scene of the crime. Did he have handcuffs in his back pocket, and was he ready to read me my rights?

Well, none of the above.

"You've got a taillight out. Get it fixed."

CHAPTER SEVEN

I will, Detective. I'll do that. I didn't even realize it was out. I just never look at my taillights. I'm sorry—"

"Easy there. It's not as if you committed murder or anything. I just wouldn't want someone to run into you, in case your other one would go out—since you never look at them." I could see by the way his lips spread open in a grin that he was teasing me, and I felt sure his Frank Sinatra eyes were twinkling with the same glee.

"Right. I'll take care of it tomorrow."

"Speaking of murder . . ." He stood to his full height, and I poked my head slightly out the window so I could still see his face while I waited for him to finish his thought. He looked over at Susan's apartment building and then back down at me. "Do you *live* in this neighborhood?"

I was glad he apparently couldn't imagine me living in such an area. But if I didn't live here, what possible reason could I give him for my presence? Except that maybe I *did* commit a murder. Since no other ideas came to my addled mind, I opted for the truth. "No. No, I don't live here, but I knew that Susan Reed did, and I just . . . well . . . I just morbidly wanted to see where, I guess." Okay, so it was a partial truth.

He didn't carry a badge for nothing. "You sure that's all? You just wanted to see the outside of her building."

Hearing him state it like that made me realize how ridiculous it sounded. But before I could try to redeem myself, he spoke again. "Want to see the inside too?"

"Wha—?"

"I don't know why you're really in the neighborhood, but I'm here because I need to check for something in her apartment. Why don't you come in with me, and then I'll escort you home. This isn't the best place for a woman alone at night, in case you haven't heard. There's been a rash of break-ins, with the perps getting bolder and bolder all the time."

I heaved a huge sigh, as if I'd just been told my best friend was not dying of cancer, after all. So Susan could have been killed by a mere burglar, not a lover or a boss. Not, in other words, Larry.

It was only beginning to grow dark, so I didn't really think I had anything to fear about driving out of the neighborhood on my own. But Kit would commit murder herself, and I would be the victim, if I passed up a chance to go inside Susan's apartment. "Well, yeah. That's . . . that's a good idea," I said. But oh, if only Kit were here. She could make such good use of a visit to Susan's living quarters. Especially with Culotta on the premises, would I even know where to look for signs of the love nest Kit was sure existed?

I rolled up my window and got out of the car, using my remote to lock it. Then I pushed the button again and heard the reassuring sound of my horn that confirmed it was locked.

Detective Culotta was wearing his teasing grin once more. "Let me guess. You always open the mailbox again, after dropping a letter in—to make sure it really went down."

"Sure; doesn't everyone?"

With the same confidence that made me know he would never doubt a United States Postal Service box, he grabbed my elbow and steered me across the street and into Susan's apartment building.

Once inside, he said, "Follow me. Hold on to my coat so I know I haven't lost you." He put one hand at his waist, presumably to have it near his gun.

Suddenly I wanted to be anywhere but Susan's apartment. And I knew there was no place Kit would rather be.

We climbed one flight of stairs and headed down a dimly lit hall. He stopped at a door blocked by yellow tape. Police Line Do Not Cross. The brass numerals on the door declared it Unit 201, but the last digit had come unhinged and hung upside down, making it look like some obscure mathematical notation. As he began to put the key in the door, I let go of his suit jacket. He immediately took his free hand and reached back for mine.

Did he really think someone was going to snatch me away?

We ducked under the police tape, and he led the way into the apartment and closed the door behind us. "Wait here." He flicked on the overhead light and did a quick check around the tiny apartment, never having to completely leave my sight. "Looks like we're alone," he said.

But I hardly heard him and was only vaguely aware that he seemed to keep one eye on me while he was rummaging through a small desk in the corner of Susan's living room. Even though I was half-afraid Susan's killer was hiding in the closet and would leap out with an ax in his hands, I felt protected by Culotta.

But the minute he'd turned the light on, my eyes had landed on a framed photo on a table next to the front door, the kind of table more suited to a sizable foyer. Or any foyer at all, for that matter. A mere throw rug constituted the only entryway Susan had. But maybe the table gave her a feeling of spaciousness even as it swallowed up more room than she could spare. Her apartment couldn't have been even half as big as my own rabbit hutch, as Tom calls it.

And was the photo standing in the center of that table an attempt to claim a life, a man, she couldn't really have? I couldn't take my eyes off it. For the first time since I'd left my office, I was glad Kit wasn't with me. That photo was nearly as painful as the two bullets ripping through Susan's body must have been. I put my hand to my heart, as if I could protect Kit through some weird osmosis.

It was a picture of Susan and Larry, all glammed up, sitting at a table with drinks in their hands, smiling widely at whoever had taken the picture.

The frame was cheap; Kit would have picked up on that immediately. Susan's too-black hair looked freshly dyed. Her white skin and dark-red lipstick gave her a Lily Munster look, only not nearly as alluring. But she'd clearly made an attempt to spruce herself up. Larry had his arm casually around Susan's shoulders. She had her elbow on the table, her chin resting in the palm of her hand. She was wearing a silver charm bracelet and an oversize hexagon-shaped watch with a brown leather strap.

I almost buckled over, feeling sick to my stomach. No matter what Kit had already told me, I hadn't been prepared to actually see Larry and Susan in some kind of nonwork setting, especially one where they looked so damn happy.

I've known Larry since we were all in high school together. I was on their first date with them, after Larry had timidly asked me if I thought Kit would go out with him. With my encouragement, he asked her to a movie, and his best friend, John Davenport, and I accompanied them—because I knew Larry was too shy to be alone with her.

And from the beginning, Larry and Kit seemed to go together like love and marriage. If either of them had been capable of an affair, I would have deemed Kit more likely—

and only because she has a daring streak that makes Evel Knievel sound like a scaredy-cat.

But Kit and Larry have always known what a good thing they've had: a rock-solid marriage at a time when most of our peers (me included) are on their first or second divorce. I think from that first movie date, I've known I share Kit's best-friend status with Larry. But that's been okay with me, as long as it's Larry I'm sharing her with.

I remembered when he wanted to propose to Kit, how he'd had me ferret out what ring she would want. He wanted to surprise her, but even more, he wanted to thrill her. He already had the ring tucked safely in his underwear drawer when he asked her father for his blessing, because Larry was going to marry Kit whether anyone else liked it or not. She had become his reason for being.

They built a home and family and life together that *no one*, let alone the homely, trashy Susan, was going to put asunder. Granted, Susan and Larry both looked happy in the picture, but maybe the booze in the glasses they held accounted for Larry's giddy smile.

I tried hard to hang on to my positive thoughts about my friends' marriage, but the truth was, anyone could have thought the same about David and me. On the surface we, too, appeared to be the perfect couple. And look how that ended.

I hadn't even realized Detective Culotta was standing close behind me until I started to smell a hint of some kind of manly cologne.

"So was she having a thing with your friend's husband?" he asked.

I turned to face him. "Larry is also my friend. He and Kit are my *best* friends." I'd attempted to sound indignant; but instead, I came across like a spoiled child choosing friends to come to my tenth birthday party.

"Good for you." Culotta's blue eyes bore into mine.

"And no, of course she wasn't having a thing with him. She worked for him, that's all."

It suddenly occurred to me that Detective Culotta might have brought me here to get my reaction to this photo. And how *had* I reacted, during my reverie? Surely it had been only a moment or two, but I felt like I was returning from a week's trip to hell.

"Whatever. But I bet your friend Kit won't be putting this picture of her hubby and his secretary on her mantel. I hear Kit James is a real spitfire."

"She wasn't his secretary," I said.

Whatever her job title, I fought to believe she was *not* his lover, in spite of this tacky photo. I probably had dozens of similar photos of myself with Tom Haskins, and he was far from my lover. But when I looked at the picture again, I couldn't quite recall the last time I had seen Larry look so happy.

"Are you done here?" I asked. "I really need to get home."

***

When I pulled into my own apartment complex, a regular Ritz-Carlton compared to Susan's Motel 6–caliber abode, I gave a wave toward Detective Culotta's car so he would know he was free to leave. But instead, he pulled up beside me and got out of his car. Again the tap at my window and a motion for me to roll it down.

But who was he to tell me what to do? So I just opened the door and got out.

"I was thinking maybe we could go for a cup of coffee somewhere," he said.

Okay, a lot of women would agree Dennis Culotta is an attractive guy. Especially if they like rugged-looking men who wear signs around their necks stating *I don't take any shit*, then he is the one for them. Under totally different circumstances, the kind where he wasn't a detective investigating a murder that might implicate my best friends, I might have enjoyed his company. If I weren't so nervous around him and terrified that I'd say the wrong thing, then a cup of coffee might have sounded good. But I was, and it didn't.

"I'm sorry; I have a busy night planned." Surely macaroni and cheese and TV constituted busy.

"Maybe just a—"

"Well, to tell the truth, I'm really not looking to get involved. My divorce was—"

He interrupted me, the palm of his hand facing me as if he were about to take an oath. "Whoa—I'm not asking you for a friggin' date. I've got some questions, and I thought you'd prefer not to go down to the station *or* have a police officer come into your home."

Thank goodness it was dark so he couldn't see my cheeks turning crimson. I felt humiliated. But it was my fault, not his. "Oh, of course. How dense of me." That didn't cover my stupidity, but it would have to do. "But what questions? What could you possibly need to—"

"Do you want to come with me or would you rather talk here at your place?"

"Well, certainly not here in the parking lot." I slammed my car door shut and headed to the door of my building.

He followed.

CHAPTER EIGHT

N ice place," Dennis Culotta said. He stood at the front door of my apartment for a few seconds before entering. His practiced eyes swept my small living room before coming to rest on a pile of socks mixed in with washcloths on one end of the couch. I had retrieved them from the dryer two days earlier and had yet to match the socks up. When my mother warned me not to leave clothes lying around the house, she should have added that you never knew when one of Chicago's finest would follow you home. Or one from Downers Grove.

"This your kid?" He was seated on the couch already, his coat removed and tidily laid across the back cushions. On the coffee table were several photos of Emily that I was planning to make into a collage for her birthday.

"Yes, that's Emily. She lives in California and is still trying to make it big as an actress. She has time; she's still in her twenties. But luckily, Luke—that's her husband—works in computers. I'm not sure what he actually does, but he does it well and earns enough to be his wife's patron."

"Can you prove any of this?" Detective Culotta looked up from the couch. His face was serious. His legs were really long, and if we lived together, I would have moved the coffee table farther away from the couch to accommodate him.

"Excuse me?"

A wide smile spread across his face. "Ms. Pankowski, relax. I don't need your life story. I just have a few questions that might help the investigation."

"Oh, of course." I felt foolish once again. And guilty. That was probably normal, I decided, when a policeman was in your living room, sitting on your couch, cramming his long legs up against your coffee table.

"Lots of people feel nervous around the police. Why don't you take your coat off and sit down. I won't take up much of your time." He reached into his inside jacket pocket and produced the same black leather notebook he'd used at Kit's house. He removed the attached pen and flipped the notebook open to a clean page.

I shrugged off my coat and joined him at the other end of the couch, carefully sitting on top of my pile of clean laundry. "What do you want to know?" I faked a calmness I was sure he could see right through.

"Relax." It was more an order than a request. Boy, he was good. "Let's start with how well you knew the victim. Susan Reed."

"Well, I didn't really know her at all."

"But you had met her?"

"Yes, at a couple of parties Kit and Larry gave. Company things. We never really talked much, just party conversation."

"Did you like her?"

"I didn't know her well enough to like or dislike her."

He hadn't written anything yet, but held the pen poised above the little blank page, focused and ready to strike.

Suddenly he shook his head. "Come on, Ms. Pankowski. Valerie. You know if you like a person or not."

"She seemed okay, I suppose. I'm sorry, but I really didn't form an opinion."

He snapped the book shut. "Seems like you didn't like her."

"I didn't say that."

"Was it because your friend, your *best* friend, didn't like her?"

I stood, for no reason other than he was making me angry. But was I allowed to ask a policeman to leave?

"Problem?" he asked. He was clearly not disturbed by my sudden movement.

"You seem to want me to say that Susan Reed was a bad person, that I didn't like her. Well, I've told you; I just didn't know her. Do you form opinions of people instantly?"

"Every time."

"Well, good for you. Now we can all sleep safely in our beds. All I know is that Susan Reed seemed like a lonely sort of woman. She wasn't overly attractive, and she had a slyness about her that I found uncomfortable. She wasn't a person you could warm up to. At the few parties we attended together, she made little attempt at small talk, and I found her rather unfriendly."

When my little outburst was over, I realized Culotta had retrieved his notebook and was busy scribbling down my words.

"Good grief," I said. "What are you writing?"

He gazed up at me, and his blue eyes sparkled. "I'm just making a note of the opinion you suddenly seemed to have formed."

I sat back down on my pile of laundry and waited for him to ask me if I'd murdered anyone lately.

"Tell me about Larry James," he said instead.

Many years ago, when I discovered my husband's first affair, I rushed over to Kit's for consolation. For an *everything is going to be all right* hug. For a comforting *it's not you, it's him* pat on the back. But Kit wasn't home at the time, and so I ended up pouring my heart out to Larry. I will always remember that he sat with me for over an hour and listened to my pathetic ramblings, saying nothing. And when I was all cried out, he said, "Do you want me to beat him up for you?" The sincerity of his offer made us both laugh.

Larry is the least violent person I have ever known. But with no father or brothers to fight for my honor—my father is dead, and my brother lives half a country away—I tucked Larry's offer away in the corner of my heart. I know I will never take him up on it, but I feel reassured that someone is willing to fight for me.

I also know if I really wanted David beaten up, Kit would be a far better slugger.

"Larry is wonderful, Detective Culotta," I said. "He's a dear, sweet man who wouldn't hurt a fly."

Culotta stopped writing immediately. "Are you defending him?"

"Does he need defending?"

"Where were you on Saturday night, April 5?"

"I was . . . I was with Kit. We were together." Geez, the room suddenly felt too warm, and it wasn't a hot flash. I dreaded his next question.

"What were you doing?" *That was the question I dreaded.* His pen was poised again, ready to jot down my alibi.

Damn, I needed Kit. She'd make up something plausible with a lot of witnesses that wouldn't incriminate us in any way. We were competing in a fly-fishing competition. We were in a parade. We were in the Bulls' locker room.

But we hadn't been doing anything illegal on Saturday night. We had simply been doing what most normal women do when they suspect their husbands of cheating. I steeled myself to tell the truth. "We went shopping," I said instead.

"Shopping?" His pen was not moving.

"Yes, aren't you going to write that down?"

"I think I can remember it."

"Good for you." I stood again. "So is there anything else?"

"Not for now." He reached for his coat and stood up. "Valerie, don't leave town, okay?"

"Huh?"

"Just kidding. A little police humor."

"Funny." I took the few short steps from the couch to the front door. "By the way, Detective, what time was Susan killed?"

"Between six thirty and nine." His blue eyes penetrated mine. "So, I guess you and Mrs. James are off the hook since you were . . . er, shopping, right?"

"Right."

It was impossible to tell if this was more of his damn police humor or if we were suspects. After I closed the door behind him, I leaned my back up against it and breathed deeply for the first time since he'd entered my home.

My immediate thought was to call Kit and brief her on my lie. But just as I reached for the phone, it rang. The shrill sound was like a land mine detonating on my kitchen counter. Was Culotta like Columbo, always asking just one more question?

Without my glasses, I couldn't read the caller ID, but I tentatively picked up the phone.

"Mom!" It was Emily. Dear, sweet Emily.

"Hello, darling." I took a seat on the couch in the same spot Culotta had just vacated.

"Mom, I'm at a casting call. I have a few minutes, and I thought we could catch up."

"Anything exciting?"

"Diner Number Two at a restaurant in SoHo, New York. It's a new sitcom that'll be out next year. Two three-word lines and two camera pullbacks."

"Sounds exciting."

"Hardly, Mom," she said, but I could hear the enthusiasm in her voice. "From what I've read of the script so far, I doubt it'll be the next *Friends*. But it's a job. They already cast Diner Number One, and that comes with a close-up."

As always, I was filled with admiration for my daughter. She is a brilliant actress, and if Hollywood knew what it was doing, she'd be walking the red carpet every year. But the reality is, she often goes months without any work at all, and the parts she does get usually never make it to the screen.

"Oh, they just called my name; I gotta go. Wish me luck. I'll call later in the week. Love you."

"Love you, too, honey. And love to Luke. Knock 'em dead. Tell them your mom thinks you should have your own sitcom." I heard her giggle before she hung up.

Then I dialed Kit's number. I was already picturing Culotta racing over to her house, his arm out the window as he put a flashing light on the roof of his car. I even checked my kitchen clock to see if he'd had enough time to get there.

"Kit," I said, when she answered the phone. "Thank goodness you're home."

"It's nine o'clock on a Monday night, Val. Why the hell do you sound so surprised to find me home?"

"Shut up and listen. Culotta was here. He asked me what we were doing Saturday night. I told him—"

"Wait a minute. Culotta was there? Where there?"

"In my apartment." I realized I would have to come clean about driving over to Susan's place. And she wasn't going to like it.

"What the hell are you talking about? Why would Culotta be in your apartment?"

"Okay, listen carefully. After I left work tonight, I drove by Susan's place on Lamont—"

"What the—"

"Will you just listen? This is important." I envisioned Culotta pulling into Kit's driveway, kicking in her front door as he flashed his gold shield, and ordering her to hang up the phone—before I could brief her. "He was here, okay? I'll explain later. But the important thing is, he asked what we were doing on Saturday night and I told him we went shopping."

I expected an explosion on the other end, but for maybe the first time in her life, Kit remained completely silent.

"Are you there, Kit? Did you hear me? We went shopping, right?"

Still no answer. Then, a few seconds later, a baby-voiced Kit said, "Okay. Shopping. Got it."

"Because it's really important, Kit. I lied to the police."

"Big deal." Grown-up Kit was back. "That asshole Culotta should be doing the job we pay him for, not harassing you."

I was touched by her concern for me, and she seemed, for the moment at least, to have forgotten to blow up about my going to Lamont Street without her. But I was sure it would come. "Okay, then," I said. "So we agree. When he talks to you, we were out shopping on Saturday night."

"No problem."

A nagging thought suddenly popped into my head. "By the way, after I left your house Saturday night, what did you do? Before you picked me up later?"

"Ya know, Val, you've got some nerve going to the skank's apartment after you read me the riot act when I suggested doing the very same thing."

"And don't you see how right I was? Culotta was there, almost waiting for me. It would have been much worse if we had both shown up."

"I don't see how. Look, Val, I gotta go. I took a sleeping pill, and it's starting to kick in. Let's talk tomorrow."

Before I could protest, she hung up. An hour later I was in bed, flipping through the TV channels for something light to watch. I decided to forego my usual *Law & Order*, lest I come across any characters who had lied to the police. I didn't want to know the repercussions. I settled on an old *Will & Grace*. I had seen it at least twice, but it still made me laugh. During the first commercial, in which a cartoon family of mucus, complete with suitcases, settled in some poor slob's chest, it occurred to me that Kit had never answered my question.

What had she done after I left her house Saturday night?

CHAPTER NINE

Susan Reed's death was ruled a homicide, committed by an unknown assailant or assailants. That was no surprise.

But when I read a brief follow-up story in the local paper the next day, it was as if I were hearing about it for the first time. Even though Susan and I had never been friends, I felt a sudden stab of pain over her violent demise. In the paper, Detective Dennis Culotta was quoted as saying robbery had been ruled out as a motive and the police were asking anyone with knowledge of the crime to contact him at the Downers Grove Police Department.

I was at my desk reading the article and munching the remains of a cherry Danish when I became aware of Tom Haskins standing behind me.

"Anything new?" he asked.

I read the brief article again, this time aloud, and then put the paper down to wipe my sticky fingers on a napkin.

"How do you know Dennis Culotta?" I swiveled my chair to face him.

"Who says I know him?" Tom was already heading back to his office, so I jumped up and followed him, like a reporter determined to get a quote.

"*You* did. In fact you said he was a good man."

Tom sank down into the leather chair behind his desk. He let out an exaggerated sigh as he reached into his drawer and took out a cigar encased in an aluminum cylinder. "Just when did I—"

"You said it, okay? I'm just curious how you even know him."

Tom took his time removing the cigar, striking a match and waving it across the tip of the Cuban. I watched as it emitted clouds of blue smoke that seemed to fill the small space around his desk. I had long since given up reminding him not to smoke in the office. His defense is centered on the fact that he owns the office building and it is, in fact, his second home. Ergo, in his own home he can do whatever the hell he likes, and no law or written policy is going to tell him otherwise.

I placed my hands on the edge of his desk, refusing to budge. Refusing to even wave away the offending smoke that was making my eyes water.

"Okay, okay," he said, when it was clear I wasn't going anywhere. "I play poker with him once a month, have for years."

"How come I've never heard of him?"

"You ever hear of Buckteeth Boranski?"

"No."

"See? I've played with him for the past two decades. I didn't realize I had to clear my poker buddies with you, Valerie."

"So what's he like?" I changed my approach and plopped down into his visitor's chair.

"As you probably guessed, he's got a prominent set of chompers, hence the name—"

"Not him, you idiot. Culotta. What's Dennis Culotta like?"

"Oh, he's decent enough. Good player. Not as good as me, of course, but okay."

"Did you know he's investigating the murder of Susan Reed?"

"Yeah. So it said in the paper. What's it to you?"

I decided not to mention Culotta's little visit to my apartment. Tom is funny about things like that. Sometimes he gets all big-brotherish and thinks my entering a convent is a good idea. "It's nothing to me," I said. "Just curious. Larry's pretty beat up about it."

"Understandable." I watched as he gently tapped the end of his cigar into a Waterford ashtray. The cut glass, a gift from one of his many girlfriends, was far too beautiful to be used to collect ashes. "Now here's what I want you to do," he said.

"Yes?" I sat up a little straighter, like the reporter ready to hear something good.

"Get Billie to bring me some coffee. And quick."

***

"They haven't released the body, so no funeral scheduled yet," Kit said. "But don't you think I should pay a visit to what's-her-name's mother? Ya know, since I'm the wife of the boss and all that crap?"

"I think that would be very nice," I said into the mouthpiece of my new hands-free headset. I was driving to the office on my way back from a quick trip to Subway, armed with sandwiches for Billie and me. Tom had taken Perry to a business lunch to meet a prospective client. A woman. A rich, attractive woman, who could apparently be won over by either Tom or his nephew, or both.

"I don't give a shit about being nice," Kit said. "I just thought she might know something about her daughter and Larry."

I hadn't told Kit about the photograph I'd seen, since I knew she would use it as proof of her husband's affair. Plus, I had almost convinced myself it was completely innocent, and I didn't want her undoing my good thoughts.

"Kit, do you really think the woman is concerned about who her daughter had an affair with? Her daughter's dead, for Pete's sake. This woman has lost her only child. But I do think you should visit her. That's a good idea. What does Larry say?"

"Ugh. Who cares what Larry says? He's almost catatonic. So, what time?"

"What time what?"

"What time do you want to go see the woman?"

"Me? Why me?"

"Oh, Val. Don't be tiresome. Ya know I can't do this stuff by myself. Just come with me. And please save me the effort of talking you into it."

I rounded the corner and turned into our small parking lot. She was right about that. It would be an effort on her part, and in the end we both knew I would go. My immediate fear was that Mrs. Reed might say something innocent about Susan and Larry that would cause Kit to initiate another murder, and in that case, it was probably better for all concerned that I be there.

"Okay, pick me up at six. But listen, call the woman first and tell her we're coming."

"Okay. What should I take?"

That is the sort of question I would normally be asking Kit, not the other way around. She could write a book on the right gift for every occasion, even meeting the mother of your husband's suspected lover—a lover who just happened to have been murdered.

"Hmm, not sure if I know what's fitting." I pulled into my parking space.

"How about Godiva chocolates? They seem appropriate, don't you think?"

"A little too festive."

"Okay, then I'll stop by Walgreens and pick up some chocolate-covered cherries."

***

On the drive to Marjorie Reed's home, I used the time to ask Kit once more what she had been doing the night of the murder, after I left her house about six thirty and before she picked me up after eleven o'clock.

"Why do you keep asking? What do you think I was doing?"

"I have no idea; that's why I'm asking."

"And why are you asking?"

"Because Culotta will ask you at some point. He asked me, so he's sure to ask you too. And by the way, don't forget we went shopping."

We stopped at a red light, and Kit retrieved her glasses from her purse so she could study her phone for directions to Marjorie Reed's. The light changed to green and she moved forward. "Geez," she said. "This neighborhood is worse than her kid's."

It was indeed a depressing street, lined with small, unkempt houses too close together, most in need of major repair.

Kit slowed her BMW to a crawl and inched her way over the numerous potholes. "Can you see any house numbers? We're looking for twenty-three thirty-four."

"There," I said. "Look, it's painted on the mailbox."

Marjorie Reed's house was lit from the outside by a gaslight that gave off little illumination but did set her home apart from her neighbors by giving a semblance of style. Her two small front windows were covered on the inside by white vertical blinds. Even from the outside I could see they were plastic, but they were clean and straight, and my Realtor eyes saw that if I could pick up her little house and move it to a better neighborhood, I could probably sell it quickly as a promising fixer-upper.

The woman who answered the door carried the same features as her house. Poor-quality makeup, but artfully applied. She had honey-blond hair that was probably colored at home, but the shade was flattering for a woman well into her sixties. I didn't notice the cane tightly held in her right hand until she used it to indicate that we should enter her home.

"Mrs. Reed, I'm Kit James. We spoke on the phone. And this is Valerie Pankowski. She's a . . . friend of the family's."

"It's good of you to come by," Marjorie Reed said. Her voice was firm and gave no indication that she was in mourning for her daughter.

Once over the threshold, we found ourselves in a small living room. The furniture was old and worn, but I was filled with admiration that she had arranged her meager possessions into a cozy ensemble.

"Can I get you ladies something? Coffee, soda? I have a little sherry, if you like."

Her cane now indicated we should sit, and I took the faded floral armchair. On the table beside me were several pictures, but I noticed none of them seemed to be of Susan. There was a mixed-breed dog almost smiling at the camera, an old picture of a serviceman in uniform, and a baby who didn't look happy about being photographed. Well, maybe the baby was Susan.

"Nothing for me," Kit said. "Thank you, though." She perched on the end of the couch farthest away from me, and we both watched Marjorie Reed hobble to the remaining armchair.

"I'm so sorry about Susan," I said, as soon as she was seated.

"Thank you," Marjorie said. Her eyes were clear, and there was no sign of sorrow. Regret maybe, and a little anger. But no tears. "Let's just hope the police find whoever did this terrible thing. Do you have children?"

"Yes, a daughter in California. I can't imagine—"

"Mr. James called twice," Marjorie said, addressing Kit, and I was glad for the interruption. "He's been so kind. Everyone has. I was so glad Susan worked for such nice people. She loved her job."

"No doubt," Kit said. "And I'm sure she was good at it."

I heard a man's voice talking in the background. Since the television was not turned on, I assumed it was the radio. Marjorie looked at me, twisting her head a little as if to hear better. "It's my gardening show," she said. "I don't have a garden to speak of, but I like to keep up."

"Me too," I said, even though I wouldn't know a petunia from a potato.

"The police say they have no leads," Marjorie said. "I can't imagine who would do such a thing, can you?" She was addressing Kit again.

"It's a wicked world, Mrs. Reed."

"Marjorie; please call me Marjorie."

"If you need help with anything, please let us know," I said.

"I will."

Our conversation lapsed while the man on the radio educated us about spring planting.

"We won't take up any more of your time." Kit rose from her chair.

Marjorie and I rose in unison, and I reached out to steady her as her cane wobbled on the faded carpet. Kit reached out to shake her hand, and I put my arm around Marjorie's shoulders to help her balance.

"Did Susan have a boyfriend?" Kit suddenly asked. Her lack of subtlety was not lost on the older woman.

Marjorie gave a little smile. "No." She looked down at her feet, which were encased in comfy slippers.

"Oh." Kit retrieved her purse, her actions making it clear that we had done our duty and our visit was over.

"Mrs. Reed," I said, "is there someone to help you? Do you have any relatives or friends close by?"

"I have all I need, my dear," she said, looking me in the eye.

Out of sheer habit, I reached into my purse and gave her my Haskins Realty business card. "Take this." I placed it on the coffee table. "If you need any help, with anything, please call me."

"Thank you," she said, but her eyes were on Kit, who was already at the front door.

"Me too," Kit said. "Call if there's anything my husband's company can do for you."

***

"Why were you so mean?" I asked Kit, as soon as we were back in her car.

"Mean? What are you talking about?"

"That woman just lost her daughter in a horrible, horrible way. No matter what you think of Susan, that woman deserved a little more compassion."

"Oh, *please*." Kit flipped up her turn signal. "That woman is just like her daughter."

"Well, I think you are wrong. In fact, I thought she was the complete opposite of her daughter. We should have stayed longer and . . . Well, it looked as if the only reason we went there was for you to find out about Susan's love life."

Kit looked across at me, and her perfectly shaped eyebrows rose in astonishment. "That *is* the only reason we went there. What did you think? That I wanted to learn how to trim my rose bushes?"

"Oh, Kit. Sometimes you are so—"

"Hey, Valley Girl, it's still early. Wanna go get a couple of chocolate martinis?"

"Forget it, Cruella de Vil. Just take me home."

"Lunch tomorrow?" She pulled up to the curb outside my building.

"Not sure what I'm doing. I'll call you."

"Okeydokey," she said. As I opened the passenger door, she suddenly leaned over and kissed my cheek. "Don't be angry with me. I'll have Larry send her a big fat check tomorrow."

***

Later, as I brushed my teeth, I thought of Marjorie Reed. In her faded little house and her worn clothes, she was somehow still an elegant, classy woman.

I wondered if I'd judged her daughter too quickly. If I'd known Susan Reed better, I might have seen something of her mother in her.

When I was ready for bed, I padded to my little kitchen to make a cup of cocoa. I probably hadn't had cocoa since I was nine, and it was a poor substitute for Kit's suggestion of a chocolate martini. But we do what we can. As I was digging into the hardened cocoa powder in the bottom of the can (apparently, this was the actual can used for my last partaking of the chocolaty beverage), my phone rang.

"Hello." I wedged the phone under my chin as I continued my digging.

"Mrs. Pankowski? This is Marjorie Reed. I just wanted to thank you again for coming to see me tonight. I hope I'm not calling too late."

"Not at all." I put down the can and turned off the burner under the pan of hot milk.

"I'm sure Mrs. James thought she was doing me a great kindness, but I found her offensive."

"I'm sorry. This whole thing has been upsetting for everyone, and Kit isn't the most diplomatic person in the world." Defending Kit was automatic after all the years of running interference for her. "She means well, Mrs. Reed. Please don't take what she said personally."

"She hardly said anything, except to ask me if Susan had a boyfriend. I was so taken aback. Why would she ask such a question?"

"I think she was just trying to get a feel for Susan. But it was rude, and I'm sorry if she upset you."

"Not for you to defend her, my dear," Marjorie said, sounding much like my own mother. Or Tom. Or even Larry sometimes. "Not that it's any of her business, but Susan didn't have a boyfriend as such. And she'd hate me for saying this, but there was someone she was smitten with. I wouldn't call him a boyfriend, exactly. If you want my honest opinion, he was probably a married man. She never told me his name, and she certainly didn't bring him around here."

"Ah." I poured the warm milk into a coffee mug on top of the dried-out cocoa.

"I never married Susan's father," Marjorie continued. "He was a married man too. His wife and children never knew of Susan's existence."

"But she knew her father had another family?"

"Yes, I told her that much. Probably not the best thing to do, but I wanted to tell her some of the truth. Funny thing is, her life was a big secret to me. We were never especially close."

"And you had no idea who the man was that Susan . . . loved?"

"No. I didn't really want to know, and I suppose I shouldn't have been surprised to think she would follow in my footsteps."

I pictured Marjorie's cane and how unsteady she was with her footsteps. But at least she was alive. Unlike her daughter.

CHAPTER TEN

Kit was sitting on my living room couch when I awoke the next morning. I was so happy to see the cardboard Starbucks cup she had raised to her mouth—and even happier to see the matching one that was undoubtedly mine on the coffee table—that I almost didn't question her presence.

Almost.

I peeked into the kitchen and glanced at the microwave clock. Six o'clock. I'd slept later than usual. In my youth, nothing short of an air-raid siren could get me out of bed on a first attempt at this hour. But somewhere between my fortieth and fiftieth birthdays, I'd begun getting up with the birds, or before. "What on earth are you doing here? And how did you get in?"

"Uh, with the key you gave me the first week you lived here?"

"Oh, that. Yeah."

I rubbed my eyes and then grabbed my latte. I took a sip, noting that it was still hot enough that Kit couldn't have been here long.

I took a second to appreciate her agility at entering my home without my hearing. Of course I didn't linger on that thought for fear I might wake up the next day to find Charles Manson in my kitchen icing a Toaster Strudel. "But why? Why are you here?" I asked.

"Gee, it's good to see you, too, girlfriend. And you're welcome. For the coffee. Any time."

"Cut the crap. It's too early. So what's up?"

"Larry, for starters. He left for Carbondale about an hour ago—some audit he has to do. Or so he says."

"Well, at least we know he's not meeting Susan Reed," I said.

She laughed, even though I had not meant it as a joke.

"Seriously, Kit. What's wrong with him going downstate for an audit? He's done that a zillion times."

"Nothing's wrong with it. In fact, everything's right about it. I realized as soon as he left that Brad would be working in their office without Larry today. Ya know, Brad can maybe . . . maybe shed some light on some things for us."

"For you, Kit. Shed some light for *you*. Count me out. I've already lied to a police detective who is breathing down our necks. There's a murderer on the loose out there. And all I want to do is sell houses and get ready for my daughter's visit."

At the thought, my tummy did a little leap of anticipation. Luke had a computer seminar to attend the following month, and if Emily was between parts, she was going to come just hang with me for a whole week. Shopping. Lunches. Movies. Museums. I was beside myself with excitement and determined to have my apartment looking like a show home (as much as an apartment can) and all set up to accommodate her every need. And I'd have reservations made and tickets bought.

Not that I didn't think she could get a part too tempting to turn down, but I couldn't bear the thought of not having my time with her. We were also going to drive up to Door County and spend Mother's Day with my mom. If possible, she was even more eager about Emily's visit than I was.

I squelched my excitement about my daughter and focused on my friend. "And what exactly is the point of seeing Brad?"

"I want to see if he confirms what friggin' Ellen said. Ya know, about Larry and the skank."

I looked into Kit's eyes, which peered at me above her mocha. "Kit, why don't you just move on? Ellen is a fool. She didn't tell you anything except what she suspects." If I hadn't been hanging on to my coffee for dear life, I would have used my fingers to make air quotation marks around the word *suspects*.

"You owe me, Val," she said.

"Huh?"

"Steve Byer's notebook?"

She had me there. A mere thirty-six years or so ago, my fifteen-year-old best friend Kit went with me to the principal's office to explain that I hadn't swiped Steve Byer's notebook from his locker in order to copy his geometry, but rather as a prank, as a way to get him to chase after me. Okay, so it wasn't my most brilliant idea, and no one could accuse me of being a *mature* fifteen-year-old.

But afterward, Kit had talked me into making the first move and meeting the consequences head-on. "It's the only way Mr. Sikes will believe you, Val. If he has to call you to his office, he'll never believe anything you say."

It turned out, for once, that her logic was correct. I got off with a mild if humiliating scolding. And of course Steve Byer and I never made eye contact again.

As Kit's finger traced the Starbucks logo on the side of her cup, I nodded. "You are so right," I said. "I do owe you." While it hadn't exactly been a death-row confession, it was one of those memories of Kit as my savior. And I knew she'd do it all over again. "Give me fifteen minutes." I turned and went into my bedroom to dress.

***

We were alone in Larry and Brad's office. It turned out Kit had a key to that too. (Did she have a large metal ring in her purse that held the key to every door in Downers Grove?) We had about fifteen minutes to snoop before Brad Parkinson let himself in with his own key. And we had just enough time between hearing a noise at the door and his swinging it open to get ourselves seated on the plush waiting-room couch before he entered the outer office. He looked surprised, and why wouldn't he?

We picked up our Starbucks cups—new ones we'd gotten at the drive-thru—from the magazine-laden table in unison and then stood up, as if we'd been practicing the routine before Brad's arrival.

But Brad spoke first. "Kit! I don't think Larry's coming in today." He crossed the room, and Kit extended her cheek for a kiss.

Every time I saw Brad, I was struck all over again by how attractive he was. *That's* how attractive he was. He carried his age well. I decided his wife shopped at a different luggage store, judging from the way she looked when we'd seen her just a few days ago.

"I know," Kit said. "We just wanted to talk to you for a few minutes. You remember Val."

"Of course. Just let me get some coffee started—seems like I'm the first one here. Then we'll go into my office." Brad's shock at seeing us seemed to have evaporated, and his manner suggested there was nothing out of the ordinary in our early-morning call.

"I'm sorry. I should have brought you a Starbucks," Kit called after him, as he made his way to the coffee maker in the far corner of the office.

"No, it would be wasted on me. Too strong. Can't drink it."

"*Wimp*," Kit silently mouthed to me.

I held my finger to my lips to shush her, even though she hadn't made a sound. I had never regretted following Kit somewhere as strongly as I did right now. And that was saying something.

As I watched him, I fought the urge to whisper to Kit. Instead, I kept to myself the thought that with his athletic build, Brad looked like anything but a wimp.

After he'd gone through his coffee-making motions—I pitied him not having a Billie to do it for him—he waved us into his office.

"I don't have long, I'm afraid." He checked his expensive-looking watch, as if to confirm his time was short. "I have several candidates to interview for—"

"That's why we're here," Kit said. "Because of Susan. I'm sure it will be hard for you to replace her."

I thought he looked like Kit must be kidding, but before I could try to figure out why, he spoke again. "Yeah, I guess Larry liked her. But—as much as I hate to speak ill of the dead, especially someone so recently dead—I never . . . thought Susan was right for us. Not from the very start." He removed his suit jacket, revealing a starched blue pin-striped shirt and an elegant tie that looked as if it cost a day's pay.

"Then why did you hire her?" Kit didn't hide her irritation, and I wanted to assure her Brad wasn't to blame if Larry was having an affair. And I wanted to remind her it was a big *if*.

But I remained silent as Brad jerked his head back a little and carefully placed his jacket on a wooden hanger in the closet behind him. He seemed to be cautiously choosing his words as he spoke, which was understandable since he'd known Kit for decades. "I didn't, as a matter of fact. Larry did. We'd both interviewed her earlier, along with a lot of other candidates. The job market was stronger then, and we didn't have the selection that I expect we'll have now. Anyway, I thought I'd made it clear to Larry that I didn't want Susan, that I didn't trust her or the circumstances under which she'd left her previous job. But Ellen and I went on a short vacation, and I returned to find Susan behind the front desk."

He stopped speaking, and a smug look spread across his face. He actually raised his blond eyebrows in a gesture that indicated Susan had nothing to do with him, that she was, so to speak, Larry's baby.

I wished for a second that Dennis Culotta would suddenly appear and shoot holes in Brad's recounting. And then it occurred to me that maybe our favorite detective had already done just that.

"So." Brad rubbed his hands together like a used-car salesman who has just sold the old clunker on the lot. "Can I get you ladies some decent coffee?" His smile was one of the million-dollar variety, and I unexpectedly had a little sympathy for Ellen.

"No, thanks," I said, as Kit shook her head.

"I'll be right back."

As soon as he'd gone through his doorway, Kit said, "Oh, this is going to be good. Ya know, it's the best idea I've ever had, coming to Brad. He knows something. I can tell."

"Well, we'll see," I said. I knew Kit was trying to get Brad to talk about the alleged office love affair, but I was more interested in how quickly he disassociated himself from Susan's hiring. Almost as if he were hanging Larry out to dry.

Brad was back, and I hoped he hadn't heard any of our exchange. I didn't see how he could have returned so quickly without at least spilling coffee on himself. Must be those long legs and the big strides they could take, I decided. He sat down and took a sip. "Now, where were we?"

"You didn't trust Susan," Kit said. "Why not?"

"It was mostly a feeling, and I'm not big on intuition, believe me. I leave that up to you women. Not to be sexist."

He studied our faces, as if to see if he'd offended us. "But the job she had before us was with Allen Craigmore. Allen's an acquaintance in the business. Poor guy got into some kind of financial trouble and was really struggling to get things right, and it seemed to me that she up and quit on him right when he probably needed her most. And I don't know—it's been over a year ago now—but I recall thinking she sounded snotty about it. Like what could he do for her anymore."

Kit and I sat silently and waited for him to continue, which he did.

"I know, I know, she probably had to take care of herself," he said, "but I just didn't hear the kind of loyalty or decency that I was looking for in someone Larry and I were going to hire. We're a small family here—except during tax season, of course. We need to be able to trust our staff."

"Is that all?" Kit asked, but I knew what she really meant was, *did you think she and Larry had a thing going?*

He shrugged. "Let me just say that nothing Susan ever did while she was working for us led me to change my opinion."

"What do you mean?" Kit asked.

He looked from Kit to me and back to Kit. "Nothing, really. Nothing specific. I never really got to know her that well; Larry did all the supervising and stuff. So I just never had a reason to think about her, period." Again, it was Larry's problem, not his.

I wondered if Kit, like me, thought he seemed evasive. Like he realized who he was talking to or the repercussions of insinuating something unsavory about a murdered person.

He glanced at his watch and stood up, this time with an air of dismissal. "Sorry, ladies, but I do need to prepare for my first interview."

"So this time *you're* doing the hiring, eh?" If I didn't know her and her suspicions better, it could have passed for Kit's wry humor. But I did know better, and so I heard the bitter edge in her voice.

"Larry just doesn't seem to have the heart," Brad said. "I mean, it probably seems to him that he just went through this process. I'm happy to do it this time."

As he spoke, he was guiding us to the front door. He opened it for us and then said good-bye, as if he couldn't get us out of there quickly enough. I heard him close the door behind us before we'd taken one step toward Kit's car. As we walked down the sidewalk, we had to make room for Blondie and Big Red and several more women (no doubt the temporary "drudges" who worked for Larry and Brad during the tax season).

"Okay, tell me what you think," Kit said, as soon as we were back in her BMW.

"Well, for starters, I think it's odd he never questioned why we were really there."

"I told him, dummy. We were there about what's-her-face."

"But he didn't ask *why* we were so curious. He just started spilling his guts about what a bad choice Larry had made. Surely you noticed how he's so completely innocent. According to him, he hardly noticed Susan's presence around their office."

"Yeah, that wasn't good," Kit said. "There's only six people in that company. How do you *not* know one of them? And another thing: I don't believe he let Larry make the decision to hire someone without his approval."

"Exactly."

"Ya know, I really expected him to clam up. The good ol' buddy system and all that shit."

"Right. He certainly took the time to let us know he wasn't in the office loop. But at least he didn't confirm what Ellen said." Then, hoping to spare Kit from reliving Ellen Parkinson's accusation, I hurried on. "Did you notice how he suddenly couldn't wait to get rid of us?"

"I should have known he wouldn't blab," Kit said. "He realized he'd said too much already and was getting Larry into some hot water with the wifey."

"Well, are you at least satisfied?"

"What do *you* think? The Parkinsons are useless. We're going to go see Mrs. Allen Craigmore, if there is one."

"*Mrs.* Allen Craigmore?"

"Yeah, the *wife* of Susan's last employer. Something tells me I have a better chance of getting the information I want from the *wife*."

I knew I should tell Kit about my phone call from Marjorie Reed the previous night. But I decided to wait a bit and see what developed.

CHAPTER ELEVEN

When I finally got to my office, around nine, I was greeted by the smell of coffee wafting through the small workplace, as if Juan Valdez himself had just delivered freshly picked beans in a sack he carried on his back. Before I could even remove my trench coat and turn on my computer, Billie put a steaming mug of the java on my desk.

"Bless you, Billie love." I eyed the mug with *Haskins Realty* stamped on both sides.

"Tom's in Vegas. He left on the red-eye this morning. Back in a couple of days. Perry's got a dental appointment."

"Teeth whitening?"

"Of course."

We both smiled, and Billie took the visitor's chair across from my desk.

"Billie, do you know Allen Craigmore?" On my drive to work, I had formed a plan to ask Tom about Susan's former employer. It might have been tricky, since Tom invented the cat-and-mouse game (he was always the cat, and he liked to make his mice work for information). But it occurred to me Billie probably knew as much as, if not more than, Tom.

"I know the son, Zach Craigmore. We went to high school together."

"What about the father, Allen?"

"Never met him. He had an accounting firm, I believe. Like your friend Larry. I heard it went belly up a year or so ago. Bad business."

"How so?"

"If I remember correctly, he bilked some clients." Billie sipped her own coffee and peered at me over the top of her mug. Her look suggested there was no doubt she remembered correctly.

"Really?" I picked up my own mug and took a sip. (Sorry, Starbucks, you are good, but you ain't no Billie.) "I heard Susan Reed worked for him, before she went to Larry's place."

"Correct."

I recalled Billie's earlier confession about knowing Ms. Reed and tried to sound innocent as I asked, "So how did you know Susan?"

Billie sat back in the chair. "Zach is a musician, used to play at Zio's. I was there a little over a year ago, and we had a drink between sets. Susan Reed came in with a couple of girlfriends, and Zach introduced us. He told me she worked for his father."

"Where's Zach now?"

"He split a while back. Moved to LA, I heard. We were never close friends, but he's a good guy. You know, one of the really cool kids in school."

"What did you think of Susan?"

"Not much. She came over to our table, and Zach was kinda forced to introduce us. But she wasn't exactly setting the world on fire, if you know what I mean."

I debated telling her about Kit's suspicions of Larry and Susan, but before I could respond, Billie spoke again.

"Rumor was, Susan was having a thing with Zach's dad."

I put my coffee mug down. "Are you serious?"

"Unbelievable, right?"

"Right."

My impulse was to get Kit and drive over to see Allen Craigmore immediately. But since I was apparently the only Realtor on duty, it would have to wait a little bit.

"Where did you hear this?" I asked, although I didn't really need confirmation. Billie was a fact-checker. She didn't waste time on idle gossip. "From Zach?"

"Oh no, not Zach. He wouldn't tell me something like that. I heard it from a couple of other people, reliable people. You know, when the whole scandal went down."

"Scandal?"

"Like I said, his dad, Allen Craigmore, was charged with stealing his clients' funds. Misappropriation is the official term, I think. Probably the reason Zach left town."

"I can't believe I never heard about it."

"Val, he wasn't exactly Bernie Madoff."

***

As soon as Billie returned to her desk, I called Kit and relayed all I'd heard.

"Hot damn!" She sounded thrilled to think Larry wasn't Susan's only alleged conquest.

"What did you know about Allen Craigmore's business?"

"Me? Why would I know anything?"

"Kit, I'm not accusing you of masterminding the whole thing. I just wondered what Larry said about it."

"Who knows? Probably he yammered on about it. Who listens? The accounting world isn't as riveting as you might think, Val. But we should definitely pay a visit to Allen Craigmore's wife, Barbara."

"How do you know her name?"

"Ah!" I could almost see the twinkle in her eye. "I found the Craigmores in Larry's Rolodex. Thank goodness he's still in the Stone Age and doesn't keep everything on his phone."

As she said it, I glanced at my own Rolodex sitting importantly on the corner of my desk. It's my own Stone Age lifeline. If I lost it, I'd have to kill myself.

"So," she said, "why don't you come by this afternoon—"

"The earliest I can leave is three o'clock."

"Good enough. We'll go see Barbara Craigmore, and then I'll fix you dinner."

It occurred to me that I hadn't heard my friend in such a buoyant mood since this whole business began, and it seemed like a good time to get her to answer my nagging question.

"Kit, one more thing. You never told me what you did on Saturday night, after I dropped you off at your house and before you picked me back up."

There was the briefest of pauses before she answered. "Nothing. I just watched TV and waited for Larry. When he didn't come home, I called you."

"Oh good." Relief coursed through me.

"*Desperate Housewives.* Two episodes. Really old ones I had recorded. Susan fell down multiple times, and Edie had multiple orgasms."

My relief evaporated just a little. That was way too much information.

***

I worked like a maniac until two thirty, not stopping for lunch. Perry returned to the office, his snowy-white teeth setting off his manufactured tan to perfection. Tom called to tell me he was staying at Caesars and I could reach him on his cell phone, but he was in a poker tournament and I should call only if the place was on fire, which it better not be or he'd strangle me with his bare hands when he returned.

My last call, before I left to pick up Kit, was from my mother. She wanted to go over the menu for Emily's visit.

"Does she like carrots with her pot roast? I can't remember. I know you never did."

"Mom, it's a month away." Suddenly I wished I hadn't mentioned the visit, in case a job materialized for Emily and she couldn't make it. I should have waited until it was a certainty.

"You never would eat carrots, which is probably why your eyesight is so poor."

"My eyesight is fine, Mom." I squinted to read the time on my watch. "For my age," I added in defense.

"It's atrocious," she said, "and age has nothing to do with it." As I said good-bye, I pictured my mother, with her near-perfect vision after all these years, and even though I agreed with her, I didn't say it. Clearly, I had inherited my father's eyesight, or maybe I should have just eaten my carrots.

On the drive to Kit's house, my phone rang. I prayed silently that it wasn't a customer with some job-related task that would delay my sleuthing with Kit. "Valerie Pankowski," I answered.

"Dennis Culotta."

"Oh, how are you, Detective?"

I almost sailed through a stop sign and wondered if it was defensible if you were actually speaking to the police at the time of your violation.

He skipped any niceties. "We need to grab a cup of coffee soon. I have a couple more questions for you."

"Well, I guess that would be okay." I felt a little twinge of something or other forming in my tummy.

"How about now?"

"Er, not good; I'm on my way to an appointment." My twinge turned to guilt at once again lying to the police, and then it turned to fear that he had checked our alibi and found it nonexistent. I pictured Dennis Culotta making the rounds at the mall, showing pictures of Kit and me.

"I'll call you later, around five," he said.

"That would work."

Dennis Culotta hung up before I could say good-bye.

***

Kit had called Barbara Craigmore to introduce herself and ask if we could stop by. As I drove down her street in the pricey Hinsdale neighborhood, I checked for competitors' For Sale signs. There were none.

The Craigmore house was a large Tudor. Barbara Craigmore answered the door. She was a handsome, rather than beautiful, woman. Good bone structure, flattering makeup, soft brown hair cut in a short bob. She wore a dark-red suit, not exactly what you would wear at home in the late afternoon. Well, at least not what I would wear.

"Hello." She extended her hand to shake ours. Then she stepped back, making way for us to enter.

"Thank you so much for seeing us," Kit said.

"Not at all, although I have to go to work in about thirty minutes. I hope that's not a problem."

"What do you do?" I asked.

"I'm a Realtor. Century 21," she said. And then, as if to prove it, she did what all Realtors do: she produced two business cards that she pressed firmly into our hands.

"Me too," I said. "Haskins Realty in Downers Grove." My own business card materialized, and Barbara accepted it with a little smile.

"I know Tom Haskins," she said. "You're a small company, right?"

"Miniscule, compared to Century 21."

"You have a lovely home," Kit said. She was clearly out of the realty loop and didn't like it one bit. "We won't take up much time. We just have a rather delicate matter to discuss."

"No problem," Barbara said, as if delicate matters were a normal part of her day. She led us into a formal living room with a cathedral ceiling and mammoth furnishings. "Sit, please." She indicated one of the two off-white couches. Her home exuded class and a lot of money.

Kit took a seat. "Okay, we'll get right to it. We're here about Susan Reed. You know she was murdered, right?"

I watched in fascination as the *so nice to have you in my home* look slipped from Barbara Craigmore's face, replaced by a hardness that made her look instantly older and not nearly as classy.

She straightened the hem of her skirt and inspected her manicure. "I read about it. Why do you want to see me?"

"This Susan person worked for my husband, Larry, ya know." Kit paused. "I'm not sure how to say this, so I'll just say it. I suspect they were having an . . . affair." I could see it was difficult for Kit to mouth the words to a stranger, and I almost grabbed her hand in support.

A little of the softness returned to Barbara's face. "Really." She made it sound like a confirmation rather than a question.

"Yes, and I wondered what you could tell us about her." Kit stopped short of asking if Barbara had been in the same boat she found herself in, but it was more than implied.

"Okay, here goes." Barbara rose and walked over to the large white-brick fireplace that dominated the room. She had her back to us as she studied a silver-framed photograph on the mantel. It showed a young boy, presumably her son when he was little.

"Susan Reed worked for my husband, yes. Allen got into some difficulty. Bad decisions were made. He started moving money around. Problem was, it wasn't his money to move. More bad decisions. Finally, a lawsuit brought about by some of his more influential clients. A total nightmare. Financial ruin." She turned back to face us. "But that's not what you wanted to know, right?"

I watched Kit nod silently.

"Was Allen having an affair with Susan Reed?" Barbara voiced Kit's question. "Yes, he was. I don't know why, or for how long, but I do know that it ended as soon as the money dried up. Allen's business was ruined. His remaining clients had left, justly so, I might add. Stupid thing was, I don't even know why Allen needed to do what he did. We had enough money; we lived very well."

She returned to sit down on the couch across from us, and a pleasurable whiff of perfume floated our way. "It wasn't just Allen's career that was ruined; it was our entire family." She glanced at the photograph on the mantel. "Our family broke up. My son was too disgusted with his father to stick around. He moved to California. I hardly ever see him now, and when I do hear from him, our conversations are strained. Our *relationship* is strained."

"Did Susan have anything to do with your husband's business . . . problems?" Kit asked.

"Oh, she had everything to do with it. The blame ultimately lies with Allen, of course, but until she arrived on the scene, our life, our family, was perfect. But he was mesmerized by that little witch. And now . . . now I work as a Realtor. I was forced to get a job for the first time in years." She said it without self-pity, just stating a fact, and I felt a little admiration for her. I couldn't imagine this woman moping around over something her husband had done, no matter how bad.

"I struggle to pay the bills," she continued. "I have a little money of my own. A trust fund left to me by my parents, but it won't last forever. There's no life insurance, you know, not for suicide."

The word *suicide* floated between the two couches, waiting for one of us to grab it. I caught it with both hands.

"Suicide?"

"Oh yes," Barbara said. A sardonic look appeared on her face, followed by one of almost glee. She was about to place the cherry on top of the sundae. "Didn't you know?

Allen killed himself. Such a noble gesture. So much money he saved the taxpayers by not going to trial. Such a nice thing to do for his family. To save Zach and me further embarrassment."

"We had no idea," I said. "I'm so sorry. If we'd known, we—"

Barbara waved a hand in the air, as if dismissing an unwanted salesperson. "It's okay. No one knew, really, except the immediate family. I tried to keep it as quiet as possible. For my son, mainly. He'd suffered enough embarrassment. But the truth is, I am tired of covering up for Allen. We all have to move on, don't we?"

Kit and I both nodded.

"We didn't have a funeral; why waste money on that?" Barbara's face had grown red and contorted with anger. "No obituary in the paper. Allen had very few friends at that point in his life, and our family is small. Since Allen saw no need to say good-bye to his wife and son, I didn't think he deserved any kind of farewell."

Kit and I nodded again. It was clear we'd unleashed some buried rage in this woman, and I almost felt as if we were doing her a favor.

"So, back to our sweet Susan," she said. "Yes, I knew she was murdered, and I'm not one bit sorry. You know, I never was involved in Allen's business. Too much shopping and tennis and far too many expensive lunches with my girlfriends. I always thought accounting was boring. I never knew how fascinating it could be."

Then Barbara Craigmore stood up, indicating this was as much as she was going to say. Indicating that if her husband hadn't killed himself, she might have done it for him.

She glanced at her watch. "I really have to get to an appointment. Mustn't keep the buying public waiting. I'm sure you understand." If I had known her for more than fifteen minutes, I would have given her a hug. She looked as if she could use one.

At the front door she shook our hands again, as if we had just finished transacting business instead of listening to a complete stranger lay out her troubled life. We said our good-byes and headed to the car.

On the drive back to Kit's house, we didn't say a word, and as I pulled into her driveway, I remembered Dennis Culotta.

Kit unbuckled her seat belt. "Aren't you coming in? I think we need a drink," she said.

"I don't think so—"

Uncharacteristically, Kit didn't argue. Instead, she leaned over and kissed my cheek. "Okay, Valley Girl. Thanks for going with me. You're a good friend."

"I'll call you later," I said, "after I finish doing some stuff at the office."

I didn't tell her about the phone call I was expecting from Detective Culotta.

CHAPTER TWELVE

I didn't go back to my office. Instead, I drove to the nearest Starbucks, where I sipped a latte in the parking lot and pondered the growing list of lies I was telling my best friend. Among other people. As I did so, I realized I wasn't the only one who could lie. Maybe Kit hadn't really been home watching reruns of *Desperate Housewives* when Susan was murdered. Or maybe Larry hadn't really been at a church and a bar.

Like the best friend she is, Kit seemed to read my thoughts and called my cell phone right that minute.

"Hello?" I said, expecting to hear the stern voice of Detective Culotta.

"Hey, Val. You at the office yet?"

"Uh, not quite." I tapped my steering wheel and glanced at my Starbucks cup in the drink holder. At least it wasn't a lie, but I decided in the future I would come clean with Kit. This was just plain wrong.

As if to validate my decision, Kit said, "Val, I lied to you. And I'm feeling horrible about it."

I remained silent in my shock at our shared wavelength, even though I usually take our like minds for granted.

"Val?"

"I'm here. What are you talking about?"

"Val, I wasn't really—"

My phone cut out with a beep I knew to be call-waiting. But I'd experienced it so rarely, I still wasn't clear how to access it. The fact that my reading glasses were buried in my purse didn't help. I pushed the *talk* button and realized I'd made a good guess when I heard Detective Dennis Culotta's voice.

"Ready for a cup of coffee?"

"Yes." Again, I glanced guiltily at my Starbucks cup. I made a mental note to make sure it was nowhere in sight when I met up with him.

He proceeded to tell me our meeting would be at a Starbucks just a few blocks from my present location. I had to give him props for suggesting a Starbucks. I would have pegged him for a Folgers man, although I definitely wouldn't have held that against him. Not with all his compensating traits, his blue eyes topping the list.

I was halfway to the other Starbucks when I remembered I'd had Kit on the other line when Detective Culotta called through. As compelling as her imminent revelation seemed, it hadn't been able to overcome my inability to keep track of two phone calls at a time. I often bemoan how one call always knocks the previous one out of my consciousness until it's too late to get back to the first party.

Well, as eager as I was to find out what truth she had to reveal, and as relieved (and irritated) as I was that the lying between us hadn't been one-sided, I'd have to wait for enlightenment. Detective Culotta had just come into view, standing on the sidewalk outside of Starbucks, apparently awaiting my arrival.

As I pulled into a parking spot in front of him, I hurriedly turned my phone off and tossed my trench coat over the drink holder and the coffee it held.

Culotta didn't even say hello, but simply nodded before turning and leading the way. He was, however, gentleman enough to place our order and pay for it, even though he didn't ask me what I wanted.

He placed two caffè americanos on the table and sat down across from me. "I need a receipt," he said.

"Didn't they give you one?"

"Not for the coffee." His tone made the word *dummy* unnecessary.

But I knew what he meant. Still, I said, "What are you talking about?"

"Val, Val, Val. I'm pretty sure you weren't with your friend Saturday night during the time in question. But if you—or better yet, if she—can come up with a receipt from your shopping spree—"

"I said we were shopping. I didn't say we bought anything, did I? You've heard of window shopping, haven't you?"

I wasn't sure where my tough-girl act was coming from, but I hoped it masked my rapid heartbeat and churning stomach.

He simply stared at me, while my mind raced through its library of *Law & Order* episodes. Had I ever heard of them searching TiVo or DirecTV records? *Could* it be proved that a person was watching a certain show, or at least that it was playing on a particular TV at a particular time? Specifically, could *Kit* prove *she* had been watching *Desperate Housewives*?

"Let me give you a piece of friendly advice," he said at last. And I did actually see a friendly flicker in his eyes. "Don't you let those friends of yours drag you into their dirty laundry. Or worse." His words doused the friendly flicker.

And drowned my bravado.

"What do you mean? Are Kit and Larry in trouble?" I didn't think I could feel any more frightened if it were Emily or my mom he was talking about. And no wonder. Larry and Kit are family to me.

"They've been . . . shall we say . . . less than forthcoming. Which always makes me wonder *why*."

I didn't know how to respond. So I said nothing.

Detective Culotta took a long swig of coffee, but his piercing blue eyes never left my face. "If I were you, I'd encourage them—if they're guilty of nothing—to come clean. About anything and everything. And if they are guilty . . . We'll find out, so it doesn't really matter what they do."

It didn't sound like a threat, really—more of a promise.

And I believed him.

He peered at his watch and then back at me. "You hungry?"

It wasn't the most romantic dinner invitation I've ever had, but I was pretty sure that's what it was. The friendly flicker had reappeared.

Still, I had to be sure. I just couldn't take any more dark thoughts about my best friends right now. "I'm sorry," I said. "I'm done talking about Kit and Larry. You'll have to take your concerns up with them because—"

"I'm done with them too. For now. I was trying to ask you if you'd like to have dinner with me. No work talk from me, but you can feel free to talk about yours."

The flicker had become a twinkle, and I realized I liked his blue eyes best when they twinkled.

"Sure," I said. I felt my cheeks suddenly flush, as if I'd just been asked out by my secret crush. Which I guess I had.

***

I don't know why, but I insisted on driving my own car. I don't think I wanted to know what it was like to ride inside a police car.

92

He told me how to get to his favorite restaurant—one I'd never heard of, so I thought *this ought to be good*—but the directions went in one ear and out the other, as my mother used to say. Any directions that have more than two steps always do that with me, and so I just followed him as intently as if he were leading me to a place where harm could never befall me—or my friends.

I soon learned Detective Culotta was just full of surprises, the first one being his restaurant of choice. As I drove behind him, noting he never went so much as a mile over the speed limit and—unlike everyone else in Chicagoland—never raced through an intersection at the sight of a yellow light, I saw vaguely familiar surroundings. And sure enough, he soon pulled into the parking lot of a restaurant called Mancino's. But the small building with the new facade was definitely the old Barney's, the hamburger joint where I worked in high school.

I decided it was maybe the subsequent coursing of nostalgia flooding my mind that made me feel all gooey and . . . well, young and flirty. I fought the urge to act on those feelings.

"This used to be a hamburger place called Barney's," I said, while we waited to be led to our table in the quiet establishment. "But that was a lifetime ago, Detective."

"Yeah? My friend Joe Mancino opened this last year. Steaks to die for. And by the way, call me Dennis."

"Okay, Dennis. I wonder if my boss knows about this place. He's all about steaks."

"Oh, he's not *all* about steaks." Dennis Culotta laughed heartily, and it was contagious.

"Yeah, Tom's pretty passionate about whatever he likes. Poker, too, I suppose."

"You got that right. How long have you been with him?"

The hostess came to lead us to our table before I could answer, and by the time we were seated with our menus, we found ourselves talking about the changes I'd seen in

Downers Grove over the decades. Dennis, I learned, had lived here only fifteen years.

He'd moved up from Indiana when he married a Chicago girl. "And she *was* a girl," he said, as if I might find the term offensive. "She was ten years younger than me and acted twenty years younger."

He shook his head, but I had the feeling the disgust he displayed was aimed more at himself than at her. I imagined he wasn't the type who was used to being guilty of poor judgment.

"Where is she now?" I asked, assuming she was no longer Mrs. Culotta.

"Don't know. We divorced six years ago. I heard she remarried." He had opened the large menu and appeared to be studying it as he spoke. But he sounded a little wistful, and it made me think it wasn't exactly what he had hoped for.

"Kids?" I asked.

"No. No kids. Although I would have liked that." I tried to imagine a couple of miniature Culottas running around with gun holsters and little black notebooks concealed under their Gymborees.

"Yeah, well, kids are nice," I said. Big revelation.

His eyes came over the top of the menu. "So what about you? How long have you been divorced?"

"About a year."

"Ah, you're just a rookie."

Before I could respond, a large man wearing a sparkling-white chef's jacket appeared at our table. His head was bald, his fat cheeks rosy, and his top lip covered by an unruly black mustache. He looked like he should have his picture on every pizza box in America.

"Dennis!" He extended a hand to be shaken.

Culotta rose instead and gave the guy a bear hug. "Joe!"

"So," Joe Mancino said, his arm still around Culotta's shoulders. "You finally got a girl to go out with you."

"This is Valerie," Culotta said.

I wasn't sure what pleased me more: Joe Mancino referring to me as a girl or the look of pleasure Culotta displayed while he introduced me.

"Pleased to know you, Valerie. Here, what are you doing with these?" He snatched our menus from us. "These are for the public. For friends, I cook something special." He snapped two fingers in the air, and a young waiter appeared. "Get a bottle of Laetitia Pinot Noir over here, pronto." The waiter disappeared, and at Joe's urging, Culotta took his seat.

"Where'd you meet this guy, Valerie?" Joe leaned close to me. "No, don't tell me. Just watch him; that's all I'm saying."

At some private joke known only to him, he burst into a gale of laughter, and before he left our table to head toward the kitchen, he gave Culotta's cheek a hearty pinch. It was an endearing sight and the first time I had seen Culotta caught a little off guard.

He placed his red napkin on his lap. "That was Joe."

"So I gathered. Impressive."

The young waiter appeared and poured our wine. A few minutes later he placed a plate of antipasto, big enough to feed half of Sicily, on the table. Before we had time to sample even a small portion, the waiter delivered two bowls of scampi nestled among creamy-white pasta ribbons.

"So how do you know Joe?" I took a sip of wine.

"We go back." He tucked the red napkin into the collar of his shirt and ate heartily.

"Indiana?"

"Come on, I thought we agreed to talk about you, not me."

I didn't point out that that wasn't our agreement at all. We'd just agreed not to talk about "the case."

But for some reason, from somewhere in the recesses of my addled brain, came the strangest response from me. "Barbara and Allen Craigmore," I said, as if announcing Academy Award winners.

"What?"

"Have you questioned—"

"Valerie, I thought we agreed not to discuss the case. I really just wanted to take the night off and have a little dinner."

"So you know about them?" I felt a little shocked at his lack of surprise. "You know Susan once worked for Allen and had an affair with him too—I'm sorry, that came out wrong. I meant as well as who-knows-how-many other men. I did *not* mean Larry James." I gulped my wine, wanting to bite off my tongue.

"Don't worry; I got it." He took a roll out of the basket on our table and began breaking it into small pieces.

"Did you know Allen Craigmore committed suicide?" I hoped that would get his attention.

He reached across for the butter dish and scooped a large chunk onto the end of his knife. "Yep."

"Well, good." I sat back in my chair. *Take the night off,* my ass. Dennis was definitely still on the clock and seemed to be doing a thoroughly good job of grilling me, without even asking any questions. "So, Dennis," I said, "have you seen any good movies lately?"

My role of police informant was over for the night.

CHAPTER THIRTEEN

When I walked into my apartment, I noticed I had four phone messages. That reminded me my cell phone was still turned off, and when I turned it back on, I saw I had six missed calls and two messages.

All from Kit, I learned.

After listening to her demands for me to call her back as soon as possible, I did just that.

"Val, what the—"

"Sorry, Kitty Kat. I'll explain, but we really, really need to talk."

"That's what I was trying to do, ya know. First, I have to fess up—"

"Fine. But you gotta hear me out too. I've been talking to Den—Detective Culotta—and he thinks you or Larry or both of you are lying."

"That's just it, Val. We are. At least I am."

I sighed, thinking my worst fears were about to come true. "Tell me, Kit. 'Cuz Culotta's wanting store receipts to prove we were shopping. I'm hoping you can *prove* you were at home watching *Desperate Housewives.*"

"I can't. Because I wasn't."

Suddenly I didn't have the energy to even sigh. So I simply waited for my friend to continue.

"I was out driving. After you left, and Larry didn't come home, I couldn't sleep. So I just went for a drive."

"Where'd you drive to?"

"Hell, I don't know. Just around. I nearly stopped by your place, but I knew you were probably sick of me by then." That part didn't ring true. I doubted Kit ever thought she could sicken anyone.

"Okay, the truth is," she continued, as if reading my thoughts, "I just wanted to be gone when Larry got home. You understand that, I know." That made more sense. I could recall feeling the same thing when my ex-husband was coming home from one of his many so-called late nights at the office. The last thing I wanted to do was be the little wife waiting at home for him.

"Yeah, I understand," I said. "But you should have told me. And by the way, whenever you feel like that, come over to my place. Don't drive around by yourself late at night."

"Thanks, Valley Girl. But I don't think there will be a next time."

Well, she'd fessed up to me; I had to return the favor. I dreaded turning my Kitty Kat into a mad tiger, but I had to do it. "Um, Kit?"

"Yeah, so what did you want to tell me?"

"I just had dinner with Dennis Culotta."

"You did *what?*"

"I said I had dinner with Dennis Culotta. We went to Mancino's. Remember Barney's when we were kids? Now it's Mancino's. It's nice, Kit—"

"Stop right there! You had dinner with Culotta? How in the hell did that happen?"

"It was crazy. He called me and asked if we could meet for coffee, and from there we went on to Barney's, I mean Mancino's. Remember how good the hamburgers—"

"Wait, wait. What the hell are you telling me? You were on a *date*?"

I had to stop and think about that. "No, no, it wasn't a *date*. He just wanted to ask me a few more questions, and so we had coffee, and then that turned into a dinner—"

"Valerie, has it escaped your mind that this man is investigating a murder? And ya know his number one suspect is my good-for-nothing husband."

"Well, not exactly . . ." I decided it probably wasn't a good time to point out that she and her good-for-nothing husband were running neck and neck in the suspect race.

"What did he say about me?" she asked.

"Well, he doesn't really seem convinced we were out shopping on Saturday night."

"Did he say that? Does he have some way to prove we weren't shopping? How can he prove it?"

"Calm down. He can't prove a thing. But he's very smart, Kit—"

"Oh, he's no Einstein, let me tell you. If he was doing his job, he'd be looking someplace else for what's-her-name's murderer instead of hounding poor Larry."

"What do you mean? Has he questioned Larry again?"

"Not face-to-face. But since Larry had a little fling with the skank, Culotta's surely checking out the ridiculous alibi he came up with."

"Look, we don't know that Larry had a fling. And for all we know, Larry really was at a bar—"

"And a church," she said.

"Okay, yes, and a church—"

"It's ridiculous, Val. I don't know why he didn't throw in the circus as well."

"Let's talk about this tomorrow, can we? I'm exhausted and really need a long, hot bath."

"Val, you didn't . . . did you?"

"I don't know what the hell you think we did. But it was just dinner. And now I need to go. I'll call you tomorrow."

I hung up on a disgruntled Kit. But I really had to mull over her new alibi. And more important, I wanted to relive my evening with Dennis Culotta. I turned on the faucet of my bathtub and poured a generous amount of vanilla-scented bubble bath under the running water.

Did Dennis Culotta really suspect Larry, or even Kit, of murdering Susan Reed? It was hard to tell if his invitation to dinner was because he found me fascinating or because he wanted to grill me about my friends. And even though he insisted we not talk about the case, it hadn't stopped me from blabbing everything I knew. But if *he* knew anything, he wasn't letting me in on it. So rather than feeling pleased that my tax dollars were being well spent, I felt disappointed that I still had no idea where his investigation was going.

As I slipped into the fragrant water, I completely forgot about Susan Reed and let my mind drift back to Mancino's.

When our meal was over, Culotta had tried to pay the bill, but Joe Mancino gave him a wounded look, followed by another bear hug, followed by a pinch on both cheeks. As Joe said good-bye to me, I braced for a similar pinch. But instead, he gently took my hand and kissed my fingertips. It was an elegant gesture from that giant who looked as if he could crush my hand as easily as if it were a clove of garlic.

At my car, Culotta and I said our good-byes. There was no touching. When I was safely buckled into my seat, he leaned into the open car, one hand on the roof of the Lexus, one hand on the door frame.

"Thanks for a nice evening, Valerie."

"Thank *you*," I said.

Then he leaned back and closed the door firmly. As I drove away, I noticed he remained standing in the parking lot and even waved as I turned the corner. I had the distinct impression he was going back inside for a nightcap with his ol' pal.

***

"You have a spring in your step, Val." This from Perry. He looked exceptionally dapper this morning in a navy-blue suit, expertly cut, with a silver vest underneath.

"And you look quite marvelous," I said.

"Why, thank you." He didn't quite nod in agreement, but it was implied. "By the way, a Dennis Culottes called for you. He left a number."

I took the pink slip Perry handed me.

"So, who is he? New client? Selling or buying?"

"It's Culotta. And neither. Just a guy I know."

I checked my watch. It was eight thirty. From the message, it appeared Culotta had called at eight. I had to admit I felt a little knot of excitement seeing his name, even if Perry had reduced him to a woman's divided skirt. I took my phone out of my purse and headed for the door. There were two missed calls, both from Detective Culottes, that I had apparently missed while I was charging my phone at home.

"Back in a few," I said to Perry, and then I returned to the privacy of my car, saying a silent thank you to the genius who invented cell phones.

Culotta answered after only one ring, and I took that to mean he was waiting by the phone.

"Hi," I said, hating how breathless I sounded.

"Valerie. Something I forgot to mention last night."

His tone caused me to straighten up immediately. My sweet image of Culotta with a red napkin tucked into his shirt was replaced by one of him poised and ready to handcuff someone.

"Okay," I said.

"Larry James's alibi doesn't check out."

"Huh?" I felt as breathless as I sounded.

"Yeah." I didn't think the pleasure I heard in his voice was from recalling our shared pasta. "The church crap?

Forget that; no one remembers him. And the bar? Someone possibly remembers seeing him around eleven o'clock or so, but can't say for sure when he got there."

"I see." I wasn't sure what he wanted me to do with that information.

"So, you find any receipts from your little shopping excursion?"

"I think I already told you. We didn't buy anything."

"Right." He stretched the word like a rubber band about to snap. "And I already told *you*, don't get dragged into anyone's dirty laundry."

"Why are you even telling me this?"

"Just want you to be up to speed, that's all."

"So now I'm up to speed. If you don't mind, I have a job to do, much like yourself. So I'm going to say good-bye."

"Okay, good-bye. And by the way, I had a lovely evening."

I ended the call and sat with the phone in my hand for a few minutes, not sure whether I was angry or thrilled. There was a lot to think about.

Why was Culotta giving me status updates? Were Larry and Kit really where they said they were? And why the hell would Perry wear a silver vest to work?

***

"Kit, I really wish you'd told me the truth from the beginning," I said. We were having lunch at Hofbrau, a cute little German restaurant in Naperville.

"I felt silly. And I wanted to protect you, Val."

We held our iced-tea glasses in midair and burst into laughter.

"Okay, okay." I put my glass safely back on the table. "That's possibly the most dramatic thing you've said all— well, this week at least."

"I didn't think you'd believe me. And then I started to worry that if I didn't tell you what I did, you'd come up with something much worse on your own. Let's face it, there's only so much *Desperate Housewives* any sane person can watch."

"Why wouldn't I believe you? I understand perfectly," I said. I had to stifle a whimper as I again remembered the overpowering need to be gone when my then-husband returned from a place he should never have been.

Kit grabbed her Dooney & Bourke and pulled out her wallet. "This is on me," she said.

I reached out and touched her arm. "You know you can always talk to me, right?"

She looked over at me and gave a sigh. "Valley Girl, I know that. Look, you're my best friend in the whole world. You know everything about me. But I just . . . I just had to be alone for a little while."

I nodded slowly. All the humiliation of my ex-husband's infidelities came flooding back. Most of it I had shared with Kit, but there were some things I had to keep to myself. I shuddered, remembering a lacy pair of women's panties I'd found scrunched up in the back seat of his car. I'd never told anyone that. I hadn't even brought it up to David. It was just too much.

"Okay," I said. "Got it." And I really did.

CHAPTER FOURTEEN

You'll never guess who I found on Facebook."

"Kit, I don't care if you found Elvis Presley. I told you I don't have time for that."

Speaking of time, I glanced at the bottom right-hand corner of my computer. Two o'clock. Kit must have raced home from our lunch and gotten right on her computer and Facebook. Which is exactly why I didn't want to get involved with it. I could tell she had become as addicted to it as Emily and Luke, who also kept hounding me to join or sign up or whatever it is you do with Facebook. I recalled their last visit and how they sat next to each other on the couch, one with eyes glued to an iPad, the other with eyes on a smartphone, while we all supposedly watched a movie together.

"Susan Reed. I found Susan Reed."

It took a minute to sink in, and then I spoke. "Okay, I do care. Just what are you seeing? And I thought you couldn't see anything if you weren't their friend?"

"Ya know we're all linked to Kevin Bacon, so I suppose it was only a matter of time before six degrees would lead me to Susan."

"You mean six degrees of separation?"

"Whatever. See, there are different levels of Facebook privacy, like some people let you see their stuff if you're a friend of a friend. And some people, like stupid, slutty Susan, let *everyone* see their stuff. Everyone on Facebook, at least. I don't know why I didn't think of it earlier, but I just decided to check—"

"Kit, I don't really care *how* you saw something about Susan Reed. I just want to know if it's anything good."

"Huh. Susan Reed? Something good? The two don't go together, Val."

"Okay then. Forget good. Did you find anything useful?" I was keeping an eye on my own computer screen, waiting for the website I needed to open so I could add a new listing.

"Not sure yet. I'm going through some pictures, and some of them have that stupid slut in them. I'll call you back when I'm done looking . . . That bitch!"

I figured she'd just seen something on her computer screen she didn't like, but I couldn't ask her. She'd hung up. I replaced my phone in its holder and tried to turn my thoughts back to my newest listing.

But it was too late. Kit had stolen my attention span for work like a pickpocket slipping a wallet away from its owner. I turned my computer off and stood to leave for the day.

"Leaving already, Valerie?"

It was Billie.

I turned and faced her. "Yep. I'm at a good stopping point." It's always a good stopping point when you can no longer concentrate, right? "Bye."

"Did I hear you say the name *Susan Reed*?" she spoke to my fleeing back.

I stopped in my tracks, not sure whether to reprimand her for eavesdropping or see if some sleuthing on her part had turned up some new information. After a brief hesitation, I pivoted and looked at her. Yep. She had something, all right. It was stamped on her face in her smug expression.

"Spill, Bill."

***

One-half hour and one bombshell later, I was on my way to see just what Kit and Facebook had to offer. I doubted it could match what Billie had served up. But halfway between my office and Kit's house, my phone rang. I knew better than to even try to decipher the number of the caller when I was driving.

"Valerie Pankowski," I answered.

"Mrs. Pankowski, this is Marjorie Reed. I hope you don't mind me calling."

It was startling enough to hear her name, but the shakiness of her voice made me even more uneasy. I pulled over to the curb, wanting to concentrate on what Marjorie had to say and also surmising I probably was not going to Kit's just yet, after all.

Sure enough, Marjorie had other ideas for me. "Do you think you could stop by sometime?" she asked, before I'd found my own voice.

"Yes, of course. What is it?"

"I'd rather talk about this in person, if that's okay with you. Can you come over?"

"When?" I asked, hoping both that she would say *now* and that she would give me more time to collect myself. I recalled our previous phone call and the fact that I still hadn't shared that information with Kit.

It also occurred to me for the first time that I certainly should have shared that phone call with Dennis Culotta. How had I not done that? It wasn't that I was trying to hide it from him. Or maybe I was, maybe I was afraid it would point right to Larry—or Kit. Oh, if only Marjorie Reed would tell me she'd learned the married man was not my pal Larry.

"Right now, if you can," she said.

I hesitated only a second before assuring her I'd be there in less than fifteen minutes.

***

As I pulled up to Marjorie Reed's shabby house, I noticed a crack in her venetian blinds snap shut. Was it me she was watching for? What was she so eager to tell me?

I felt like a Little Leaguer facing the Yankees. I should have brought Kit in on this. Then again, I knew Mrs. Reed wouldn't have had a word to say to my best friend.

The front door opened before I was even out of my car. I smiled at the woman whose infirmity made her look old beyond her years, and I marched up the walk to her. Maybe if I acted brave, I'd feel brave. We exchanged hellos as I entered the house.

She offered me the familiar floral chair and then used her cane to hobble over to her own spot on the couch, where a permanent impression on the cushion testified to the many hours she'd sat there. She heaved a loud sigh as she lowered herself and then leaned her cane next to her against the arm of the couch. "You must wonder why I wanted you to come."

I merely nodded at her understatement.

"I think I know who my daughter was having an . . . was in love with." She grasped her cane back in her hands, but it was obvious she was doing it for moral support and not because she had any intention of getting up off the couch. Movement seemed so difficult for her, I had a feeling she changed positions as little as possible. I wondered just what was wrong with her.

Maybe that's why I changed the subject. Or maybe I was afraid to hear what she was going to say next. "Are you feeling okay?" I pointed to her cane.

"Yeah. I mean, as good as ever, I guess. My hips bother me. I have lupus, you see. I don't know if it's that or the medicines I've taken for it, but my hips have been shot for some time. I have trouble getting around—or doing just about anything—without help."

She obviously felt sorry for herself, and who could blame her? "I'm sure you miss your daughter's help among many, many other—"

"Huh! She never helped me." Her eyes took on a troubled, faraway look, as if she were reliving an unpleasant experience. "She was too selfish to give my problems a second thought—a first thought, even. The truth is, I'm better—" Suddenly she quit speaking, and her eyes registered a return to the present once again. "I didn't ask you to come here for a pity party." She gave a short, joyless laugh.

"Why *did* you ask me here?"

"Like I said, I think I might know who Susan's . . . love interest was, and I thought you would want to know. If you don't already." She wore a look of satisfaction, one that was almost smug, in fact.

I was afraid of her answer.

But she gave it anyway. "Mr. James. Larry James. Susan's boss. No wonder his wife was so mean to me. As if it's my fault they—"

"What makes you think that? What makes you think it's him?" My voice had lost any hint of sympathy I might have been showing her before. I squirmed in my chair and felt myself beginning to perspire. I was afraid to hear what kind of proof she was going to present, afraid it would be convincing.

"Oh, I can just tell by the way he's treating me. He came to see me, that night after I called you on the phone."

"But did he say he and Susan were having an affair?"

"Not in so many words, but he said a lot of wonderful things about my daughter, sweet things. He saw a Susan I surely never saw. Love is blind." She gave a snort. "It seems to me only a man who was—anyway, he gave me a lot of money too. I don't think people just go around doing that with dead people's relatives unless those dead people were special—"

"Oh, is that all? His wife *told* him to give you some money, to help you out; she felt sorry—"

Marjorie Reed tightened her grip on the cane again as she interrupted me. "A mother knows. And also I found a note in her apartment. It was obviously from someone she was involved with, and I matched the handwriting against Mr. James's check. I'm sure they were the same."

"What did the note say? Do you still have it?"

"No, I tore it up. I didn't want the police or anyone to see it and think badly of Susan. It was clear that it was someone who was sneaking to see my daughter; it told her when he could get away and where to meet him. Why, I think he probably passed it to her at work, like a naughty schoolboy passing a note to his girlfriend in class."

I couldn't tell if she found that disgusting or cute. Her tone of voice indicated the former, but her look was almost tender. Maybe she was having a fond memory of her own past with a married man, Susan's father.

I didn't mind interrupting her reverie. "Well, I'm far from convinced that the note was from my friend Larry James," I said. "And the police would not be happy to know you tampered with evidence."

Was I trying to scare her off, keep her from reporting anything that could incriminate Larry? Or Kit? Was *I* tampering with evidence? Or intimidating a witness?

"That's why I'm telling just you, not the police. I thought you'd want to know." She sounded surprised to think she might be wrong.

But she was.

CHAPTER FIFTEEN

I sat at a Starbucks and sipped my mocha that had grown lukewarm. It was the first place I'd found where I could be alone—or at least not with Kit—after leaving Marjorie Reed's house. My phone beeped from within my purse like a spoiled child wanting my attention. I reluctantly pulled it out, knowing the beep meant I had a message.

I was wrong. I had three messages. All from Kit telling me to get over to her house. To rush over to her house. And finally, to get my ass over to her house. I slowly drained the last of my mocha. Kit clearly wanted to share what she had found on Facebook. And I really wanted to see it. But I wasn't sure I wanted to see *her*. In the past few hours, I had been given too much information, none of which I wanted to share with Kit. And all of which made me uneasy about Larry again.

Foremost, if not first, there was Marjorie Reed's claim of finding a note from Larry. I still doubted it was from him, if it even existed at all. But why would she go to the trouble of making up such a story to incriminate Larry? Since her daughter's death, he had been nothing but generous to her. So why pick on him? Why even mention the note? Was it her way of steering me away from the murderer? Someone she knew and was covering for? Herself, even? She said she hadn't told the police, and I wondered why not. If she was going to the trouble of incriminating Larry, surely she would have told the police rather than me.

Suddenly the *Law & Order* theme song burst through my thoughts. I watched in awe as my phone vibrated on the table in time to the music.

I didn't plan to answer it, but the middle-aged thug sitting at the next table (who clearly was not a music lover) gave me a look that said *you better pick it up, lady, or eat it*. I picked it up.

"Val, what the hell are you doing? I need you to see this. Get over here."

"I just have a few things to wrap up." I smiled sweetly at the guy next to me. He threw a mean look my way, as if we were in the public library and I was speaking too loudly. "I'm leaving the office in ten minutes. Promise." Another lie to my best friend. And what if she'd already called the office and been told I wasn't there? I shook my head in disgust at myself.

"Okay, hurry. You are gonna love this."

I dropped the phone into my purse. She thought *she* had news. I inched my way past the crowded tables, careful to avoid upsetting the gangster wannabe who was now deep into his *Guns & Ammo* magazine. Kit's proclamation that it was a dangerous world came flooding back to me. But at Starbucks?

I drove slowly to her house, taking the longest route I could find. I needed time to convince myself that the right thing to do was not tell her about my conversation with Marjorie Reed. Since I really didn't believe it anyway, I saw no reason to give Kit any more ammunition.

But then there was my little chat with Billie. That might be another thing entirely. I still needed to decide what to do with that information.

***

I'd had a feeling when I said, "Spill, Bill," she would do just that. And I should have known I wouldn't like what she would spill.

"Val, I'm not a gossip," she'd said. "You know that, right?"

I sat back down in my desk chair and thought about how to respond. Technically, Billie doesn't gossip. Not in the normal sense of the word. But she knows a lot of people, and a lot of stuff, and with a little prodding on my part, I have often gained useful information from her. But I wouldn't call it gossip. Not exactly.

"Val, you do believe that, right?"

I gave in and nodded in agreement. Clearly, it was the only way she was going to tell me whatever the hell it was she had to say.

"Okay," she said, as if we had just agreed on the rules for a duel at dawn and she was about to slap my cheek with her glove to get things started. "When I heard you talking about Susan Reed—"

I pursed my lips.

"Valerie, this office is a cracker box. I'd have to be stone-deaf not to hear you."

"Okay, it's small. We hear stuff."

"So." Billie sat down in the visitor's seat across from my desk. "I thought you might be interested to know that I saw her in a restaurant one night not long before she was murdered."

"What restaurant?" As if her naming the establishment would prove anything.

"Zambino's." She sounded as if I should be surprised. "Do you know it?"

"Go on." I nodded like I had my own table there. Of course I didn't know Zambino's. It was new, and reportedly they had live jazz and fabulous drinks with names no one could remember. The closest I would come to Zambino's was reading about it in the arts section of the newspaper.

"So, anyway, I was there one Friday night with a few girls. Girls' night out." She stopped talking for a second, staring at me hard, as if I might not get the concept.

"Girls get together at night and go out. I got it, Bill. What's the significance?"

"Okay. Here's the thing. Susan Reed was there. And she wasn't alone."

I felt a little chill creep over me. Quickly, I began straightening an already-straightened pile of contracts on my desk. "Hmm," I said. "Well, no law against that, Bill."

"Aren't you curious who she was with?"

Normally, I love Billie. I really do. She has helped me out of so many work-related jams and probably saved the lives of Tom and Perry by preventing me from killing them. But right now she was just plain annoying. "Okay, so tell me, for Pete's sake."

"Larry James."

"Really."

"Yes." She leaned in close to me. "And I have to tell you, they were awfully chummy, the two of them."

"And just what the hell do you expect me to say? They were business associates. They worked closely together. What is wrong with that? Do you know how many times I've had dinner at an overpriced restaurant with Tom Haskins? Is that wrong too?"

A little smirk appeared on her face. "Val, I never said it was wrong. I know you and Tom have been out in the evening. And probably he's kissed you on the cheek and held your hand, and put his arm around you—"

"Damn right he has." And it was true. Tom and I had been in similar circumstances. When I was in the throes of my painful divorce, I had more than once used Tom's shoulder as a place to rest my head and cry. But it was hardly what I would call romantic.

"Okay then," Billie said. "So it was nothing. All I'm saying is, I saw the two of them, and I know Kit is your best friend—"

"And Larry too—"

"Okay, and Larry too. It's just what I saw. It has to go no further. I'm sure Kit knows all about it, anyway."

***

As I drove to Kit's, I wondered why Billie had waited to tell me about seeing Larry and Susan together. Deciding there could be any number of reasons, I reminded myself that she's not a liar. If she said she saw them, then she did. How she interpreted it was another matter entirely. Either way, this little nugget didn't need to be tossed Kit's way. Not yet. Her gun was waiting to be loaded, and this would be the bullet with Larry's name on it.

My phone rang again when I was halfway to Kit's house. I began to form an all-too-automatic lie about still being at the office, certain the caller was Kit, but then I just let it go to voice mail. It had occurred to me how close I was to the Downers Grove police station, and I decided to make my way there. I had no idea why, but it seemed preferable to going to Kit's and not telling her all I had found out.

I pulled into the parking lot, surveying a row of cars in search of Dennis Culotta's. It was a large, dark sedan in need of a car wash. I steered my car into the empty spot next to it. The other four cars in the lot all displayed the emblem of the Downers Grove Police Department. But Culotta's car was unmarked, unless you counted the words written in the grime on his back bumper. *I wish my wife was this dirty.* I smiled to myself, wondering if the author had known he was violating police property.

A desk sergeant pointed down the corridor and sent me in the direction of Dennis Culotta. He was alone in the detectives' room, sitting at one of four desks, a phone in his right hand and a pen in his left. Because he was not wearing a jacket, I saw a holster and gun strapped on his right shoulder. Somehow it looked chic against his crisp white shirt. He looked up as I stood in the doorway and motioned for me to come in and take a seat. He showed no surprise, as if he had summoned me and I had come running.

"Good," he said into the phone. "Thanks; I'll be waiting." He put down the phone and leaned forward on the desk, rubbing his hands together. "Valerie. What's up?"

I sat down and wondered the same thing. *What* was *up? Why was I here?*

"Oh, you know. I was in the neighborhood. Just passing by. Thought I'd see some of my tax dollars at work." I chuckled, but he merely leaned back in the chair and refused to share my joke.

"Okay, ma'am. This is the detectives' office. As you can see, I'm the only one here right now. The others are on stakeout or arresting people."

"They left you in charge of the phones?"

"Yes. As you could tell when you came in, I was busy doing police work."

"Impressive."

"You bet. I was speaking to a Mr. Chin. Local guy. No priors. Clean sheet. We were discussing egg foo yong and bird's nest soup."

I stared blankly at him, but suddenly a wide grin spread across his face. "Dinner, Valerie. Or late lunch. Whatever the hell time it is. Mr. Chin delivers."

"Oh, that's good."

"I can call back and double the order."

"No. Really, I have stuff to do. I was just passing by."

"So you said."

"And I was wondering if you have any leads in the case."

He leaned forward. He picked up a pencil and tapped the eraser end on the desk. "Valerie, I'm not sure I can pass on police information to a civilian. Don't think that would be right. But how about you? You got any leads you can pass on to me?"

"Of course not," I said. I was suddenly filled with a desire to find out if Marjorie Reed had shared her note story with him. "But I was visiting with Susan's mother."

"Yeah? And how is she doing?"

"She's fine. Well, as fine as you can be when your daughter has just been murdered. You know, she was babbling about stuff, and I wonder if she isn't a bit . . . well, a bit . . ."

"Nuts?"

"No, not nuts. Well, not exactly. She said some stuff that didn't make sense. Have you spoken to her recently?" Any guilt I felt at claiming that Marjorie Reed was less than stable quickly evaporated when I recalled her lame attempt to pin something on Larry.

He didn't answer for a moment but increased the speed of the tapping pencil. His eyes bore into mine. "Is there something I should know?"

I wondered if he could hear my heart beating. I knew I could. What in the hell *was* I doing here? If anyone was nuts, it was me.

"Dennis, I don't know anything. And I should go." I stood up and hooked my purse over my shoulder. It felt as if we had matching holsters.

He rose too, and I realized I'd forgotten how tall he was. How blue those damn eyes were. "Valerie. If you have any information concerning a crime, you realize it is your duty to report it. Right? Withholding information is a serious business."

"Yes, of course I know that." I turned to leave. "It was nice seeing you."

"Yeah, remember what I said. If there's something I should know, you better tell me now."

"Right." I took a step toward the door. "Well, there is something."

He had a smile on his face; one of his front teeth was a little crooked, but it matched his overall ruggedness. "Tell me."

"Okay. You might want to check your back bumper. A little crime has definitely been committed."

As I headed back down the corridor, I heard him say, "I'll call you. We'll do dinner."

Again, it wasn't exactly the most romantic proposal I've ever had, and he certainly seemed to take a lot for granted. But it would do.

CHAPTER SIXTEEN

Kit opened her front door before I was out of my car, and she began yelling at me when I wasn't even far enough up her long, winding sidewalk to hear her. But I could make out the gist of it immediately and then the actual words. "What the—?"

"Kit, I have a good reason for being so late." Okay, so I had to come up with something—something I was willing to share with her.

"Yeah? I'm waiting." But she didn't wait more than the few seconds it took her to say, "What good reason could you possibly have for putting off what I'm about to show you?"

What she was about to show me was obviously so good that her mood lifted visibly—and audibly—by just speaking those last six words. It lifted so much that she dismissed my excuse before I even finished giving it.

"I decided to stop by and see Detective Culotta, since it was on my way here, to see if there was more he could tell me—us. But there wasn't; he just—"

"Screw Culotta. Not literally, of course. Then again . . ." Her devilish grin attested to her good mood. Whatever she'd found on Facebook made it impossible for her to stay mad or even irritated at me right now, no matter how late I was, no matter that I'd talked to Culotta without her. Again.

I followed her upstairs to the bedroom that used to be their son's, a room Kit has turned into her office, even though the only office-type work she does is pay bills. She also, come to find out, trolls Facebook. A Chicago Bears pennant hanging above the closet door gave the only hint to the room's past life as a teenage boy's sanctuary. Kit had two chairs placed in front of the sleek glass-and-metal desk that held her laptop. She guided me to the black leather ergonomic chair on rollers and then sat down on the dining room chair she'd brought up for the occasion.

She tapped a key to dismiss her screen saver—a wedding photo of their son and his bride taken with Kit and Larry—and in its place appeared a screen with a photo of Susan Reed in the upper left-hand corner. I barely had time to notice a mane of straight black hair and a red ruffled blouse before Kit began paging down. "I want you to start from the beginning, though thank God I didn't read them in chronological order," she said.

"What are you talking about?"

"Patience, Val. Patience is a virtue; didn't your mom tell you that?" Spoken by the most impatient woman I've ever met. And if only she knew what my mom really thinks of her, not that my mother bothers to hide her disdain that well. But Kit's too sure of herself to ever seem to notice any negative vibes coming her way from my mom—or anyone else. Kinda the opposite of me, whom she has more than once accused of being too sensitive.

So I sat patiently while she paged down, down, down, then back up, and then down again. While she searched for the right spot, she multitasked, resuming her sales pitch for Facebook where she'd left off earlier that afternoon. "Val, I don't know why you are so stubborn. See how easy this is?

You can connect with so many people this way. Even the dearly departed." Her laugh sounded macabre. "Here, start reading here." She tapped the computer screen with a French-manicured fingernail.

But before I could scoot in to read anything, she began to read it out loud herself. "*Sending my love your way, L.*"

My stomach churned, and I pushed my way in to read the words myself. I saw what it actually said, with the built-in name in bold blue letters preceding the words Susan had posted:

Susan Reed *Sending my love your way, L.*

How could Kit be smiling? Wasn't this the proof she was looking for, that Susan and Larry had a thing goin' on?

But smiling she was, as she repeatedly flipped up the screen and, apparently choosing only a few of many such posts as a sampling for me, read aloud, "*Wondering why you aren't calling me, L. Growing dangerously impatient, L.* Then there's this one: *Family is everything to me.*"

Kit turned toward me and raised her eyebrows, as if I might shed some light on what Susan had meant. I shrugged and returned my eyes to the computer screen. As far as I could tell, Larry was being incriminated more with each entry Kit read, with each "L" as in Larry that she read aloud. Was that what was making her so happy? Proof that her husband had been having an affair with Susan Reed?

"*Coming to a theater, er, coffee shop near you soon,*" Kit continued reading Susan's Facebook posts. "*Make that coming to your office.*"

"To his office? She *worked* in his office," I said. "Of course she'd be—"

"Exactly. That should be your first inkling that maybe 'L' isn't Larry." Suddenly I understood why Kit was beaming. She was showing me vindication, not incrimination. But I was no longer so sure Larry deserved vindication. In fact, quite the opposite.

"More of the same, more of the same." She was whipping upward with the Facebook pages. Then I saw this:

Susan Reed *I'm serious, Liam. We need to talk. I know you are reading this.*

"Liam?" I asked.

"Exactly. Liam! Not Larry; Liam!"

Well, no wonder she was glad she had read the entries starting with the most recent. She'd known right away the "L" stood for Liam. How like her to get a kick out of watching me think the "L" was for Larry.

And if it weren't for what I'd heard from Marjorie Reed and Billie, and what both Kit and I had heard from Ellen Parkinson, I *would* have rejoiced along with her at Larry's proven innocence. But as it was, I had to fake it. "Well, you must be so relieved."

"No *I told you so*? What's up, Val? You were Larry's biggest advocate, and all you can manage is *you must be relieved*?"

"I mean, I'm just glad you're relieved." I rolled back from the desk and stood up. I hated Facebook more than ever. Oh, I was glad it was bringing my friend relief, or more accurately, pure joy, over her husband's exoneration. But I also *trusted* Facebook less than ever because I was quite certain something *was* up between Larry and Miss Susan. Maybe Liam was Susan's pet name for Larry. Maybe—

"Val, what is it? Do you know something you're not telling me?"

I had a split second to decide whether to allow myself the luxury of the confession I so wanted to make. But it was just too soon. I needed to talk to Larry again first. "Kit, when have I ever not told you something?"

"There was the time—never mind, Valley Girl; let's go celebrate. I have a bottle of vintage pinot with our name on it."

I followed her to the kitchen, and once we were sipping our wine, I spoke without really thinking. Big mistake. "Well, Liam is a pretty unusual name, and Susan's circle of people wasn't that big. We might be able to find out just who this Liam is."

Kit furrowed her brow. "Why? Why would we want to bother? Val, you don't still think we need to prove Larry's innocent, do you? What's up with you? You were the one trying to convince me—"

"I don't think any such thing. Sorry. I just don't shift gears as fast as you, that's all. I was still thinking in terms of solving her murder. But you're right. That's not our job."

"It could be, ya know."

"What? Why?"

"Whaddya mean *why*? Why the hell does Larry spend hours chasing a golf ball? Because it's *fun*. And it would be fun to try to solve her murder. Besides, we've proved pretty good at it, ya know."

Suddenly I shared Kit's feeling of relief. At least a little. Surely *she* didn't have anything to do with Susan's demise or she wouldn't suggest we try to solve the murder. Not that I ever seriously entertained that notion (did I?). Still, I knew Kit might not like the truth after she dug it up. But how could I tell her that? "Count me out. Larry didn't do it; that's all I care about. I'm a Realtor, remember? *Not* a detective."

"What about me? What am I? Just a housewife?"

"Oh, Kitty Kat, if there's anyone who's *not* just a housewife, it's you. Cheers." I held my wineglass in the air until she finally reached up with her own and clinked it.

***

As I climbed into my car, I debated whether to go to Larry's office. Uneasy about driving any more than necessary after drinking even one glass of wine, I decided against it. Instead, I backed out of their driveway and then called his cell phone.

"Larry, sorry to disturb you—you are at your office, aren't you?"

"Yes, Val, why?"

"Never mind. We need to talk."

"Maybe next week, after tax season?"

I didn't answer until I completed my left turn at a busy intersection. "No, not next week. Tonight."

He sighed. "Tonight. Okay, tonight. I'll stop by before I go home. But that's not going to make your best friend very happy."

"I don't think either one of us wants my best friend to know we're meeting, Larry. Not yet, anyway."

The silence that followed made me wonder if we were disconnected. "Larry? You there?"

"Yes, I'm here."

"Don't say anything to Kit, okay?"

"Of course not."

And then there was a silence so loud I knew we were disconnected.

I drove home in dread.

***

I hadn't been home long when the buzzer rang into my apartment from the building's outer lobby. That alone deepened my suspicions about Larry. Why was he hightailing it over, ditching his all-important tax work, unless he was scared about what I had to say?

Deep in thought about that, I pushed the buzzer in my apartment long and hard, giving him ample time to make it through the door to the inner lobby that would have come unlocked at my bidding. Only when I heard a loud rap on my apartment door did it occur to me that I should have made sure it *was* Larry and not some modern-day Downers Grove version of the Boston Strangler.

But it was quite the opposite.

It was the police.

It was, to be specific, Detective Dennis Culotta.

"Oh. It's you." I felt a sudden urge to throw up, and then the nausea was replaced by stomach cramps and I began to perspire—an all-too-common condition of late. "What are you doing here?" I stood in place, the door still only partially open, as if by refusing entry I could make him disappear—before Larry really did arrive.

"Aren't you going to invite me in?"

"Oh! Detective—Dennis—you should have called first. I . . ."

"You what?" His eyes pierced mine, and I knew there was no lie I could tell him that would pass for the truth.

So I said nothing.

"You didn't announce yourself when you popped into my office today. Fair's fair." His blue eyes twinkled, but I was in no mood to appreciate them. I had to get him out of here before Larry showed up.

But he was making that difficult, the way he just pushed—albeit gently—past me and made his way to my couch, sinking into it as if he intended to stay for a good long while.

"Is this a social call?" I asked.

"Why? You gonna report me for police misconduct if it isn't?" Again, the twinkle that had charmed me before simply scared me now. Who knew *what* he would suspect if Larry appeared. *When* Larry appeared.

"Seriously, Dennis, this is a bad time for me. I've had a longer-than-long day." I stayed by the front door, as if I could will his return to it. Then I would push him out as gently as he'd pushed his way in, and I'd pray to God he'd get out of the neighborhood before Larry pulled onto my street. I glanced at my own watch. It was only nine o'clock, still early for Larry, if his recent schedule, at least according to Kit, was any indication. Then again, he no longer had Susan—

My thoughts were interrupted by the sound of my buzzer. The relentless sound of my buzzer, as I continued to ignore it.

"Aren't you going to answer that?" Dennis Culotta asked. The twinkle disappeared from his eyes, rendering them a different shade of blue. A darker blue. A probing blue.

I avoided his gaze and ditched the subtlety. "Really, you need to leave, Dennis. And next time, call first."

"What if the next time isn't a social call?"

Was he mocking me? Threatening me? I didn't really care, so great was my relief as he stood up.

But sheer terror replaced the relief when I opened the door for him, for what I hoped would be his hasty exit.

There, on the other side of the threshold, looking trapped at the sight of Dennis Culotta, stood my friend Larry James.

CHAPTER SEVENTEEN

L arry!"
"Val."
"Mr. James."
"Detective Culotta."
"Larry."

Detective Culotta shot me a look of amusement. "Okay, let's not go through that again. I think we've established who we are."

"Larry," I said again, apparently not ready to end the round-robin. "What in the world are you doing here?"

"You said to drop by."

I stared at him. I felt numb. Should I introduce him again? Detective, meet Prime Suspect.

"Taxes, Val," I heard Larry say. "Remember? You wanted me to look over your return. You said to drop by any time."

I was so relieved, I nearly collapsed. But instead, I grabbed his arm and pulled him into the room. "Do you believe this guy?" I faked a grin that would have guaranteed me Miss Congeniality in a beauty pageant. "An accountant who makes house calls."

Culotta grimaced. "Yeah, he's a regular TurboTax on legs."

"Larry, sit down," I said. "I appreciate your coming over. Detective, will you excuse us?"

"Sure; I wouldn't want to delay a citizen's paying her taxes."

"Right." I let out a laugh that was way too loud.

The two men passed each other in the tiny space between my front door and the couch, staring at each other like a bull and a bullfighter.

"So," I said to Culotta when he reached the doorway, "was there something in particular you wanted?"

"It'll keep. Have a nice evening, ma'am." He turned to give Larry one last look.

When I closed the door behind him, I leaned against it and had to reach for the doorknob to stop myself from sliding down to the floor.

Larry stared at me from the couch as he loosened his tie. His expression said something like *what in the hell was the lead detective on Susan Reed's murder case doing in your living room?*

"Well, that was awkward," I said, when I was finally able to speak.

Larry took off his jacket. "Got a beer?"

Relieved to have somewhere to go, I took the few steps to my kitchen and took two Heinekens from the refrigerator. I had a passing thought, as I unscrewed the caps, that it was strange I even had beer in my apartment. I probably hadn't bought beer more than twice in the past thirty years, but on a recent trip to the grocery store, I had plunked a six-pack into my cart.

I handed one bottle to Larry and took a major swig from the other. I had forgotten how good cold beer tasted. "So, Larry." I took a seat at the other end of the couch. "We need to talk."

He took a long swallow and turned a little to face me. "Er, don't you think you should first tell me what that was about?"

"Huh? Oh, that." I waved my Heineken toward the door. "You mean him?"

"Yeah, I mean him. You insist I come over and when I get here, I find you entertaining the police."

"Oh no, it's not what you think. I had no idea he was coming over."

"Val, you're not seeing him, are you?" Larry's eyes widened.

"What do you mean? Of course not. Why would you think that? He probably was just in the neighborhood. Look, I had dinner with him last night, okay? It was nothing. We just sort of bumped into each other, and one thing led to another—"

"Dinner? You had dinner with him?" He took another long pull on the bottle of beer, and I suddenly felt like a rat for cheating on him with Culotta.

"It was nothing—"

"I don't like him."

"Well, no, of course not. Why would you? But he's . . . interesting. Once you get him away from the job."

"Still don't like him."

"I know, Larry. But really, we have much more important things to discuss than Dennis Culotta."

"Okay, so let's discuss."

***

I told him about my visit to Marjorie Reed. I told him about the note she had supposedly found and then destroyed. I told him she claimed he wrote it.

He gave a short laugh, put his beer on the coffee table, and rubbed his hands over his face.

"You didn't write a note, did you?" I asked.

"No."

"That's what I thought. But what worries me is why she wants to incriminate you."

He retrieved his beer, took a couple of long swallows, and then returned it to the table. "She's a crazy bitch, Val, like her fucking daughter."

I was shocked. I don't think I'd ever heard Larry—dear, sweet, mild-tempered Larry—utter such harsh words about anyone. "I thought you liked Susan."

"I did. But I was a fool, Val. I didn't really know her at all. Got another one of these?" He waved his empty bottle, and I hurried to the kitchen for a full one.

"That night," he said slowly, "that night she died? I told you I was at a church, and that part was true. I was at a church. But I never went inside. I went there to meet someone. Do you know who Liam Fitzpatrick is?"

I nodded. Our notorious Chicago politicians are as well-known to any citizen who reads the front page of the *Chicago Tribune* as the Bears are to those who read the sports page. The Fitzpatrick dynasty was as famous as that of the Daleys. As a state senator, Richard Fitzpatrick had earned a reputation more for influence than integrity. Upon his death, a few years back, his son Liam was elected to the seat.

Liam. Ohmygosh. *Liam*, as in Kit's Facebook discovery. Could there be a connection, or was it a mere coincidence? After all, Liam was an Irish name, and there were plenty of Irish guys in the Chicago area.

"You were sitting outside the church with Liam Fitzpatrick?" I asked. It seemed as unlikely as if he had been saying the rosary with the pope.

He nodded. "Does that surprise you?"

"Yes. I didn't know you were friends with our state leaders."

"I'd hardly call it friends. But I've come across Liam a few times. Republican fund-raisers, boring rubber-chicken dinners. You know how Kit loves her Republican party."

"Don't remind me." Like all good friends with opposing views on major subjects, Kit and I stay away from politics. She is a red-state kind of gal, whereas I keep my options open, straddling the line between red and blue.

"He's not a bad guy," Larry said, "at least if you compare him to his father."

I nodded, not familiar enough with either the father or son to comment.

Larry continued. "Okay, here's the thing. Turns out Richard Fitzpatrick was Susan's father."

It took a while for that to sink in. My mind struggled with the image of that handsome, stately man having an affair with Marjorie Reed. "You're kidding," I said. But clearly he wasn't. "So that means Liam was Susan's half brother."

"Got it in one." Larry almost smiled. "Somehow—I swear I don't know how—Susan dug up her roots."

"She probably found out from her mother."

"Possibly, though she told me her mother refused to discuss it. And no wonder. I don't think Marjorie wanted to rock the boat. Turns out Richard Fitzpatrick, being such an honorable guy, had been sending Marjorie money every month up until his death. When he died, the money well dried up. His family knew nothing of Marjorie or Susan. But somehow Susan found out who her father was. She was never shy about getting what she wanted, and I'm guessing she wanted back pay plus a little increase. When Liam turned her down, she wasn't happy, and her badgering turned into blackmail."

So Kit's big find of the "L" on Facebook did make complete sense. "You mean Marjorie knew what her daughter was doing, but didn't want to go public?"

"Probably."

"But how did you learn all this? I'm guessing Susan didn't tell you."

"Actually, she did. Not long after she started working for me, she told me she was trying to find out who her father was and wanted my help. But I didn't have a clue how she should, or even *whether* she should, go about searching.

Next thing I know, Liam wants to meet with me. So we met in front of the church, and he asked if there was any way I could calm Susan down."

"What did you tell him?"

"What could I tell him? Susan was a headstrong girl. But I told Liam I'd see what I could do. I don't think I sounded very convincing. And as it turned out, I never got the opportunity. After Liam and I had our little chat, we went our separate ways. I went to the bar. I don't know where he went. But as they say, the rest is history. Susan was murdered that night, and I never got a chance to speak to her again."

"What were you planning to do?"

"Good question. Hence the bar and one too many drinks. I guess I wanted to warn her. The Fitzpatricks are not a family to mess with. Even by Chicago standards, they are corrupt. Liam has huge political aspirations. Plus, he's big in his Catholic church, and a little sister born out of wedlock to his father wouldn't have exactly thrilled the congregation. Not to mention how it would tarnish his father's legacy. Truth is, when it comes to political power, he's not half the man his father was, and riding his daddy's coattails is part of his gig."

I could see Larry's bottle was almost empty again, and I went back to my fridge for another. When I returned, I remained standing and forced myself to ask him what I had to ask him. "Larry, were you having a thing with Susan?"

He looked up at me, his face weary. "Val. How many times? I was not having an affair with Susan Reed. I liked her, yes, in the beginning. She had a spunkiness about her. She was tough. Wanna hear something funny?"

"Always." I took my seat again at the end of the couch.

"She kinda reminded me of Kit at that age. You know, that bravado Kit was born with. I've always admired that about Kit. She's never afraid of anything."

I almost told Larry that if he planned on living for the foreseeable future, he better not share his comparison with

Kit. But surely he knew that. I took a sip of my own half-finished beer and then heaved a big sigh. "Okay, Larry, since we are dishing here, let me tell you what I know. Two people have told me they've seen you and Susan having cozy dinners."

He didn't look alarmed; in fact, he looked almost bored with the subject.

But still, he asked, "Who?"

"Ellen Parkinson, for one. Actually, she said lunch, not dinner, and I think she could have been drunk at the time. So she probably doesn't count."

"And the other?"

"Billie Ludlow, from my office. You remember Billie, right?"

He nodded, a little less bored this time.

"She said she saw you and Susan having dinner at Zambino's."

"True. We were there one night. I told you, Susan wanted my help. I was her shoulder to cry on. We were together more than those two times. Funny thing was, that last time, we were kind of celebrating. Susan told me she couldn't explain but that she'd found out who her father was and even discovered she had an inheritance coming. At least she was telling the truth, sort of."

"You didn't insist she tell you who her father was? After you'd been helping her?"

"I told you, I didn't really help her. I didn't know how to go about something like that. I knew Kit would and almost suggested Susan talk to her. But somehow I knew they were a little too much alike. I didn't want to end up in the middle of that. So I just listened to her a few times, about how hard it had been to grow up without a father and to not even know who her father was, and how her mother was a selfish bitch."

"Funny. Her mom seems to have thought the same about *her*. Yet they weren't completely estranged." I sank back on the couch.

"I don't think Susan dared to alienate her mother completely because I think she always hoped she'd tell her the truth. And I guess she finally did."

"Hmm. Well, I'm just glad you weren't having an affair. I never really believed you were." And I don't think I did. Not *really*.

"Val, you've known me a long time. I admit some guys go off the rails, but you know me. I love that crazy wife of mine. I just got a little too close to Susan, even though it was nothing romantic. Only problem I seem to have is convincing Kit of that."

I thought of the picture on Susan's table and doubted an absence of romantic feelings on her part. But I believed Larry about his own intentions. "Actually, I think you are off the hook, with Kit at least." I told him about Kit's Facebook discovery, and he smiled.

"You two are quite the detectives."

"Hey, that was all Kit, not me. I wouldn't know Facebook from face paint." It sounded like a remark my mother would make, and we both chuckled. "Ask her about it when you get home; she'll be glad to show you how clever she is, I'm sure."

He finished his beer and stood up. "Speaking of which, I guess I better go." He grabbed his jacket. "You're a good pal, Valerie Pankowski. I'm glad I told you all this stuff. I feel so much better." He put his arms around me and gave me a hug. "But do me a favor. Be careful with that detective. He likes you, it's easy to see. I don't want you hurt."

Culotta's face suddenly appeared before me, and I released myself from Larry's grip. "You've got to tell him everything you just told me," I said. "Don't you see? It will clear you completely. The police have to know all about Liam and his father; they—"

"Hey, Val, how stupid do you think I am? Culotta already knows."

***

I felt jubilant after Larry left, my shaky faith in my good friend completely restored. I had a nagging feeling, however, that Culotta had let me down. Cheated on me somehow. How dare he know stuff and not tell me?

As I gathered the empty beer bottles from the coffee table, my phone rang, and I realized for the umpteenth time how useless caller ID is for me since I rarely have my reading glasses handy. Maybe I need one of those chains to wear around my neck. I set the bottles down on the kitchen counter and picked up the phone. "Hello?"

"So how'd the taxes come out?"

It was Culotta. I walked to the window with the phone to my ear, expecting to see him leaning nonchalantly under a streetlight with his phone to *his* ear. Of course there were no streetlights within my line of vision, and no sign of him, but I still pictured him watching me from somewhere. "I've got a couple of Heinekens in the fridge. Want one?"

"Are you trying to bribe an officer of the law?"

"Dennis, I have one question. Why didn't you tell me you knew all about Liam Fitzpatrick? And why haven't you arrested him?"

"That's two questions. But the answer is the same for both: none of your business."

"But I've been so worried about Larry; you could have let me know you had cleared him."

"Who said I cleared him?"

"But surely the evidence—"

"Whoa! Listen to me, Valerie Pankowski, and listen good. You know nothing about the evidence. I'm telling you for your own good—stay out of this. Go sell some houses, get your hair done, or whatever the hell it is you do all day. But stay out of this."

"Hey! You called me."

"Yeah. Even I can make a mistake once in a great while. And I'll take a rain check on the beer."

He hung up.

CHAPTER EIGHTEEN

I gotta go. I'll call as soon as I'm done here."

"Val, no, wait. I'm not done telling you about my talk with Larry—"

"Kit, Barbara Craigmore is here."

"What do you mean? Where are you?"

"At a showing for Realtors of a new house on the market. I'm still in my car, but I just saw Barbara Craigmore go in through the front door."

"Oooh, that could be good. Ya know—"

I turned off my phone before Kit could finish, but I knew she wouldn't be upset with me. We both had our priorities straight. And our priorities remained anything to do with Susan Reed, even though we were sure Liam was her murderer.

I felt charged as I climbed out of my car and headed up the driveway to follow Barbara Craigmore into the brick two-story that was unlikely to sell any time soon, given the current housing market.

I entered the spacious foyer and began to case the joint. I smiled at myself as I realized I was confusing my new avocation with my vocation. Switching the jargon of my thoughts back from Mickey Spillane lingo to Realtor-speak, my eyes wandered up the winding staircase and took in the detail of the crown molding and dentil work before scrutinizing every female Realtor in sight. No sign of Barbara. But she must still be on the first floor, I decided.

I wormed my way through to the kitchen/family room combination that was so large I thought it might even have a bedroom tucked away there somewhere. My eyes combed the group milling around the appliances that were concealed behind cherry wood that matched the cabinetry. Then my gaze moved across to the floor-to-ceiling stone fireplace, where I spotted Barbara, still standing tall among her peers even though she was bent over, plugging one ear and pressing a phone to the other. She was about a block away, but I was by her side in an instant.

She seemed to sense my presence, although I thought I was nonchalantly perusing a flyer I'd picked up from the marble coffee table. "I'll call you later, Zach. I gotta go," I heard her say, before she wiggled her orange handbag off her shoulder just enough to deposit her phone in it.

"Barbara, hi." I pretended to be surprised to see her but felt like my performance fell flat.

"Valerie." It had been only about forty-eight hours since Kit and I had stopped by her house, but it looked like the forty-eight hours had been hard on Barbara Craigmore. She had dark circles stamped under her eyes, and she hadn't washed and blow-dried the bed head out of her light-brown hair.

"So, what do you think?" I turned my attention to the mammoth fireplace and rubbed my hand over one of the cool stones.

Barbara ran her own hand through the back of her unruly hair. "As grand as it is, I'm not sure the seller is going to reap the benefit."

"I hear you. Too many stone fireplaces and still not enough credit to go around."

She laughed a little and stepped closer to me. "Not to mention too many Realtors," she whispered. "Have you ever seen this many?"

"Not since I was at a convention in Las Vegas. Long time ago."

She smiled again, and then it struck me that she was giving me her business face. There was no joy in that smile, but it probably came automatically when she was on the job. "I guess I better start taking some notes." She dug in her large leather purse and retrieved a pen and small notepad.

"Yeah, that's what they pay us for." I took my own pen and pad from my purse. "By the way, have you heard any news about the murder?"

She had her pen poised to start making notes, but she stopped and glared at me. "What the hell does that mean?" There was no trace of her fake smile.

"Oh, nothing, really. Just that the police have been busy interviewing Larry and Kit James. They even interviewed me; can you believe it? I just wondered if they had talked to you."

"Why should they talk to me?" I knew she was lying, if for no other reason than I had complete faith in Culotta's detective skills. Barbara Craigmore would have been high on his list for investigation.

"There's a Detective Culotta in charge of the case—"

"Look, Valerie, I have another appointment—"

"Barbara, we didn't really finish the other day—"

"Oh yes, we did. Please excuse me."

I watched, stunned, as Barbara made her way through our fellow Realtors, out of my line of vision—and presumably out the front door.

It was probably just as well. I had no idea what I would have said to her if she'd let me continue. I'd just had the feeling there was more she could tell me.

Suddenly I felt certain of it.

***

"So you and Larry are all fine?"

"Yep. Liam saved our marriage." Kit placed a steaming mug of coffee in front of me and joined me at the counter. "I wonder why Barbara didn't want to talk to you."

I wondered, silently, why Kit was so quick to believe Larry. Oh, I believed him. But it had been hard for me to picture him having an affair. Kit was the one who had been determined to prove that, and it was unlike her to give up so easily. Liam or no Liam. But I felt relief to hear I could continue to count on the steadfastness of their marriage—and our Sunday brunches.

"Val? Did you hear me?"

"Oh, sorry, no; guess I was spacing it." I took a sip of coffee. "Wow—this'll help me focus."

"Too strong?"

"Mmm . . . not sure that's possible. But strong enough, that's for sure. So, what were you saying?"

"I said I think we need to talk to Liam ourselves."

"Don't you believe Larry? Don't you think Culotta can bring this one home?"

"I don't know. I have a feeling, a suspicion—"

"But I thought you said—"

"I believe Larry. I believe he wasn't having an affair with Susan. But I'm damn curious about her. I mean, I was intrigued before, I suppose, though I couldn't enjoy it like I can now that I know she wasn't screwing my husband. But to think her father was Richard 'Dickhead' Fitzpatrick . . . that's some good stuff, ya know."

"Kit, we're not writing for *People* magazine—"

"We could, ya know. They use people from all over to give them stories—"

"Now *you're* the one who's not focusing. Drink up." I tapped her coffee mug and then watched as she put it to her lips.

After a few more sips, during which she seemed to be concentrating so hard on something that I didn't want to interrupt her, she spoke. "Do you really think Liam murdered Susan?"

"Well, I would think Dennis, er, Culotta, Detective Culotta, would have arrested him if it was a clear-cut case. But who else would want Susan *dead*?"

Kit practically spit her coffee at me. "Can you count that high? For starters, probably everyone we've met who is connected to her. And who knows how many enemies and frenemies she has that we haven't met."

"What do you mean, everyone we've met? Who? And more important, why?"

"Val, her own mother didn't seem sorry to see her gone. And certainly if she thought Susan was going to screw up any potential income from the Fitzpatricks, that's motive enough for Mommy Dearest, wouldn't you say?"

"Yeah, I guess."

"And Barbara Craigmore. You said yourself how weird she acted with you this morning. And why? Your only connection to her has been Susan Reed. Questions about Susan Reed's *murder*, to be more specific. And telling. Besides, she told us herself she blamed Susan for her husband's business schemes and legal troubles."

"Yeah, but—"

Kit never liked to be butted, and she spoke right over me. "Even Ellen Parkinson. Ya know, Brad Parkinson worked with Susan too—all day, every day. And he seems just a bit too eager to distance himself from that fact. So just because Larry wasn't having an affair with Susan doesn't mean his partner wasn't."

"What about you, Kitty Kat? You had motive, considering you thought at the time that Larry was having an—"

"Very funny, Val. But seriously, it could have been any one of those people. And as you point out, your boyfriend hasn't arrested Liam."

I rolled my eyes. "Not that we know of. And thank God it's not our problem to solve," I reminded her.

"But it can be," she reminded me.

"Kit, all we care is that it's not Larry. And it's not. Why would we—"

"I told you why. Because it'll be fun. C'mon. We'll start with the most obvious, the stone we haven't turned over yet. I'm gonna call Liam Fitzpatrick right now."

***

Only Kit could manage to get us an immediate appointment with a state senator. Of course only Kit had the guts to drop Susan Reed's name to his assistant, insisting he mention it to Liam Fitzpatrick before turning us down.

And so late Friday morning (when I should have been working), I found myself riding in my friend's BMW on a trip to Springfield, Illinois, where we were to meet with Senator Fitzpatrick on his lunch break. Thank goodness my boss was still out of town and wasn't likely to show up in the state capital to yank me home and—in his opinion—out of harm's way.

"The fields look awfully wet," Kit said, as we buzzed down Interstate 55. "Farmers are going to be late planting corn this year."

Where did that come from? Kit is as city girl through and through as I am. I changed the subject to the one at hand. Namely, what the hell we were going to say to Liam Fitzpatrick. "We can't just ask Liam about Susan, can we? Didn't he think he was talking to Larry in confidence?" I asked.

Kit dismissed my ethical concerns. "Humph. Like Larry needs to care what Liam Fitzpatrick thinks of him from behind bars."

"But I thought you said he might not have done it? What about all the other suspects?"

"Odds are."

My friend didn't seem to be in the mood to talk about the subject at hand. I could only hope it was because she already had a plan.

***

"Mrs. James, good to see you again."

"Thank you. This is my friend, Valerie Pankowski."

Liam Fitzpatrick extended his hand to shake mine. "I don't believe we've met."

"Valerie is a Realtor in Downers Grove. Haskins Realty."

"Ah yes, I know Tom Haskins. I believe we've shared a single malt on occasion. What can I do for you ladies?" He began walking and beckoned with a wave of his hand for us to follow, but his long strides were hard to keep up with. This man did not have a minute to waste.

I recalled pictures I'd seen of his father, and although Liam was an attractive man, he was a watered-down version of the original. He was probably six feet tall, with reddish-blond hair and dark-brown eyes. His navy-blue suit was impeccable and displayed a tiny United States flag on the lapel. Flags of the United States of America and the State of Illinois stood in the corner of his office, and Fighting Irish of Notre Dame memorabilia and photos of his family adorned the shelves behind his desk. Well, not all his family. Not Susan Reed.

"What can I do for you?" he repeated.

I glowered at my friend, who was suddenly speechless. I refused to fill the silence, to answer Liam's question. This was Kit's idea; she could tell him what he could do for us.

But in spite of my resolve, I soon felt compelled, as always, to fill the silence. "We wanted to talk to you," I said inanely. Then I glared at Kit again, willing her to speak up.

And speak up she did. "Mr. Fitzpatrick—"

"Please. Call me Liam," he said with the polish of a politician, which is to say without any real warmth. "Sit." He

141

took a seat behind his desk and indicated the two chairs facing him.

"Liam, I'll get right to the point," Kit said. "You're busy, and so are we. I know you met with my husband, and what you told him was very disturbing, to say the least."

For a brief second, Liam looked as if he might jump out the large window behind him. But he quickly composed himself. "Your husband assured me my words would go no further than him," he said, no longer bothering with even a fake warmth. He picked up a Mont Blanc pen and twirled it between his fingers.

"Telling a spouse doesn't really count, ya know." Kit looked him squarely in the eyes.

"And her?" He pointed the pen in my direction. "Your husband has two wives?"

"Look. Let's not get sidetracked. My husband came under suspicion of murder because you chose to involve him just hours, maybe minutes, before Susan Reed—your sister—was murdered. What's up with that?"

"My half sister. Maybe. And what do you mean, *what's up with that?* Like I knew she was going to be murdered?"

"Maybe."

"Mrs. James." Liam sounded as if he were talking to an impudent child. "Let me be perfectly clear. This is a private matter. There is no proof Susan Reed was related to me—"

"Not now, anyway," Kit said.

"Mrs. James, this meeting is over. It was inappropriate for you to even come here today. I don't know what you expect me to do. I have nothing more to say to you. And I would advise you in the future to stay out of my family's business. The consequences could be unpleasant." He threw the pen onto his desk and stood up.

Following his lead, Kit and I also stood. "Nice chatting with you, Senator," she said. "Give your wife my regards."

I watched in fascination as the color in Liam's cheeks turned to match the red in his hair. "Leave my wife out of this."

"I was merely asking you to pass on my regards. I'm not planning a girls' weekend in Mexico."

I could see that Kit was enjoying the exchange. But for me, it was like watching a boxing match, not that I ever watched one, and knowing someone was going down for the count at any second.

I hoped it wouldn't be Kit.

CHAPTER NINETEEN

Liam Fitzpatrick's assistant escorted us out of the building in a polite yet don't-let-the-door-hit-you-in-the-ass kind of way. It was clear we had ruined Liam's day.

"Was he threatening us?" I asked Kit, as soon as we were back in her BMW.

"You mean his little *unpleasant consequences* speech?" She snickered.

"Exactly."

"I have to hand it to him," Kit said, almost as if she admired him. "He's not owning up to having a little sister."

"And as you pointed out, it's very convenient that she's dead."

Kit put on her Chanel sunglasses and turned the key in the ignition.

"You really got him going when you mentioned his wife," I said. "Do you even know her?"

"We've met a few times. Fancy is superrich; her family is in oil. We were seated next to each other at a five-hundred-dollar-a-plate dinner—"

"Wait a minute; did you say *Fancy*?"

"Yeah, Fancy Fitzpatrick—"

"Are you kidding me? Is that her name?"

"Val, surely you've heard of her. She's high society. Big-time."

"Ah, well, you know how I avoid high society. And did you really pay five hundred dollars for dinner?"

"Of course. When your husband is a brilliant accountant, you can go to as many fancy-schmancy dinners as you like." She tapped the side of her nose with her index finger, indicating—what? That she and Larry were scamming the GOP?

We rode the three hours back to Downers Grove with Kit filling me in on all the society I'd missed, high and otherwise. When we finally got to her house, it was nearly seven o'clock. I declined an invite to dinner and climbed into my own car. I had to get home and at least check my e-mails for any work-related issues, a task I had to do on a computer. When it came to my phone's keyboard, I was still, well, all thumbs.

I pulled up to my reserved parking space in the back of my building and felt a little thrill in the pit of my stomach when I saw Culotta sitting on the hood of his car with his feet resting on the fender.

I got out of my own car. "Hey! Visitors are supposed to park in the designated spot. Over there, clearly marked."

"Really? Someone should report me to the police." He jumped down and came toward me, opening the door to my building like a real gentleman. "You eaten?"

"No." As I passed by him, I realized I was famished.

"Wanna grab a bite?" he asked.

"I guess I could do that. Although this *is* a work night." I waved the magic fob on my key ring past the electric eye at the inner door, and then Culotta opened that too.

"It's only seven fifteen," he said. "I wasn't planning on us hopping a flight to New York."

"Okay. A quick bite would be good." I caught a glimpse of his grin in the illuminated hallway.

Upstairs in my apartment, I gave him a Heineken while I checked my makeup and ran a brush through my hair. When I returned to the living room, he was finishing his beer and reading my latest issue of *Time* magazine.

"So, where you been all day?" he asked.

"Working, lunch with Kit." I was becoming accustomed to not truthfully answering his many questions.

"That must have been a helluva lunch."

"Okay, why do you want to know?"

"Just asking a simple question."

"Let's just go." I grabbed my jacket. "I'm famished."

We drove to Barone's for pizza. I've been there many times and love it. But on a Friday night it was crowded, and I silently groaned as we entered. I knew it could take hours to be seated. Culotta took my hand and led me through the crowd waiting for tables. When we had pushed our way to the bar, he snapped his fingers in the air toward the bartender. Within three minutes, the manager appeared, a kid young enough to be my son, and led us to a table at the back of the room.

"Thanks, Gino." Culotta pulled out a chair for me.

"No problem; enjoy your dinner."

"Wow," I said, when Gino left. "That's impressive."

"You said you wanted quick. Just trying to keep you happy."

My mood lightened a little, and I grinned. Maybe he wouldn't ask me any more questions that I didn't want to answer.

"So, really, where were you today?" he asked, as soon as he was seated.

I put down the plasticized menu. "Dennis, I don't think we can be friends if I have to report my whereabouts to you. You make me feel as though I am a suspect."

He didn't say anything for a moment; clearly, he was taking time to think. "Okay, fair enough."

"Thank you." I picked my menu back up. "I'll take pizza with everything." It wasn't until after my wine arrived and I'd had a few sips that I began to relax.

As we ate our hearty slices of pizza, Dennis relayed some funny stories. One concerned a poker game when Tom got a royal flush.

"Oh, *please*," I said, interrupting him. "I've heard this story a million times. Tom considers it the most exciting night of his life."

"Valerie, it is a big deal. Uh, no pun intended. But we've played for a lot of years, and I don't recall anyone having had that hand."

"Well, if you want to see it again, the cards are in a shadow box on the wall in Tom's office."

Gino was suddenly back at our table. He put another mug of beer in front of Dennis and a fresh glass of wine down for me.

"So," I said, as soon as Gino was gone, "how's the investigation going?"

"Ah, I'm not allowed to ask you questions, but you can ask me. Is that how it goes?"

"Totally different. You can ask me if I sold a house today, or this week, or this month."

"Did you?"

"No. I'm getting close, though. What about you?"

"I haven't sold a thing."

"Come on; you know what I mean."

"You got any properties in Springfield?"

I took a big gulp of my wine. I could feel a flush spreading over my face. "What are you talking about?"

"See, I know you and Kit James took a little jaunt to the state capital today."

"How the hell do you know that?"

He leaned back in his chair. "Valerie, I'm a detective. I detect things."

"Well, if you already knew, why do you keep asking me?"

"Just wanted to see if you'd fess up."

"If you must know, Liam Fitzpatrick is an acquaintance of Kit's."

At that, Dennis laughed. "That's a good one, Valerie."

"What's so funny about it?"

"Oh, let's just say I had a phone call this afternoon from a very pissed-off senator who described Kit James as anything but an acquaintance. Now tell me the truth. Why did you go there? What the hell do you think you are accomplishing by getting in the middle of a murder investigation?"

"So you admit Liam Fitzpatrick is being investigated?"

His cheery laugh had completely disappeared, and I had a glimpse of how he would interrogate a real suspect. But not me. Surely not me.

"I've told you, I won't discuss the case. It's strictly police business."

"Except for my involvement in it, right?"

"You shouldn't be involved. Unless, of course, you have something to do with it."

"You know I don't."

"Do I? You took a three-hour drive for a five-minute conversation with one of the main . . ."

"Suspects?"

"I never said Senator Fitzpatrick was a suspect. I'm just wondering why you and Kit James found it necessary to go see the schmuck."

"So you don't suspect him?"

"Should I?"

Dennis Culotta was as frustrating as the therapists portrayed on TV, answering every question with another question. Well, I had a question of my own. "So that's the reason for this little dinner? You want information?"

"I want you to leave it alone. I don't know how many times I have to tell you."

I wiped my mouth with my napkin and threw it on the table. I was being overly dramatic, but I didn't know how else to derail his train of thought.

He took my wrist and held it. "I'm not playing games, Valerie. Leave this alone."

"Do you know who killed Susan Reed?"

I watched a slow grin spread across his face. "Do you?"

"I think I had better get home. I have an early start tomorrow."

He released my wrist. "No problem. Gino, bring me the check."

***

I was home by nine. Dennis escorted me to my front door and left. I felt tired and used. On the surface, it appeared that Dennis enjoyed my company, but it seemed every conversation involved him pumping me for information and then telling me to keep out of things.

If he was as good at detecting as he claimed, he should know everything I knew and more. And if Larry was being honest, then Culotta was aware Liam Fitzpatrick was Susan's half brother. Also, even amateur digging into Susan's past would have revealed that Allen Craigmore was Susan's lover before he killed himself. So what did Culotta want from me?

Well, I was planning to check my e-mails, have another glass of wine, and not think about Dennis Culotta and how he rattled me. I had my reading glasses on, so when my phone rang, I checked caller ID before answering.

It was Kit.

"Okay, before you say anything," I said, "let me tell you I just got home from Barone's. Culotta and I shared a pizza."

"Oh, Val, you didn't tell him where we went today, I hope." Kit sounded almost as rattled as I felt.

"Didn't have to. He already knew. Seems Liam called him."

"Son of a bitch."

"Which one, Liam or Dennis?"

"Both."

"Well, Dennis was a little angry. He read me the riot act for interfering. Kit, do you think maybe we should stay out of—"

"We've had a stroke of luck." Her voice had returned to almost normal, excited now instead of rattled. "The Junior League is having a big luncheon tomorrow, a fund-raiser for the homeless or something equally noble. All the usual worthless muckety-mucks will be there. I was invited weeks ago but didn't even respond. So here's our chance to talk to Fancy Fitzpatrick. She's some kind of big shot in the fund-raising world, naturally. She'd do more good if she'd just donate what she spends on makeup each month. Anyway, we'll go and seek her out."

"Oh, Kit, I don't know." I knew I sounded wimpy, as if I were ready to follow Culotta's orders. His smug face appeared before me.

"Don't worry, Valley Girl. I'll just say I returned the RSVP, and hell, if they didn't get it, they can take it up with the post office."

"It's not that. I'm just wondering what the point is." As I said it, I could hear Dennis Culotta laughing at me across the table at Barone's. Once again I was filled with indignation at his bullying me.

"Point? Are you kidding me? Fancy could be the one. She has plenty of reason to get rid of Skank-o-lena. You're not going to let Dennis Culotta tell you what to do, are you?" Kit read my thoughts better than Dennis Culotta could any day. Of course she'd had more practice.

"Definitely not. It's just that—"

"That Liam Fitzpatrick thinks he's such hot shit. Makes me want to rethink all the dough I've given to the Republicans over the years. Look what it gets you. Senators who go around bumping off anyone they don't like the look of."

I ignored Kit's exaggeration. "Okay, we'll go." I *was* curious to meet this Fancy Fitzpatrick. Plus, I knew that if I didn't go, Kit would go alone, and that could be more disastrous.

I hung up and poured myself a glass of wine. After debating whether to call my mother, I decided she would probably be in bed already. So instead, I called Emily. There was no answer, but I left a message reminding my daughter and her husband that I loved them both.

Just as I was resigned to not having a conversation with anyone else for the evening, the phone rang. Tom Haskins was on the other end.

"Tom!"

"Don't Tom me. Where the hell were you all day?"

"I went to the Realtors' showing of a new listing."

"Okay, and what did you do the other seven hours?"

"That does it." I curled up on one end of the couch and took a sip of my wine. "I quit."

"The hell you will."

I smiled to myself. In the background I could hear typical Las Vegas–type noises. People talking loudly, slot machines clinking, Tom munching on his cigar.

"You're not getting yourself into any trouble without your old Uncle Tom to help you out, are you, Pankowski?"

"What's that supposed to mean?" I was afraid that somehow Tom and Culotta had spoken.

"It doesn't mean anything. Except I know how you like riding shotgun for that dingbat friend of yours. I need my best Realtor selling houses, not running up bills at Lord & Taylor."

"Come back soon, Boss." Suddenly I missed him.

CHAPTER TWENTY

It was one of those raw, rainy April days in Chicago when none of my spring clothes seemed appropriate. But neither did my winter wear. Of all times to be going to a Junior League luncheon. I knew others there would be wearing designer dresses and suits created for just such days.

I grabbed the closest thing I had to perfection, knowing it fell far short but surprisingly not caring all that much. One of the biggest advantages of being fiftysomething. There's no competitive drive to be among the best-dressed and best-looking females at any function. I was content to leave that to the Fancy Fitzpatricks of the world. As for me, well, I was happy just to be comfortable—which today translated to warm and dry.

I took my gray lightweight-wool skirt and matching jacket from their hangers and tossed them over one arm, and then I rifled through my blouses before selecting one in tangerine silk that I hoped would brighten my outfit and maybe even my day.

I was really dreading the luncheon.

For one thing, I felt we were pursuing the wrong woman. If we were going to find out who most wanted Susan Reed dead, I had decided during my restless if not totally sleepless night, we needed to find out who had told her about her Fitzpatrick family. And I'd decided that search should take us back to Susan's mother.

But I didn't have time to dwell on that. Since I'd finally fallen into a good sleep just before six, I didn't wake until almost ten, so I was going to be lucky if I could get ready and get to the office to meet a couple of administrative deadlines before Kit picked me up there.

I'd just finished putting on my mascara (okay, so I did care a little what the luncheon ladies thought of my appearance) and was slipping into my black open-toed pumps (okay, further proof that fashion still mattered at least a little to me) when my phone rang. Knowing I had no time to spare, I didn't even look at caller ID to see who I was missing before closing my apartment door behind me.

As I approached the car, my cell phone rang—no doubt the same caller. I peered at the screen on my phone as I opened my car door.

Dennis Culotta.

"Here's the thing, Valerie," he said. Whatever happened to *hello*? Wasn't it made too memorable by that Tom Cruise/Renée Zellweger movie for Culotta to simply dispense with it? "I don't want you mad at me."

I felt my heart flutter like a teenager's, and I hoped I wasn't having a heart attack. I was sure Culotta had never uttered those words before, to anyone. I couldn't imagine him caring if anyone was mad at him.

"Valerie, are you there? Can you hear me?"

That made me giggle. He sounded just like the commercial for cell-phone service. "Yes, I hear you now."

"And?"

"And what? I'm not mad at you." It wasn't entirely true. Let's face it: Culotta's a very attractive man, but it didn't take Sherlock Holmes to detect a bully lurking inside him just ready to pounce.

"Good." He sounded relieved. "So what are you up to today?"

"Work, then lunch. I really don't have time to talk." Now I *was* getting a little mad. It seemed that keeping track of my whereabouts was Dennis Culotta's chief priority. And my chief priority right now was getting to the office and finishing my work so I'd be ready for Kit to pick me up in exactly seven minutes, mainly because I didn't want to make an entrance at the luncheon. I much preferred to slink in early and hide in a corner.

"Can I call you later this afternoon, say five-ish?" he asked.

"That'll work." I still felt a little mad, but a little happy too.

***

Kit looked chic in a black Chanel pantsuit and cream silk blouse as we stood at the entrance and she searched the crowd for Fancy Fitzpatrick. Vases of delicate calla lily blossoms graced a dozen or so round tables. No one was actually seated yet, but the room was buzzing with groups of women chatting and blowing air kisses, like bubbles escaping from a bubble-making machine. Most evaporated before they hit their intended target.

As we made our way deeper into the room, a couple of women greeted Kit, and there was even one woman I knew slightly. A competing Realtor.

"Valerie, how are you, dear?"

I gazed at the unnatural blond hair and Botoxed smile as I tried desperately to remember her name. "Good," I said. *Arlene? Darlene?*

"How's Tom?"

"Great, just great."

"Give that old rascal a big kiss from me," Arlene/Darlene said.

"You betcha." I took the business card she offered me. *Marlene Sanchez*. Close enough. I felt grateful when Kit tugged at my sleeve. I smiled at Marlene and then turned toward Kit.

"Geez." Kit started to lead the way through the throng. "I hope she left some Botox for the rest of us."

"Shush," I said. "She'll hear you."

"Oh good. Look, there's Fancy."

***

Fancy was a lot of things, but fancy wasn't one of them.

I was immediately surprised that Kit hadn't even inkled to me that Fancy was, well, frumpy. Oh, she'd no doubt spent more on her outfit than I'd spent to heat the Big House the entire time I'd lived there with David and Emily and then just David. But what was it they said about a sow and a silk purse?

It wasn't just the unhidden extra rolls she carried in her midsection, either, though they were certain to frumpify the most elegant of dresses. Maybe it was the old-lady pattern of pink and purple swirls her nonelegant dress had going on, or maybe it was her perfectly coiffed hair that just didn't look natural. A hurricane wouldn't have moved a blond hair on her head. I swear, my own mother looks like Anne Hathaway compared to Fancy.

Liam Fitzpatrick's attractive face flashed before my mind's eye, and I found it hard to believe this was his wife. Not that I couldn't believe Fancy had once been a beautiful—at least adorable—young girl, probably even Homecoming or Prom Queen. She had big blue eyes and deep dimples. Even in her fifties, with a strict diet and a new do, she could have been a strikingly attractive woman.

But that train had left the station.

We edged our way to Fancy's circle, where five other women seemed enthralled by her account of working with the homeless. Kit was all but holding my hand, as if I were a two-year-old she feared might dart into the street.

"You really deserve a medal, Fancy, or at least some national recognition for all you do," I heard one of her fans say.

"Oh, Belinda, stop." Fancy waved one hand, indicating that Belinda should do anything but stop. Her other manicured hand patted her helmet of hair, as if to be sure it was still there. "Oh, Kit James. How are you?"

Kit leaned into the circle, and she and Fancy extended cheeks in each other's general direction, leaving enough space for an eighteen-wheeler to drive through. "I thought I'd come and see where all my money goes." Kit straightened back up.

"Oh, you!" Fancy took Kit's arm and led her toward one of the empty tables. "We don't see enough of you. Now, you just come and sit over here at my table. We have some catching up to do."

"Delighted, Fancy." Kit turned and waved for me to follow. "By the way, this is my pal, Valerie Pankowski. Be nice to her; she's loaded." Kit gave her wicked grin.

We took three seats at a table on the perimeter of the room, Fancy in the middle, flanked by Kit and me. Another woman approached, prepared to sit down next to Kit, but Fancy discreetly shooed her away.

"So." Fancy put her hand over Kit's. "I hear you've been rather naughty. Liam tells me you were down in Springfield yesterday."

"Yep." Kit removed her hand. "And I'm guessing he told you why."

"Of course; we have no secrets."

"Then we need to talk to you about your sister-in-law."

Fancy frowned, no doubt trying to convey confusion. "I don't have a sister-in-law. I'm an only child, and my husband has just the one unmarried brother." She continued to look perplexed, as if worried an errant sister-in-law might be escaping her memory.

"Give it up, Fancy," Kit said.

"Okay, so what about her?" Fancy visibly relaxed her phony act and stared across the table into the room. Gone was the sweet voice issuing from her marshmallow face, replaced by a harsh schoolmarm's tone. As another woman approached the table, ready to sit, Fancy waved her away too.

"Tell me what you know," Kit said.

"I know Susan Reed's mother milked my family for years, with no proof that she had a right to."

"It was actually your husband's family she was milking, ya know," Kit said. "And you really don't think she had a right?"

"No, I don't think she had a right. Married people have rights. She was a two-bit tramp. Like her daughter. She had no place in our family; she just wasn't our sort."

Kit's eyebrows shot up, but she knew she didn't have time to try to shift this woman's paradigm. "Whatever. So you knew Susan was Liam's sister."

"I knew no such thing. And neither do you." I watched a wide smile form on Fancy's lips as someone walked past the table and waved. But the smile vanished as soon as the passerby was out of her line of vision.

"When did you last see your sister-in-law?" my friend asked.

Her persistence was making me nervous. I even felt a little sorry for Fancy and wondered why she didn't call security and have us thrown out.

"*Last see her?*" Fancy controlled her shriek so that only we could hear. "I never even met the woman. You think I would entertain such a person?" Fancy moved in her chair but continued to sit on the edge, as if ready to bolt any minute. I was surprised Kit didn't take her hand to keep *her* from darting away. Instead, she seemed to hold Fancy with eye contact as strong as superglue.

"And obviously you know Susan was murdered," Kit said.

Again, Fancy moved her weight around.

Was she uncomfortable physically or mentally? I wondered.

"I read the paper," she said.

"I'm just curious if you have any thoughts on who would benefit from her death. Seems like poor old Susan was a huge pain in the ass to you and your family. It must be a relief that she's not around anymore." Kit held her stare while Fancy looked desperately around the room. She no doubt suddenly wanted to be rescued by one of her entourage.

"Kit James." A beaming smile formed again on Fancy's face, obviously for the benefit of any of her minions who might be watching. "I'm going to say this only once. You stay the hell away from my husband and my family. We have nothing to say about Susan Reed."

A waiter approached, obviously not privy to the memo advising not to come near Fancy's table until she gave the all clear. Fancy took a glass of champagne from his tray, smiling up at him the whole time. "Keep circulating," she ordered, and he scooted away before offering Kit or me a drink.

"Have the police spoken to you?" Kit asked. We both watched as Fancy took an inelegant gulp of her drink, leaving a deep-red lipstick outline on the glass.

"The police? Puh-leeze. The police don't interview people like us. We are not common criminals. But I have heard your husband—sorry, his name escapes me—was arrested. That must have been awful for you."

"He wasn't arrested, you idiot. He was questioned, and only because he did your damn husband a favor."

"Hardly what I'd call a favor." Fancy toyed with a string of pearls that was almost concealed by the rolls of fat at her neck. "Didn't Susan work closely with your husband?"

"Yes, she worked for him, but she wasn't *related* to him."

"My husband is a state senator, don't forget."

"I don't give a shit if he's the Duke of Earl. My husband got into a lot of trouble trying to help him out."

Fancy heaved a sigh. She'd said all she was going to say. Her blue eyes roamed the room, finally fixing on a tall, skinny redhead who was taking a sip of wine and talking to another woman. "Janice, Janice, over here." Fancy waved her fingers in the air.

The redhead took a final gulp of her wine and headed toward our table. I thought I saw her raise her eyebrows a little at her companion, indicating she'd been summoned and she'd better move her ass.

"Fancy, it's time to ask everyone to be seated. You're going to do that, right?" Her name tag said she was Janice Warner, and her demeanor said she was Honcho Number Two, to Fancy's Head Honcho. Whatever her moniker, I figured she'd never known Fancy to be so delighted to see her, and she wasn't sure if that was good or bad.

"Yes, I'm coming right now." Fancy hoisted herself out of her chair and upon standing, seemed to regain her composure. She returned Kit's stare again. "We're done here, anyway."

"Oh no, we're not," Kit said to Fancy's back, but only Janice Warner turned around, wearing a shocked look.

But she couldn't have been more shocked than I. "What the—"

"What the, indeed." Kit turned and looked at me.

Still stunned by the whirlwind exchange that seemed to have caused more harm than good, I began to smooth the napkin on my lap.

Kit grabbed it and tossed it on the table. Then she took my hand and pulled me up. "Get your bag. We're blowing this place."

Back in her BMW, we sat in silence for a moment. We both wondered just what we'd done and just what we should do next.

Then Kit spoke. "I'll say one thing for our dead girl: she wasn't the most popular kid on the block."

"You surely didn't expect Fancy to be inviting her to a family picnic."

"No, of course not. Ya know, I wasn't sure exactly how much Fancy knew, but apparently she knows everything."

"It kinda puts Ms. Fancy Pants high on the list of people eager to get rid of Susan, although the list seems to get longer every time we turn around. But I have a feeling that Fancy would be more than a little unhappy if the press got wind of her husband's baby sister. She likes being a senator's wife way too much."

"You're right, Val, but we need to find out from Marjorie Reed just how Susan learned the identity of the paternal side of her family."

CHAPTER TWENTY-ONE

Kit dropped me off at my office by three o'clock, and I scrambled to catch up on some paperwork. Both Perry and Billie were leaving as I arrived, so I had the place to myself. I set up two appointments to meet with homeowners on Monday morning. I also checked our roster for open houses the next day. Perry and I were scheduled for one each. When my phone rang in my purse, I glanced at my watch. Five o'clock on the dot. If nothing else, Culotta was punctual.

"Hi," I said. I kicked off my shoes under the desk. "When you said five-ish, you weren't kidding."

"Valerie, is that you?"

"Mom?"

"What's five-ish? Is it some kind of Jewish fish?"

"No, Mom, it's—never mind. I was expecting a call at five, that's all. How are you?"

"This morning William Stuckey took me to Walmart to buy some tomato plants. I'm going to plant them in that area at the back of the yard by the two trees. You know where I mean?"

"Yes. That would be perfect." I smiled gratefully at the mention of William Stuckey.

He and my mother have been friends for more than sixty years, and yet she always refers to him by his full name, as if she just met him. He was a widower who had lived in Chicago and then moved to Door County a few years before my mother. They had gone to the same high school, belonged to the same church, and eventually started playing dominoes once a week. Before my father's death, he and William Stuckey were good friends and played golf every weekend. And my father called him by just his first name.

"But isn't it awfully early, Mom? I'm surprised you found tomatoes in the stores up there already."

"We can get tomatoes year-round up here. Where do you think I live, anyway?"

"I mean tomato plants. You can't put them in the ground for a long time, can you?"

"They didn't have any yet, but I wanted to check. I'll take better care of them than the store will, so I want to get them as soon as I can. And William Stuckey invited me to lunch afterward. We went to the Bluefront Cafe. You know the place?" She sounded happy, and I was happy for her, even if I did think it was way too early to be looking for tomato plants.

"Yes. It's a good place. You want me to help plant the tomatoes when I come in May?"

"Oh, not necessary, dear. William Stuckey will help me."

I decided to change the subject. "I had lunch today with Fancy Fitzpatrick." So I stretched the truth a little.

"Who's she, a movie star?"

"No, Mom, she's the wife of Liam Fitzpatrick, our state senator."

"Democrat or one of the other bunch?"

"The other bunch."

"I should have known by that ridiculous name." My mother was a lifelong Democrat, as my father had been, and lunch with Republican wives held little interest for her.

I decided to change the subject again. "I have a date tonight." But suddenly I wasn't sure if that was a better topic. Even though Culotta had said he would call, it wasn't a sure thing we would be going out somewhere.

"Date? That's nice. Is it someone I know?"

"No, he's just someone I met at work." I wished I'd never even told her. I could almost see the worry lines form on her face. I had to decide quickly if it would be better or worse to tell her my potential date was a detective.

"What's this man's name? And where does he live? I know you modern girls like your privacy, but I think I should know where you are going, just in case something happens and I need to call the police."

"Okay, Mom." I opted for more lies. "We're going out with three other couples. I'm meeting him at The Capital Grille in Lombard. I'll be home by ten at the latest."

"Hmm. Sounds okay. Make sure you have a quarter in your shoe in case you need to use a pay phone." The idea of cell phones remained foreign to my mother, even though I had purchased one for her and paid the monthly fee. She kept it on her kitchen counter and eyed it suspiciously every once in a while, as if it were a bomb set to go off at a certain time. "Have a marvelous evening, dear."

"Yes, I will, thank you. And I'll call you tomorrow and tell you all about it."

We said our good-byes, and ten minutes later, as I was easing back into my shoes, Dennis Culotta rang. A glance at my watch told me it was five thirty already.

"You had dinner yet?" he asked.

"Er, it's five thirty. I thought I'd hold off until at least six and make a night of it."

"How about I pick you up at seven? Think you'll still be awake?"

"That would be good."

"I'm in the mood for a steak. How's that sound?"

"Capital Grille?" I suggested.

"Whoa. You know your steaks. I'll see you later."

I almost suggested that perhaps one of us should call for a reservation. Getting a table without one was all but impossible on a Saturday night. But then I remembered who my companion would be. Nope. No reservations required. One of the benefits of dining with the police.

On the drive home, I recalled my conversation with my mother and her protectiveness of me. Okay, it was a little daffy, but it was still nice that she was concerned about my safety. I reached into my purse and pulled out my phone. Time to keep up the tradition. I hadn't heard back from Emily since I'd left my message the night before, and I was eager to hear about the role she'd been auditioning for.

"Hi," I said, when she answered.

Her voice sounded as sunny as always, and I wondered if it was the weather on the West Coast. I didn't recall constant cheerfulness when she lived in Illinois. But maybe it had nothing to do with California. Maybe she was just really happy. I hoped so.

"Mom," she said. "This is so weird; I was just about to call you. Guess what? You'll never guess."

"Diner Number Two?"

"Yessss!"

I was instantly thrown back to the twelve-year-old Emily who got the lead role in the school production of *Sleeping Beauty*. David and I had gone to all three performances, marveling at our talented daughter. Even though she had slept through fifty-six minutes of the ninety-minute production, she had been center stage throughout most of the play. Dressed like a real princess in a yellow chiffon number my mother had made, she took her bow at the end with her fellow thespians. Her father and I rose from our front-row seats and applauded as if she were the leading lady in a Broadway play.

"That is so fantastic, and *you* will be fantastic."

"It's not a speaking part, you understand, but I will have to do a bit of acting when the leading man gets into a fight with another customer and bumps into my table. Plus I get paid, only scale since there's no dialogue, but I will be on camera."

"Well, it sounds just incredible."

"I know, right? I can't believe it. Luke and I are going out tonight to celebrate. What about you, Mom? What's going on there?"

I decided not to mention my upcoming date. "Nothing much. Just working incredibly hard. When do you start your job? Will you still be able to make it to Chicago next month?"

"Yes, I don't think that will be a problem. I start right away, so we should be done."

"Okay, honey. Well, I better get off the phone, but I'm really thrilled about your news. Give Luke a big hug."

***

The bar at The Capital Grille was crowded with those poor devils who didn't have reservations, or connections. Culotta and I sailed past them as the hostess led us to a cozy table for two at the back of the restaurant. As a prompt waiter handed me a menu, I realized I was starving. Only toast for breakfast, and no lunch due to our hasty departure from the Junior League affair.

"I'll have prime rib, well-done, with a baked potato and all the trimmings." I handed the menu back two seconds after I'd received it.

"Bring me a T-bone, medium rare. Same potato. And I'd like to see the wine list." As soon as the waiter left, Culotta spoke again. "I guess someone is hungry."

"No kidding; I haven't eaten all day." I took a piece of bread from the basket in front of me and tore off a piece.

"What about lunch?" He took his own piece of bread.

"Huh?"

"Didn't you say you had a lunch thing? When I called you earlier, you mentioned lunch."

"Right." I stuck my knife into the butter dish, not sure what was coming next. I *had* said I had plans for lunch, but I hadn't mentioned where. A normal person might not have remembered that, but this was no normal person.

And was his question innocent, or had he been undercover at the Junior League? A waiter, possibly, or did he have cross-dressing skills, disguising himself as an Illinois matron?

"So? Did you have lunch or what?"

I put the knife down on the table. "No," I said, with an extreme show of patience. "Dennis, do you somehow know that I went to a Junior League thing with Kit? That we left before lunch was served? That I was the only woman in the room wearing gray, and definitely the only one who wasn't wearing a two-carat diamond?"

He slowly spread some butter on his slice of bread. "I do now." He masked a smile by taking a bite of the bread, but not before I saw it.

"Okay then." I grabbed my knife and started putting butter on my own bread.

When the wine arrived, we toasted the arrival of spring. It was his surprising suggestion. We were chatting like two relatively ordinary people out on a date on a Saturday night by the time our food arrived. I told him about Emily's job. He told me his lieutenant was about to be a grandfather for the first time. I told him I thought I needed new tires. He said he'd share the name of a guy who would give me a fair price.

Over dessert, lemon tart for me and Neapolitan ice cream for him, he reminded me that it had been a week since Susan Reed's murder. "In fact, just about this time a week ago." He looked at his watch as he said it, and nodded like a television medical examiner calling the time of death.

It was hard to believe it had been only seven days. It seemed as if I'd known Culotta forever, and the murder was something that had happened in the distant past. "Can I ask how you are coming along with the case?" I spooned the last of the tart into my mouth.

"You can ask."

"Oh, for Pete's sake, forget it. You were the one who brought it up."

He signaled the waiter and ordered coffee and two brandies. I was a little irritated that he hadn't asked me if I actually wanted brandy—or coffee, for that matter.

Once again, he waited for the waiter to leave before speaking. "You know, there's an upside to Susan's murder."

"What on earth is that?"

"I got to meet you."

Maybe this was law enforcement's idea of foreplay. I wasn't sure if I was flattered or horrified. I wiped my lips with my linen napkin as I considered my response. "Really, if I lost my daughter that way, I would be thoroughly disgusted to hear the lead detective on the case confess to an upside to her murder."

"So, you don't think it's a compliment."

"No, I don't think it's a compliment. I think it's a cruel thing to say."

"You're being a little dramatic, don't you think?"

"Not at all. What next? Are you going to have the bullet that killed her turned into a pendant for me to wear around my neck?"

"Wow, that hurt." He slapped his chest as if I'd just shot him. "Or maybe you're hinting? The bullets are still considered evidence, but I'll see what I can do when the case is over."

For a moment, I forgot Culotta's macabre train of thought and focused on the murder weapon. *Where was it? Why hadn't Kit or I even discussed it?* "What kind of gun was it?" I asked.

"Bullets were from a Glock 9mm."

"Have you checked all the suspects to see if they own such a gun?"

He looked at me in mock surprise. "That's a brilliant idea, Ms. Pankowski." He slapped his forehead with the palm of his hand. "Why didn't I think of that?"

"Well, I'm only saying—"

"And while you're at it, how 'bout you run down the list of suspects for me so I can get working on the case properly. You seem to know who they are."

"Maybe better than you."

Our coffee and brandy had arrived. He picked up his drink and leaned back in his chair, scrutinizing me.

"Okay." I tore open a packet of Splenda. "Let's see, there's Brad and Ellen Parkinson, and—"

"Wait. Go back. Motive?"

"She's an alcoholic who doesn't trust her husband. He might have been having a thing with Susan. He is Larry's partner and claims he didn't like Susan, but I don't trust him." I stopped to pour some cream into my coffee.

"That all you got?"

"Hardly. There's Barbara Craigmore. Her husband, Allen, used to employ Susan. We know he had an affair resulting in a ruined business and his suicide. Barbara lost her husband and lifestyle, and apparently her relationship with her only son is hanging by a thread. She's very bitter."

"Okay, who else?"

"There's also Liam Fitzpatrick. He was Susan's half brother. He's pretty mad she showed up, not to mention she was blackmailing him, or at least attempted to. Then there is his charming wife, Fancy. She seems even madder than her husband over Susan's sudden appearance and claim to be family."

Culotta drained his brandy and began working on his coffee. "Go on."

"Well, lastly, there's her mother. If the money well dried up and Susan had anything to do with that, she wouldn't be very happy."

"A mother killing her own daughter. Tut tut tut. And you call *me* cruel."

"You *are* cruel, and this wouldn't be the first mother in history who killed her child. Money is a great motivator." Satisfied that I'd run down the list of likely suspects, I gave him a contented smile and took a sip of my brandy. "So, there you have it."

He leaned across the table. "Er, Miss Marple, haven't you left out one or two?"

"Have I?" I leaned forward so that our foreheads were only a couple of inches apart. I was eager to hear the remaining names.

"Larry James."

"Oh, come on. You know as well as I do that Larry didn't do it."

"Kit James."

"Oh, now you are really stretching. Kit has nothing to do with this."

I didn't say out loud what we were probably both thinking, that she *had* thought her husband was sleeping with Susan. Well, thank God she finally knew he was innocent. Of the sleeping *and* murder.

Culotta drained his coffee cup as I drained my brandy glass. "One more," he said.

"One more? Who? Tell me."

"You."

If I'd had any brandy left, I would have spit it out. "You're joking, right? I can't tell if you think that's funny, but it's not. I hardly knew Susan and had absolutely no motive to kill her. And besides, if you think I'm a suspect, why do you keep following me? Turning up unannounced. Calling me every five minutes?"

"You haven't heard of that police strategy? Keeping the suspect under surveillance?" His face was expressionless, and I couldn't gauge if he was serious or not.

I slapped my napkin down on the table. "I think I'm ready to leave. Early start tomorrow. Thank you for dinner."

"See now, there you go again, with your *early start tomorrow*. You're mad at me."

"Brilliant deduction, Detective Culotta. I have just one question: why do you keep telling me to stay out of it, and then discuss the case with me?"

"I didn't actually discuss the case with you. You just ran down a list of suspects, but I don't think I've actually given away any police secrets."

"You really are good. Please take me home."

We drove home in silence, and he didn't even offer to walk me to my door. I didn't know if it was that or his accusation that annoyed me more.

He did at least get out of the car and walk around to the passenger side to help me out. "Do you own a gun?" he asked.

"No, I most certainly do not own a gun. And if you worked a bit faster and spent less time following me around, you might actually come up with the weapon that killed Susan."

He smiled, the big blue-eyed smile I'd become so fond of. "What makes you think I haven't?"

CHAPTER TWENTY-TWO

K it, he's an asshole. I mean it. Unless it's police business, I won't be talking to him again, let alone dining with the shithead."

"Valerie, your language!"

"*My* language? You always talk like a truck—"

"Val, that's part of my character. It's who I am. It sounds so vulgar when *you* swear."

"Kit, will you focus? This isn't about my language. It's about Dennis Asshole Culotta. I think he's just been using me, hoping to get information from me. Which can only mean he must still think Susan's death has something to do with you or Larry. Why else would he need me? You guys are my only connection to Susan."

I hugged the phone between my ear and shoulder while I removed the uncomfortable shoes I'd worn to dinner with Dennis Asshole. I wasn't surprised Kit was so irritable. I'd probably caught her dozing on the couch during a must-see movie, her favorite Saturday-night pastime. Sometimes she rents the same movie three Saturday nights in a row before finally completing it.

"Then he must be seeing you because he wants to *see you*. It's obvious he knows Larry and I had nothing to do with Susan's death, ya know."

"I'm not so sure."

"What's that supposed to mean? Why on earth would he think there's any reason either one of us would want her dead? Aside from the fact that she was a scumbag, of course."

I realized I should have told her about the picture on Susan's entryway table. Then she'd know why they might be suspects. But if I told her right now, it would seem like I was just irritated at *her* and her know-it-all attitude, and was just trying to strike back. Regardless, I forged ahead. "Kit, I never told you about a picture Dennis—Detective Culotta— and I saw at Susan's apartment."

"Yeah?" I imagined her sitting up on the couch and pausing her movie, if she hadn't already. I could even see her throwing her comforter off, no doubt having a sudden hot flash because of what I'd just said. "Go on."

"Well, I'm sure it's nothing, but there was a picture of Susan and Larry, probably having dinner together or something. It certainly made them seem like a couple."

"Oh, Val." Kit heaved a big sigh, and I had a mental image of her pulling the comforter back over herself and lying down again, relaxing in the knowledge that what I'd told her meant nothing.

But how could it mean nothing? Suddenly *I* felt a hot flash coming on.

"Val, I bet I know the picture you're talking about. It was on that skank's Facebook page—didn't I show it to you?"

She hadn't, but I remained silent, curious and still irritated.

"That picture was taken at a company Christmas party, and I was on the other side of Larry when it was taken.

Skankface must have cropped me out of it. The only coupling she did with Larry was in her mind."

A strange mixture of relief and regret washed over me. Good friend that I was, the mixture was made up of ninety-nine percent relief for my good friends and only one percent regret that I couldn't penetrate Kit's tough skin right now. Well, I was tired. I just needed to get to bed and get some sleep. We'd start over the next morning. "I'm glad, Kit. I'll call you tomorrow."

***

"Still cranky?" my best friend's voice greeted me.

Actually, I'd been about to call *her* when my phone rang. I took another sip of coffee and decided to ignore her accusation instead of throwing it back at her, where it belonged. We were way past the age for did-too-did-not. "Kit, if we hurry, we can go to Marjorie Reed's before my open house at noon."

"And we want to do that because . . . ?"

I resisted a heavy sigh that would indicate she should know the answer. She still seemed ready to pick a fight, but as my mom always said, that took two. And I wasn't going to be one of them. We had business to conduct. A murder to solve. "I think it's important we know how Susan found out about the Fitzpatricks." I didn't add *don't you?* I didn't want to leave an opening for debate.

Not that Kit ever needed an opening. "I'm not sure that matters, or whether Marjorie Reed would even know. But sure, we can go. Pick me up?"

"In a half hour."

"You going to make sure she's home?"

"No. I want the element of surprise."

"Whatever."

We had reversed roles, and it felt good to be leading Kit for a change. Different, but good, even though I realized my zeal came from a sick need to somehow one-up Culotta.

***

Larry answered the door and handed me coffee in a stainless-steel to-go mug. The name of his golf club was stenciled in bold green and white letters on the side. "Where are you girls off to so early?"

I took the coffee and kissed him on the cheek. "Kit has a few errands, and I've got time to kill before my open house." I wasn't sure whether Larry was in Kit's loop.

He stepped back so I could enter the foyer. "I'm going to the club to hit a few. Sounds like I'm relieved of kitchen duties."

A pang of disappointment washed over me at the realization I would be missing our traditional Sunday brunch for the second week in a row, and I almost regretted my suggestion that we visit Marjorie Reed.

"Why don't you fix us some dinner later?" Kit appeared in the kitchen wearing gray pants and a black silk-blend cropped jacket, something I'm sure she had just thrown on. She always manages to make casual look elegant.

"Steaks?" Larry asked.

"Small ones," Kit spoke for both of us, and I pushed the previous night's prime rib out of my mind. Two slabs of beef in a twenty-four-hour period. I could almost hear my cholesterol yelling *yippee, a party!*

"Steak sounds wonderful," I said.

"Okay, you girls try to stay out of trouble." He handed Kit her own travel mug, and then he gave her a kiss on the cheek.

"Do you think it's odd that Larry doesn't ask you where we are going at nine o'clock on a Sunday morning?" I asked, as we settled into my car.

"He did ask." Kit buckled her seat belt. "I told him we were running errands."

"Ah, great minds. I told him the same."

"Believe me, he doesn't care. You remember marriage, don't you, Val? He does his thing, I do mine, then we meet at the end of the day and sometimes we have to lie a little about what we've been up to."

I stared hard at her profile next to me as she pulled down the visor and checked her makeup in the mirror. I was thinking how easily she had dismissed my description of the photograph of Larry and Susan.

"Yes." I turned the key in the ignition. "I remember it well."

***

The Marjorie Reed who greeted us was not the same Marjorie Reed we'd met with before. Well, it might have been the same person, but it was not the same persona. Gone was the sweetness in the voice we heard yelling from inside the house. "Hold your horses! I'm coming!" she hollered, after we rang the doorbell twice and then knocked. And when she flung her front door open, gone was the cane as well as any hint of decrepitude. And gone was any sense of welcome. "Oh, you two."

Kit and Marjorie glared at one another, and I waited for one of them to speak (since I had no idea what to say). When I realized neither of them was going to budge, I spoke up. "May we come in, Mrs. Reed? We'd like to talk with you, if we could." Okay, so I hadn't exactly turned into Kit, after all.

"What about?"

"Well, about your daughter."

"What about her?" It was obvious this woman had no intention of letting us in her house.

"Mrs. Reed," I said, "we're curious . . . about how . . . well, we're wondering how Susan found out her father was Richard Fitzpatrick."

That moved her. Literally. She stepped aside, not in welcome but in resignation. We made our way to the couch, and she followed behind. "How did *you* find out about Richard Fitzpatrick?" she asked.

"Mrs. Reed, the secrets are all coming out," I said.

"Which means they aren't secrets anymore." Kit the mean girl suddenly surfaced. Mrs. Reed seemed to bring that out in her, although I was certain it was really directed at Mrs. Reed's dead daughter.

Marjorie Reed slumped in her chair and stared at the floor. "What would *you* have done?" When she looked up at us, I saw tears spilling out of her eyes.

But I reminded myself what an actress she apparently was. *Emily could take lessons right here in Downers Grove*, I thought.

"Being a single mother back in my day wasn't as easy, or commonplace, as it is now," Marjorie said.

"Let's back up," Kit said. "Before the poor-me single mother, you were some man's mistress—a married man."

Well, I hope you feel better, getting that off your chest, I thought. But I couldn't blame my best friend. Even though she finally realized Larry hadn't had an affair, I knew the hurt she'd felt must still be fresh in her mind—and heart.

"He was leaving his wife," Mrs. Reed said, without any conviction. "He was always just about to leave his wife. But it doesn't matter. Fact is, I got pregnant, and by the time I realized that even my pregnancy wasn't going to win him away from his wife and other family, it was too late for me to do anything but try to survive."

"And so . . . ?" Kit pressed on.

"And so I made him support us."

"Child support is only fair," I said. Maybe I was a sucker, but I was starting to feel sorry for Marjorie Reed.

Kit glared at me. "Yeah, but what about these later years? Susan had grown up. And yet you were still extorting money from Richard Fitzpatrick until the day he died, weren't you? And then his son Liam."

"What else was I going to do? I hadn't paid enough into Social Security to be able to live off that. I had spent all of those years raising his daughter." Marjorie was showing the toughness that no doubt enabled her to confront men like Richard and Liam Fitzpatrick and convince them she meant business. Pay up or live with the very public consequences.

"Where did Susan fit into your master plan?" Kit asked.

"Are you kidding? She's the reason I was entitled to money."

"First of all, not forever. No father supports his daughter forever. And you were never the wife. *You* never had any rights. When did she find out about your private welfare system? And why is she dead?"

"What do you mean, *why is she dead?* How on earth would I know?" Marjorie scooted forward in her chair, and I thought maybe she was going to attack Kit. If only she'd had her cane.

"Don't tell me you don't think her death is connected to the blackmail," Kit said.

Marjorie Reed stood up and began screaming. "There was no blackmail! Don't you sit in your fancy mansion with your buttoned-up accountant husband and tell me how easy my life was, how I didn't need money from my child's father, how his wife is the only one who deserved to have the—"

"She didn't say that, Mrs. Reed," I said, suddenly realizing she probably wasn't a Mrs. Reed or Mrs. *Anything.* "Kit is just trying to figure out why someone wanted your daughter dead. The Fitzpatricks are the obvious—"

"She's their family. Family doesn't kill their own people—"

"Oooh, family members kill each other all the time. Listen to your local news," Kit said.

Marjorie Reed moved back in her chair and heaved a big sigh. "What do you want from me?"

"When and how did Susan find out Richard Fitzpatrick was her father and that he'd been paying you off all those years?"

Marjorie looked at us and seemed to decide the only way she was going to get rid of us was to answer the question. Or maybe she was just too tired to fight anymore.

But the question remained: could we trust her to tell us the truth?

"I was in the hospital last year, and Susan had to find my insurance card," she said at last. "She came across an uncashed check from Liam and . . . and I ended up telling her everything. And the next thing I knew, she was going to him for *more*. I knew I was lucky to be getting anything, and she insisted on *more*. She was such a selfish, greedy—" Marjorie stopped and erased the brief look of hatred from her face. "That's it. Now you know. And you'll have to excuse me."

She stood and left the room, apparently retreating down the small hallway to her bedroom. We heard a door close. Then we looked at each other with raised eyebrows and looks of pure bewilderment.

We showed ourselves out. What else could we do?

CHAPTER TWENTY-THREE

I'll come back about six o'clock." I pulled up in front of Kit's house, and she opened the passenger door.

"Perfect, Valley Girl. Now go sell some houses," my friend said.

On the twenty-minute drive to the Patterson Avenue open house, I mulled over our meeting with Marjorie Reed. It had left me feeling dissatisfied. We learned Susan had innocently found out about her lineage, but so what? Knowing that didn't help solve her murder. Yes, the mother was a good candidate for bumping her daughter off, but so were the Fitzpatricks.

When I reached 66453 Patterson Avenue, I parked in the long driveway as close to the house as possible, giving the potential buyers I hoped would come plenty of room to view the property, yet indicating they weren't the only ones interested in the place. I took the open-house sign from the back of my car and stuck it firmly in the front yard.

The home was a dream. In a better economy, it would easily sell within a few weeks. The owner was also the builder, and he and his pregnant wife were eager to get out from under the heavy mortgage of their forty-five-hundred square feet.

Taking the key from the lockbox hanging on one of the double front doors, I let myself in. A fabulous first impression: large tiled entryway, twenty-foot ceiling, and curved staircases to my right and left.

This part of my job I love, even though I believe open houses rarely accomplish much. But the feeling of being the only one there, trusted by the owners to sell their most valuable asset, is exhilarating.

I set up a stack of flyers on both ends of the long, curved granite counter in the kitchen. I turned on the space-age coffee maker that the owner had prepared; then I put a CD in the player and turned the music down to a barely audible level. Finally, I did a cursory walk-through of the house. You never know when even the most meticulous seller might leave a pair of underwear on the bathroom floor or the family pet might leave a present in the laundry room.

Certain everything was perfect, I poured myself a cup of coffee and took a seat on the chocolate-brown leather couch in the den to wait for the first house hunters. An hour later I said good-bye to the second of two couples who had rung the doorbell. The first couple I had immediately dismissed as having no potential as buyers. The big clue was they came on foot, and I pegged them as neighbors who wanted an idea of what their own home was worth.

The second couple showed more promise. They said they loved the place, especially the room on the second floor that housed a sixty-inch flat-screen and two comfortable couches. The owners had decorated the room with old movie posters: *Casablanca*, *The Godfather*, *Cool Hand Luke*. When the enthralled wife referred to it as a media room, I made a mental note to push it as such. In my hastily written flyer, I had mundanely called it the TV room.

After they left, my business card in hand, I poured another cup of coffee and took my seat in the den again. On the glass coffee table in front of me were several magazines fanned out like an overly large deck of cards. I took the one at the end so as not to disturb the hand: *Time Out Chicago*. Its cover boasted "Fall Fling" and "120 Things to Do in Our Great City."

I sipped my coffee and tried to tune out the music emanating from the CD I'd selected. I suddenly found it more distracting than soothing. I opened the magazine at the last page and flipped backward toward the Table of Contents. When I got to the section "Chicago Happenings," I had to put my coffee cup down, nearly missing the coaster—a huge no-no. Before continuing, I quickly turned to the cover to check the date. The magazine was six months old. Back to the "Happenings," I took my glasses out of my pocket to get a closer look.

There were several photographs taken at a dinner to raise money for the Chicago Symphony, with Fancy and Liam Fitzpatrick among the prominent guests. They appeared together in two photographs, Liam looking James Bondish in a classic tux, Fancy looking more like a Bond *mother* than a Bond *girl*. And way down in the corner of the page was a picture of Fancy flanked by two women. The woman on her right was identified as the director of public relations for the Symphony, the woman on her left was identified as Ms. Susan Reed, *friend*.

I rearranged the magazines so as not to make a missing one obvious and then stuck the *Time Out Chicago* in my briefcase. Since I clearly remembered Fancy telling us she'd never met Susan, this was definitely something to discuss with Kit, if not Culotta.

No, not Culotta. I was sick of his always being a step ahead of us. It was time to pass him up.

I didn't have time to dwell on my discovery. The doorbell rang, and I let in an Indian couple (both doctors, I quickly learned). They were followed by a family of six:

Father, Mother and four kids. I am always a little uncomfortable when there are so many people wandering around a house. But I reminded myself that's why they call it open.

By four o'clock I had given my card out to seven couples, and I was feeling optimistic that I would hear from at least one of them again. When the owners showed up five minutes later, I was happy to offer them some hope.

After I'd said good-bye and thanks, I packed up my Lexus and headed back to the office. I'd have enough time to catch up on some paperwork before going over to Kit's for my steak. High cholesterol be damned, it was starting to sound really good.

Both Perry and Billie were at their desks, not surprising for a realty office on a Sunday afternoon.

"Anyone hear from Tom?" I took a seat at my desk and turned on the computer.

Before either one could answer, my cell rang, and sure enough, the Big Guy's name showed on the screen. "Well, well, well," I said, "we were just talking about you."

"All bad, I trust." It was good to hear his voice.

"Just wondering when we're going to see you again, Boss." I winked at Perry. He had been playing some kind of computer game but punched the *escape* button as if Tom were actually standing at his desk.

"Good news for you, then," Tom said. "You can see me in about forty-five minutes. Pick me up at the American terminal. I just landed."

"Me? Tom, I just got—"

"Leave now, Val. Don't stop for shoe sales or coffee. I'm in no mood."

Before I could answer, he hung up.

I debated whether to call him back but realized it would only lead to—well, another debate. So I flipped off my computer, waved good-bye to the kids, and headed out to get the boss.

In my car, I put in a call to Kit's house. Larry answered.

"Do you think we could have dinner a little later, Lar?" I merged onto I-88. "I have to pick Tom up at the airport and presumably drive him home."

"Great. Bring him here instead. I have another steak. It'll be good to see Tom."

"You sure about that? I don't know that Kit would—"

"Kit will be thrilled."

Kit's voice suddenly boomed through the phone that she'd undoubtedly yanked from Larry's hand. "Are you kidding me? The last time I was in that dump you call an office, Tom Haskins threatened to have me arrested. Don't you dare bring that lunatic here."

"Fine with me," I said. And it really was.

Although the four of us went to the same high school, Tom's the oldest by a few years. He was a good friend of my brother, Buddy, a Naval Academy graduate and retired Navy officer who lives in Washington, DC, and they still keep in touch.

In the past few decades, Tom has become not just my boss and good friend, but a sort of surrogate older brother. We steered each other through three divorces (one for me, two for him), and he filled a certain place in my heart that was left vacant when my big brother moved on to start his own life.

Like my surrogate husband Larry, Tom is a go-to guy, someone who would beat up any bullies for me. An in-case-of-emergency guy. Yes, he can be gruff and even downright surly at times, but he is also the smartest, kindest man I know.

Socially, Larry and Tom cross paths frequently and maintain a good friendship. Kit and Tom, however, not so much. Generally, when they find themselves in the same room, they pace around like two bears in the same cave. Obviously, they're just too much alike.

Suddenly I found myself defending Tom. "Kit, if I remember correctly, that was six months ago and you had hit Tom's car in the parking lot."

"I might have touched it. I don't recall any damage."

"The bill was over five hundred dollars, Kit," Larry the accountant chimed in. He'd obviously picked up an extension. "I'd like to see Tom. Bring him over, Val, and don't take no for an answer."

"Oh, shut up," Kit said. "A *screw* costs five hundred dollars on a Mercedes. Bring him over if you two insist. But Larry, make sure we have a bottle of Laphroaig. Tom Haskins is practically an alcoholic."

***

I decided not to tell Tom where we were going until I headed the car toward Downers Grove instead of his downtown high-rise condo. "So how was Vegas? Have a good time?" I watched for my exit.

"Do I look like I had a good time?"

"Hmm, not sure. You hungry?"

He leaned back a little in the seat and pulled on the strap of his seat belt where it sat snugly across his midsection. "Hungry? Let's see. I've been on a damn plane for four hours, I consumed ten thousand packets of miniature peanuts, so I'd say no, I'm good, thanks."

"How does a steak sound?"

"Moo?"

"Oh, Tom, you're so witty."

"Hey, where the hell are you going? I don't need to go to the office."

"We're not going to the office. I'm taking you for a delicious home-cooked steak."

"Hold on, Pankowski. If you think you can throw a steak on the Bunsen burner you've got stashed in that rabbit hutch you live in—"

"No, no. We've been invited to dinner by some friends."

He was silent for just a moment, and I could see he was mentally culling all the people we had in common for who might invite us to dinner. "Geez, not Larry and the dingbat?"

"You like Larry."

"I love the guy, but—"

"Just shush. And be nice. They've got Laphroaig." I wasn't really sure what Laphroaig was, but I knew it must be good.

It shut Tom up for the rest of the ride.

***

As we walked up the driveway to their house, the front door opened and Larry and Kit appeared on their doorstep ready to greet us, like the President and First Lady welcoming foreign dignitaries.

Kit had changed into a cornflower-blue silk dress that set off her auburn hair. Larry was more casual in a golf shirt and Dockers.

"Come in. Good to see you, Tom," Larry said. He smiled and extended his hand for a shake.

Kit leaned toward Tom and kissed his cheek. "Welcome to our humble home, Tom," she said. "It's an honor to have you here."

"Cut the crap, Katherine," Larry said. "Val, do something with your friend." He put his arm around Tom's shoulders and steered him toward the living room.

"Why do I have to do something with her?" I mumbled, as I took Kit's arm and steered her toward the kitchen and away from the men.

"He looks shorter." Kit glanced sideways as Tom and Larry disappeared. "And has he gained weight?"

"Kit, you just saw him two weeks ago at my apartment."

"It's strange, but I always thought he had more hair than that."

"He's completely bald, Kit. Well, almost."

"Maybe he was wearing a hat last time I saw him."

We'd reached the safety of her kitchen, and I laid my briefcase on the granite counter.

"Yes, Kit, he's famous for his cowboy hats. And no doubt he had lifts in his shoes and was wearing a girdle." I sighed. "He's exactly the same as he was two weeks ago. But will you forget about Tom for one second? I have something to show you."

I pulled out the copy of *Time Out Chicago* and thumbed through for the "Happenings" page.

"Take a look at this." I pointed to the picture of Susan and Fancy. While I was at it, I handed her my reading glasses.

"Wow. Fancy looks like a whale."

"But do you see who's with her?"

"What. The. Hell." Kit pulled a tall stool a few inches toward her and sat down. "I don't believe it."

"Exactly. Remember Fancy told us she'd never met Susan? They seem pretty cozy here."

"No kidding. So why would the old bat lie?"

"Good question."

"What's a good question?" Larry was suddenly at the freezer, starting to fill a Waterford ice bucket. But he obviously didn't care what the good question was. He didn't wait for either of us to answer him. Instead, he smiled at me and said, "I'm so glad you brought Tom over, Val."

Kit took off my glasses and returned them to the briefcase. "Oh man, are we gonna be sucking up to Tom Haskins all night?"

"Fine with me," Tom said. He stood in the doorway, his jacket removed and a huge grin covering his face. "Kit, why don't you go first?"

***

Dinner went smoothly, considering the diners. Kit threw gibes across the table at Tom as easily as if she were tossing him dinner rolls. Tom caught most and threw them right back. Larry and I were the perfect buffers, occasionally forced to catch a roll midair and throw it over one of our shoulders.

The steaks were perfect. Kit had made a vegetable-packed tossed salad. Twice-baked potatoes stuffed with sour cream and chives completed the feast.

After we finished eating and Tom and Kit brought their debate on who the next superpower would be to an inconclusive end (Tom voted for China, Kit for India, and Larry and I abstained), the men took their three fingers of single-malt whiskey and a couple of cigars outside to the patio.

I collected some dishes and followed Kit to the kitchen. "That wasn't so bad, was it?"

"Oh, he's a dream come true, Val."

As her sarcasm floated across the kitchen counter, I looked out through the French doors to the patio. I could see the two men sipping their whiskey and puffing on cigars. Tom said something, and they both guffawed. A teenage memory grabbed at my heart: Tom, the cool senior to my awkward freshman, picking me and two girlfriends up after school in his Corvair and driving us to my brother's football game.

"It's good to see Larry laughing again," I said.

"Ya know, you're right." Kit looked up from the dishwasher, where she was filing plates. "I just wish we could find whoever it was who murdered that damn girl and we could get on with our lives. What should we do next?"

"I dunno. Wanna play cards? It's still early."

"I don't mean now, ding-dong. I mean for the investigation. What's next? What did your boyfriend—"

"You mean Detective Asshole? And he's not my boyfriend."

"Okay. Detective Asshole. What else did he say?"

I put two water glasses on the counter and cringed at the memory of my evening with Culotta. "He didn't *say* anything. I did all the talking. Oh, I am such an idiot."

Kit took the two glasses and carefully placed them on the top rack. "Seems like we have two things to cover. First, we should talk to Fancy again. And then we should find out who owns a Glock 9mm."

"Hah! You make that sound so easy."

"Shouldn't be too hard. We had to register *our* gun. Maybe there's a place we can check online."

"Wait a minute; you have a gun?" I wouldn't have been more surprised if she'd told me she had a Bengal tiger living in her garage.

"Of course. Larry bought a gun about five years ago."

Just then the patio door opened and Larry stuck his head into the room. "Val, I'll give Tom a ride home. No need for you to go all the way downtown."

"Okay," I said, "that's great." As he closed the door, the rich smell of Cuban tobacco wafted across the kitchen. "What kind?" I asked again, after Kit retrieved a can of air freshener from under the sink and began furiously spraying the room.

"It's vanilla," she said.

"Not the spray. The gun. What kind do you have?"

"A Glock 9mm."

CHAPTER TWENTY-FOUR

There she is." I pointed to Fancy, sitting, appropriately, in an overstuffed chair in a cozy corner of Starbucks. "But who's the looker sitting with her?" I moved my finger to point at a handsome young man sitting next to Fancy in a matching chair. They were engrossed in conversation. Fancy had her hand on his knee and her face just inches from his.

Kit and I had employed the element of surprise again that morning by appearing at Fancy's Chicago home at eight o'clock. The housekeeper, an elderly Hispanic woman who barely spoke English, told us *Mees Fitzy, she gone*. It took every detective skill we possessed to determine that Mees Fitzy was at a ubiquitous Starbucks in the area. This was achieved by the housekeeper holding an imaginary cup to her lips and pretending to drink, pointing at the sky (presumably looking for stars), and taking a dollar bill from the pocket of her skirt and telling us it was a buck. *You unnerstan?* I saw a bright future on a game show.

Unfortunately, she was unable to communicate the particular Starbucks where we could find her employer and shook her head in frustration when we pushed her. She'd said all she had to say.

We returned to Kit's BMW, and I watched as she took her phone from her purse and began searching for a Starbucks in the area. There were four close by, but we had lucked out and found Fancy at the second one. We arrived like two of the three Charlie's Angels, barging in and scoping out the place.

"Yuck," I said. "Surely they're not . . . she's not—"

"What? His cougar?" Kit gave a mean laugh, and I shushed her. But Fancy and her whatever were way too intent on their own conversation to notice us until we were standing at the little round coffee table right in front of them.

I cleared my throat, and they turned their faces toward us. Fancy looked shocked to see us, and her guy had a look of . . . was it fear or just concern? And were we the cause, or had he already worn that look before we approached? And either way, why? I gave myself an internal shake, settled on his look being merely surprised, and chastised myself for my melodrama. Sure, I was working a murder case, but then again, not really. I was a Realtor. Apparently a Realtor with too much time on her hands.

Or was I just determined to show Culotta I was much more than that?

Fancy spoke before I could decide what to say. "What in the world—?"

"Nice to see you too," Kit said. "Look, we need to talk. Truthfully, this time. Maybe you could excuse us?" Kit looked directly if not unkindly at Fancy's boyfriend, and then he looked directly at Fancy, as if seeking permission to leave. There was no doubt who wore the pants in the relationship, even though Fancy was wearing a kelly-green pleated skirt (something she should never wear, I knew, even without seeing her stand). Up this close, I could see the guy was even younger than he seemed from across the room. And he definitely looked a little frightened.

Fancy sighed and waved a resigned dismissal. "Yeah, go. We'll talk later."

I watched him stand and then lean down and kiss the top of Fancy's mound of blond hair.

"Bye, then," he said.

Kit and I looked at each other as he moved past us and bolted from the coffee shop.

"Okay, what do you two want now?" Fancy picked up the coffee cup in front of her and took a sip. I noticed that her hand clasped the cardboard like a manicured claw. Her nails, untouched by acrylic, were long and painted a deep red. She wore a diamond ring with a center stone of at least three carats, but the smaller surrounding diamonds looked dirty and gave off no sparkle.

"Good-looking *kid*." Kit took the seat he had vacated, and I pulled up another chair from the empty table next to us. "What's he to you?" Kit asked.

"A friend. And none of your damn business. Now why the hell are you two stalking me?" She looked perplexed for a moment. "How did you—did Marta—"

"Surprised? She no speaka da Engleesh, but she's pretty nifty with the sign language," Kit said.

"Ah, so you've taken to harassing my housekeeper now. What next? Do you plan on interrogating my hairdresser too?"

Kit and I glanced involuntarily at Fancy's stiff blond hairdo. It probably took Two Men and a Truck to get that baby in place every day. Then Kit brought us back to the matter at hand. "Why did you lie to us? Show her the picture, Val."

I rifled through my large black handbag for the magazine. I took it out and opened it to the picture of Fancy and Susan. But apparently I wasn't quick enough for Kit since she grabbed it from my hand and thrust it under Fancy's nose.

"So you never met the Reed woman, huh? The photographer seems to think you were friends. See here? It says *friend*." Kit tapped the magazine so hard I thought she would poke a hole in it.

Fancy barely glanced at the magazine, as if we were showing her a property for sale that she had no interest in. She placed her coffee back on the table and picked up a blueberry muffin, taking a huge bite. A shower of crumbs fell from her mouth, cascading past her two chins and landing on her ample bosom. "What on earth is it to you? Why are you so obsessed with me?" She raised her plucked eyebrows slightly, as if she were used to being the obsession of many people.

"Hold on to your ego," Kit said. "It's you and *this woman* we are interested in." Kit pointed again at the photograph.

"But why?" Fancy asked.

I almost wished Culotta were here, with his knack for getting people to spill their guts. Okay, maybe it was only *me* his technique worked on. But still, I would have loved to see him question Fancy.

Kit sighed in utter disbelief. "Uh . . . because she was murdered? And both you and your husband would seem to have motive?"

"I told you: you're wrong about all that. And what the hell is it to you, anyway?"

"We're just being good citizens, ya know. Might even have to make a citizen's arrest if you don't come clean."

I stifled a giggle over Kit's remarks, pushing away the image of us strong-arming Fancy and marching her out of Starbucks.

"Okay, Susan and I *were* friendly—before she claimed to be a relative. She'd helped me on last year's muscular dystrophy telethon." Fancy looked down at her pudgy knees that poked out of her skirt.

I wondered what she was thinking about, but Kit had no time to waste. "And?" she asked.

"And she impressed me as a hard worker and fun gal to be around. Humph!" Fancy looked up, first at Kit and then at me, as if I'd be easier to convince. "It's not as if we ever became bosom buddies. She was too . . ."

"White trash for you?" Kit gave a distasteful look, but I wasn't sure if she meant it for Susan or for Fancy. Probably both.

"Whatever." Fancy gave her head a little shake. "I appointed her to several different committees, and we worked well together. Until . . ."

"Until you found out she was your sister-in-law." Kit's matter-of-fact tone left no room for argument, and Fancy didn't try to defend herself. "But still you were seen with her after that." Kit tapped the magazine photo again, not so roughly the second time. It was a simple reminder more than an accusation.

"What did you want me to do? Defriend her? For your information, real life isn't like Facebook. I'd have too much explaining to do. It was easier to just . . ."

I couldn't believe it. Even Fancy was versed in Facebook, probably even had her own page or profile or whatever it was called. I made a mental note to talk to Emily about Facebook, maybe even let her sign me up.

"So why did you lie to us? Why did you tell us you'd never met Susan?" Kit asked.

"Why do you think, Miss Smarty-Pants? You're breathing down my neck as if you think my husband or I killed her. You think I'm gonna tell you I'd spent a lot of time with her?"

"You don't think we're going to find out anyway?" Kit looked at Fancy in disbelief if not disgust.

"If you were a normal person, you wouldn't even be asking such questions, any questions. There's no reason for you—"

"My husband and I had our own association with Ms. Reed, if you must know," Kit said, "and I wanted to make sure the focus didn't fall on us when it belonged elsewhere."

I was surprised at her honesty, but since she was demanding the same from Fancy, I decided it was only fair. I gave my friend a smile of approval. "What about the police?" I asked Fancy. "Were you honest with them?"

"The police?" Fancy looked bored. "The police know better than to hound me or my family. You should take a lesson from them."

"Fancy, have you not been listening to us?" Kit sounded like a frustrated mother. In fact, I half expected her to follow with one of my mom's favorite lines, one I grew up hearing all too often. *You must be deaf in one ear and can't hear out of the other.* Kit turned and faced me. "Val, maybe *we* need to fill the police in."

"Oh, why don't you two get a life? The police aren't interested in me." Her satisfied look left me nonplussed. If I were her, I would have been at least a little unsettled. Was it her money and influence that gave her such confidence? She took the last bite of her muffin and then rose from her seat and brushed crumbs from the front of her body. At least she proved me right about one important issue: no way should she be wearing a pleated skirt.

"Oh, I think the police might be very interested in you." Kit stood and headed out of Starbucks.

I followed.

***

Back in Kit's BMW, we headed toward my office, where I had left my car. Both of us were quiet, as if pondering the whole scene with Fancy. I noticed Kit's phone perched in the top of her purse, about to topple out. I picked it up to put it in a more secure spot, and when I touched it, a picture of the two of us instantly popped up.

It was taken about six months earlier at a friend's birthday party. We were sitting at a table in a Mexican restaurant, each holding an oversize margarita glass, both of us tipsy. Still, Kit managed to look as elegant as if she'd just left her stylist. I, on the other hand, looked like I'd been on a week-long tequila bender south of the border.

"Great picture of you, Kit," I said, "but a good friend would have deleted this."

"Don't be ridiculous. You look cute."

It wasn't lost on me that she didn't question my assessment of her own appearance in the photo. Then again, she probably really did think I looked cute. Isn't that what friends are for?

"Well," I said at last, "Fancy really didn't seem bothered about our going to the police, did she? Maybe we are barking up the wrong tree. I mean, we're thinking she is the murderer, right?"

"Hmm, not sure. But you are right about one thing: she didn't give a shit."

"Well, it would be interesting to see what spin Culotta would put on it. She said the police haven't spoken to her."

"She also said she'd never met Skank-o-lena."

I didn't like Kit implying I had no reason to contact Culotta. "Well, I think I'll give him a call anyway," I said. "Just in case he doesn't know about Fancy and Susan."

"It can't hurt, especially as you and Culotta have such a special relationship." She took her hands off the wheel to wrap air quotes around the word *special*. Then her face grew serious. "Yeah, you really should make sure he knows about Fancy and Susan."

CHAPTER TWENTY-FIVE

After checking my e-mail and returning phone calls from two of the people who had visited my open house the day before, I told Billie I was taking an early lunch. Tom had not arrived at the office, and I wanted to be gone before he showed up. I was going to Subway for a toasted chicken-and-avocado sandwich, and then I planned to call Dennis from my cell. First things first.

But somehow my car took a wrong turn, and then another. Before I knew it, I was on Burlington Avenue, heading toward the Downers Grove police station. Well, in person was always better than a phone call, wasn't it?

I pulled into a visitor's spot and turned off the car. Pulling down the visor, I checked my lipstick in the mirror. Then I marched into the building and up to the front desk, where a hefty guy with a marine's haircut was reading *People* magazine. "Detective Culotta, please," I said.

He barely glanced up from an article on Kim Kardashian. "Who should I tell him is here?"

"Valerie. Valerie Pankowski."

"And what do you want to see him about?"

"About—" I stopped to consider, wondering what Kit would say if she were in my place. "He'll know what it's about," I said at last.

Hefty opened his mouth and looked at me as if he were about to insist on an answer. But instead, he picked up the phone and passed along the information. Then he turned the page, where I saw an upside-down Kate Hudson in a leopard-skin bikini.

Culotta appeared, looking more like an attorney than a cop in his dark suit and tie. A good-looking attorney. I was glad I had come.

"Valerie. Always a pleasure to see you," he said. I wanted to believe he meant it, but his teasing grin left me unsure. "C'mon; follow me." He turned and led the way to his office.

If there was one positive thing I could say about him, it was that he didn't hold a grudge. There was no indication that our last meeting had ended on a bad note. "Sit." He motioned to a chair and then closed his office door behind us. "In fact, I was just about to call you and ask you for coffee or something. I don't think our last meeting ended very well."

I wanted to slap the self-righteous look off his delectable face, even though he wore it well. "Do they ever?" I asked.

He leaned back in his chair until its two front legs raised up. If I had done that, the chair would have toppled backward and I would have landed on the floor. But Culotta's chair was apparently topple-proof, and it balanced easily on two legs. "So what's on your mind?"

"I ran into Fancy Fitzpatrick this morning," I said, plunging straight into the deep end of the pool.

"Whoa." A huge grin spread across his face. "Let me guess. You want me to arrest her for causing an obstruction?"

I watched as he rocked his chair back and forth, and I found myself wishing it would fall over and he'd land on his ass.

"I shouldn't have come here," I said quietly, more to myself than to him.

Still smiling, he reached over to his desk for a pen and then returned to his precarious rocking.

He rolled the pen between his fingers.

"Okay," he said, "how about a moving violation? Her, not you."

"Okay, Culotta," I said after several seconds of silence. "Your little circus trick here is fascinating, but I have better things to do." I stood, and he immediately dropped the chair down on all four legs.

"Valerie, before you rush off, perhaps you can tell me why you came."

He almost had me there. But I made a quick decision that for a change I wasn't going to spill my guts. It had been a stupid idea to come here, to try to be of some help. He'd have to figure it out for himself. "I was just passing by on my way to lunch." I pulled the strap of my purse over my shoulder. "And by the way, I don't have time for coffee or anything else. Sorry."

"Geez." He stood up. "Not that I'm complaining, but these little sudden visits of yours are baffling. I'm beginning to think you like me."

I could feel my face grow hot as I tried to think of something clever to say. Nothing came to me, except an overwhelming feeling of foolishness.

"Let me walk you out to your car," he said. "It could be dangerous out there. Maybe Fancy Fitzpatrick has a tail on you." He came around the desk and put his hand on my elbow.

I felt the heat move down my body from his continued touch as he silently walked me out of his office. As we passed Hefty, who was still reading *People* magazine, I caught Culotta's wink in the officer's direction.

At my car, Detective Culotta let go of me and gripped the door handle as I hit the button on my remote. "It was good to see you again, Valerie."

"Shouldn't you be working on the case?" I asked. It was weak, but the best I could come up with.

"Ah yes, the case. I would, but I keep getting these damn interruptions from a cute blonde." He looked way too pleased with himself.

"Well, I'm leaving now, so you can feel free to get back to work."

He folded his arms across his chest. "So let me see if I have this straight: you *don't* want to tell me about your little visit with our favorite politician's wife?"

"No."

"Okay, then. But you're not withholding information, are you, Valerie?"

"Did you know Fancy Fitzpatrick and Susan were friends?" Suddenly it seemed important that I tell him. Not so much that he have the information, but more that I had a reason for this brainless visit. "Well, maybe not friends, but they had a relationship of sorts. Were you aware of it?"

He gazed up over the top of my head, almost as if he were dismissing my words. Obviously, he did not like his investigation questioned. And I couldn't blame him. I hated it when Tom questioned me on why I had lost a sale. Or anything else.

Nevertheless, I shook my head and persevered. "Well, were you?"

His blue eyes narrowed as he brought me back into focus. "Are you kidding me with this crap? Look, lady, do you know how long I've been a detective? I've solved more murders than you've had lattes at Starbucks, and I'm considering every angle of this case. You might not believe it, but I'm in the middle of a thorough investigation and will interview every possible suspect. Without, I might add, any assistance from you."

"Dennis, I—"

"You show up every five minutes in between selling houses and getting your hair done, and you think you know more than me? This is bullshit, Valerie. This isn't some TV cop show. Don't you dare question my judgment or my methods." He moved his gaze from my face and began staring at the car parked next to mine.

For some reason, I felt compelled to defuse him, though I didn't know whether that was for his sake or mine. "Dennis, I'm sure you're doing a great—"

"Oh, how kind of you, Valerie. Perhaps you could put a call in to my captain and recommend me for a promotion. Coming from you, that would mean so much."

"I'm just saying—"

"I told you to stay out of this from the beginning, but you just don't listen."

His clipped words stung, but it wasn't the first time. What was even worse, he was right. I moved past him and opened the car door. I don't think I had ever felt so foolish. As I drove away, I watched him in my rearview mirror. He was kicking an empty soda can across the parking lot. Hands in his pockets, head bent forward, he looked like a teenage boy who'd just lost a fight. He looked sad, but not nearly as sad as I felt.

My phone rang before I had even reached the end of the street. I took a deep breath before answering. I quickly prepared all the ways I could tell him I was sorry.

"*Pankowski!*" It was worse than I'd thought. Not Dennis calling to make up, but Tom calling to perforate my eardrum.

"Hi, Tom." I took another deep breath. "I was just—"

"Your next words better be you were just racing your ass over to this office."

"Yes, Tom, I'm on my—"

"What am I paying you for, Pankowski?"

"I was taking a lunch break, for Pete's sake."

"Lunch is for Realtors who sell a house occasionally."

"Tom, will you please stop yelling—"

He hung up on me. And the strange thing was, it felt good, since it was the very least I deserved.

***

In spite of Tom's barking, I stopped at Subway and bought a sandwich for both of us. I hoped the chicken-and-avocado would placate him a little. The good thing about Tom's tantrums is that they usually don't last long.

Unfortunately, this wasn't one of those times.

"What the hell is this?" he asked, as I placed the sandwich on his desk.

"Lunch. Toasted chicken-and-avocado. Delicious."

"Why is it wrapped in a grocery bag?"

"It's not a grocery bag." I took the sandwich, wrapped in Subway's waxy paper, out of the plastic bag. "See?" I laid it on his desk and opened the paper. "Yummy."

"Did you get it at a homeless shelter?"

"Of course not; I went to—"

"Subway. I can read, Valerie. But I don't eat sandwiches wrapped in newspaper made by a fifteen-year-old pimply kid who can't speak English."

"Fine. I'll eat two. And you are an ungrateful devil." I stomped out of his office and took his sandwich to the refrigerator in our little kitchen. At my desk, I turned on my computer and quickly started to look busy.

"Janet Holmes called," Perry said, after he was sure it was safe to speak and Uncle Tom wasn't going to beat us both with the stapler.

"Oh good," I said. She had been one of my open-house prospects. "Give me the number."

Perry put down the plastic fork he was using to eat his bean-sprout salad and handed me a pink piece of paper.

I called Janet Holmes, and we arranged to meet back at the house the next morning. As soon as we hung up, I called the owner, who was happy with the news. For the rest of the day I avoided Tom, which was easy since he stayed in his office behind a closed door. But at five o'clock the door opened and Tom appeared.

"Buy me a drink, Val," he said.

"I'm very, very busy, Boss. You know, doing what you pay me for."

"Perhaps your Internet shopping can wait until tomorrow. I need a drink."

I faked reluctance and made a big show of shutting down my computer and then shifting papers around on my desk.

"I'll meet you at Patrick's," he said.

***

Patrick's is a charming bar, dark and intimate, and a favorite spot of other local Realtors, so the gossip is always good.

Even though Tom left the office ten minutes before me, I beat him to Patrick's by fifteen minutes. I took a stool at the far end of the long bar, putting my purse on the one next to it as a reservation for Tom.

When the door opened, he made his usual spectacular entrance. It took him a good ten minutes to make his way down to my end of the bar. He stopped to shake hands with several other patrons and kiss a few cheeks. When Tom finally arrived and took the stool next to me, Patrick himself appeared behind the bar. It was an honor indeed. He normally leaves the serving to one of his many sons or grandsons.

"What's it to be, miss?" he asked me, his Irish brogue still evident after nearly sixty years in America. "And Tom, 'tis a pleasure indeed to see you." He actually put his hand over his heart as he said it. Behind him on the wall, the Irish flag was prominently displayed.

"How's it hangin', Pat?" Tom took out a cigar and lit it. I thought for a moment he'd be made to put it out; then I realized that Patrick was also smoking a fat stogie.

"So," Tom said, after two glasses of red wine had been placed before us and Patrick had gone. "What's been happening, Kiddo?"

I filled him in on the open house, making it sound as if I'd had more traffic than Grand Central Station on a Monday morning. Tom nodded, puffed on his cigar, and took a sip of wine. "So you shouldn't have any trouble selling it?"

"Probably not," I lied.

"And how's your boyfriend?"

"Huh? What are you talking about?"

"Your boyfriend. Culotta."

"Oh, Tom," I said, as coyly as possible. "You know *you* are my only boyfriend."

"Then it really sucks to be you."

"Come on; Culotta and I had dinner a few times. And to tell the truth, they didn't go well. I'm not sure he even likes me."

"He thinks you're a pain in the ass."

"Are you serious? How dare he."

"Have you been stalking him?"

"Of course not. If anyone's been stalking, it's him, not me."

"You should keep out of his way. He's a tough guy, Val. He don't play nice. Not like your old Uncle Tom."

"Of course; you are a pussycat, dear," I said. But before I could remind him of the string of brokenhearted women he'd left in his wake, a third person violated the little space between our stools. This was nothing new. Whenever I'm in a bar or restaurant with Tom, I'm amused by the number of women vying to catch his eye.

But this one was a surprise.

"Barbara." Tom got down from the stool and kissed her cheek. "Good to see you."

Barbara Craigmore looked more like she was just starting her business day, rather than ending it. Her dark-pink suit was crease-free, and her white blouse looked as if it had just come from the dry cleaner. "Hello, Tom. Val. A few of us came in for a drink. Just wanted to say hello." She motioned toward a table at the opposite end of the room, where a group of six women, probably all Realtors, were ordering drinks.

"Glad you did." Tom returned to his stool.

"How's business?" she asked Tom, pointedly ignoring me. I recalled the last time I'd seen her, at the showing, and she hadn't grown any friendlier since then, even though she did look a lot better.

"Business is great." Tom rested his cigar on a heavy glass ashtray and took a sip of his wine. "Got the greatest salesgal in Chicago working for me. What more do I need?" He tipped his wineglass to indicate he meant me. I was so surprised, I almost looked over my shoulder to see if, in fact, the greatest salesgal in Chicago was standing behind me.

Barbara gave a little laugh, waved good-bye, and headed back to her group.

"Sales*gal*?" I said, as soon as she was out of earshot. "What the hell was that?"

"It was a compliment." He chuckled. In his warped world, where he often refers to women as dames or chicks, he probably thinks *gal* is an accolade.

"Gee, I'll break out my go-go boots," I said.

Tom ignored me and turned slightly on the stool to look over at Barbara's table. "She looks good. Considering."

"Considering what?"

"Considering all Allen Craigmore put her through. I heard she's still paying off his debts. At least he had the good sense to kill himself."

"I didn't realize you knew about that."

"Word gets around, Val. It was a bad business."

"Did you know he had an affair with Susan Reed? The girl who was murdered?"

"That's what they tell me. In which case, I guess the guy *is* better off dead."

CHAPTER TWENTY-SIX

The last time I'd seen the Parkinsons together was at Larry's company Christmas party two years earlier at The Sutton Place Hotel on Chicago's Miracle Mile. It had been a lavish affair planned by Kit down to the last detail. At the time, I was still married to David, although he had been out of town doing what he did when he was out of town. I didn't want to think too much about that. I knew all too well what it was.

Kit had insisted I go to the party to keep her company, but I don't think we shared more than two minutes together. I'd spent most of the evening sitting at a table with three other couples whose names I quickly forgot. But I'd enjoyed watching Kit work her boss's-wife magic, looking gorgeous in a deep-purple raw-silk suit. Ellen Parkinson, the other boss's wife, spent most of the evening standing at the bar knocking back martinis and keeping a careful eye on her handsome husband.

Now Kit had insisted once again that I join them for a company celebration, a much smaller one. Brad Parkinson had scored a lucrative account. Rather than go out, Kit cooked her fabulous osso buco, and the five of us sat around her dining room table. But Ellen Parkinson was still knocking back the martinis.

She looked even thinner than she had the last time I'd seen her, and she'd done something strange to her hair. It was too dark, too short, and brushed back in a manly fashion. She was wearing a cheap-looking beige cotton suit over a white shirt and had applied too much deep-red blush to her sharp cheekbones.

In contrast, Brad Parkinson looked as if he'd just stepped out of *GQ* magazine. His dark-blond hair was perfectly groomed, and he had removed his suit jacket to display snappy red suspenders over a blue-and-white pin-striped shirt. As I sipped my pinot grigio, I wondered what they had looked like when they first met, nearly thirty years ago. Had Brad been as dashing back then? Had Ellen been as dowdy?

"A toast to Kit." Brad raised his wineglass. "That was fantastic. You are a magnificent cook."

"To Kit," I agreed. I watched my pal at the other end of the table, her eyes shining in the glow from the candlelight.

"Oh, stop," she said. "It was nothing."

"It was osso buco; that's not nothing," Larry said, husbandly pride radiating from his face.

"It's veal shank, for crying out loud," Kit said. "Anyone with a decent cookbook could throw it together."

"Ellen couldn't, could you, honey?" Brad said. "Ellen's good at a great many things, but cooking is not one of them."

I looked to see how Ellen would respond and watched a wicked smile form on her thin lips. I saw Brad give her an equally wicked wink, and I was filled with curiosity about just what Ellen was so good at.

"And here's to Brad," Larry said. I wondered if he'd caught the look between the Parkinsons. He raised his glass, and we all drank a toast. "Val, this guy here just single-handedly put us in the black for the foreseeable future. I don't know how he got Filex to switch accountants, but I'm glad as hell he did."

"Yep," Brad said. He looked way too pleased with himself, reminding me a little of Culotta. "And it wasn't easy. A murdered employee doesn't exactly scream confidence. 'Bout time we had some good news."

"Surely Susan's death would have nothing to do with your business," I said, although I didn't really believe it.

Brad ignored my comment and frowned. "I just wish the police would solve the murder. What the hell are they doing, anyway?"

"Ask Val." Kit stood and began stacking plates at her end of the table. I noticed she avoided giving me any eye contact.

"Val?" Ellen spoke. "What does Val have to do with it?"

"Oh, she and Culotta are dating; didn't you know?"

"Kit," I shrieked. "That's absolutely not true."

"Really?" Ellen said, before she drained her martini and held her glass toward Larry, presumably for a refill. "Is that even allowed?"

"Why shouldn't it be? Culotta and Val are both single," Kit said. Then she slowly walked around the table, adding plates to her stack. "They're a cute couple, don't you think?"

I stood up. "Kit, you are giving the wrong impression. Culotta and I are not dating, Ellen"

"Oh, come on, Val. We're all friends here. I'd call two single people having dinner on a Saturday night a date. What would you call it?" She disappeared into the kitchen, and I dropped my napkin on the table and followed her.

At her kitchen counter, I grabbed her arm and twirled her around. "What are you doing? Why would you say something like that?"

"Shush." She looked through to the dining room and smiled. "They'll hear you."

"What are you up to?"

She put the plates on the counter, took my hand, and led me out to the back hallway. "I wanted to see how Ellen reacted to your pillow talk."

"Okay, first, there has been no pillow talk. And second, why?"

"She's acting weird. Even for her. She told me before you got here what a relief it was that Skanky was no longer lurking around the office."

"Er, I would have thought you would agree with that."

"I have totally different motives, ya know. Besides, I would never say that to anyone but you, Val. Plus, she asked me ten thousand times if the police had a suspect, and who they thought had done it."

"What did you say? You didn't mention Fancy, did you? Or Mrs. Reed?"

"Absolutely not. I told her I'm going with Professor Plum in the library with a rope. She was half in the bag already, so she's probably still trying to figure out who Professor Plum is."

We walked back into the kitchen and Kit put on rubber gloves to begin washing plates.

"Ya know, I never would have agreed to spend the evening with them if I could help it," she said in a hushed tone, even after she'd turned on the faucet. "They are huge bores. She gets drunk out of her mind, and Brad can talk only about himself. But Larry insisted. Personally, I can't stand—Ellen, darling, need something?"

Ellen Parkinson stood in the doorway, her half-finished martini sloshing around in its glass. "So, you and the detective?" she addressed only me, her eyes narrowed to slits.

"Kit exaggerates." I picked up a towel and took a rinsed plate from the sink. "Culotta's got much bigger fish to fry than me."

"Really," she said. Taking baby steps, she walked unsteadily to a stool. It took two attempts for her to land her bony backside safely. "I think it's disgraceful how they don't keep us informed. But do tell, Val. Anyone we know, these so-called bigger fish?"

"It's just an expression, Ellen. I meant it generally. I know as much about the police investigation as you do." I rubbed the plate with the towel so hard that Kit removed it from me. I gave her an irritated look.

"Just trying to save the pattern on the Spode," she muttered.

"So, Val," Ellen said, "when you and the detective had dinner at The Capital Grille Saturday, you didn't discuss the murder?"

It was a good thing Kit had rescued her precious china, or I might have thrown it at Ellen. "How the hell do you know where I was Saturday?"

"Wow, so defensive! Brad and I were there too. I guess you must have missed us."

"Oh, really?"

"Yes, and you two seemed very cozy. I'm just wondering what a policeman could possibly have to say to you."

I wasn't sure what annoyed me more, the fact that she had been spying on me, or that I wasn't worthy of a conversation with a detective. "This is ridiculous," I said. "Kit, thank you for a lovely dinner, but I really must go."

"No, no, don't leave; we haven't had dessert yet," Kit said.

"Oh, dessert," Ellen said. "Val, don't rush off. This is just getting interesting. I was hoping you could fill us in a little, seeing as how the police have failed to do so. I hope I haven't made you uncomfortable." She eyed me over the rim of her glass, and it was obvious she wanted to make me squirm.

"Sorry, not interested in your little games, Ellen. Kit, I'll call you tomorrow. Tell Larry good-bye."

I could feel my face burn as I dug in my purse for my keys. I knew I was being too dramatic, giving Ellen just the reaction she wanted. I was furious at myself, but more furious at Culotta, who was the cause of it all.

As I walked to my car and hit the *open* button on my remote, I made myself a promise that I was done with the whole damn thing. Susan Reed's murderer could go free, for all I cared.

I kept my promise all the way home, but when I pulled into my parking spot at the back of my building and saw Culotta sitting on the steps leading to the back door, I knew it might be a hard promise to keep.

I took my time getting out of the car and walked slowly to the back-door entrance. Culotta looked up, but he wasn't smiling.

"It's over, Valerie," he said.

"Oh, for Pete's sake, you came all the way here to tell me that? Look, Dennis, we are not a *couple*, so telling me it's over is ridiculous—"

"C'mere," he said, patting the empty spot next to him on the concrete step. "Has anyone ever told you that you are the worst detective in the whole world?"

"I'm a Realtor, not a detective. And what the hell does that mean, anyway?"

"It means that when I say it's over, I'm talking about the murder case. Not this little—whatever the hell this thing is." He made a swirling motion with his fingers, taking aim at both of us.

"Oh." I sat next to him on the cold step.

"Valerie, don't you want to know what I came to tell you?"

"Not really. I don't give a damn anymore."

He stood up. "Okay, then. Sorry I bothered you."

I watched him walk to his car, and I believed he might really get in and drive away if I didn't yell at him. "Okay, stop. Tell me."

"We made an arrest. We got the murderer."

"Are you sure?" I asked. I had no reason to doubt him. I'd just kind of figured Kit and I would get there first.

"Oh yeah, we even got a confession."

I stood up. "Dennis, get back here."

CHAPTER TWENTY-SEVEN

I had Barbara Craigmore pegged as the killer from the beginning." Culotta sat on my couch, his long legs stretched under the coffee table. I had invited him up for a drink, even though I was out of Heinekens and the only alcohol I had in the house was a sickly sweet zinfandel I'd opened months ago. He winced as he took a sip.

"So you already arrested her?"

"Yep. Today, at her house. She's got a good attorney. Maria Sweeney. She used to be a DA, so she knows her way around the courtroom and the law."

I sat down on the edge of the cushion next to Culotta and took a sip of my wine. After the fine pinot I'd had at Kit's, it tasted even worse than I'd expected.

"I saw Barbara just last night," I said. "Tom and I were having a drink at Patrick's, and she stopped by to say hello."

"I didn't know you two were friends."

"Oh, believe me, we're not. It was Tom she was interested in, not me."

"Yeah, Tom's a good guy."

"You think so?" I paused, to give him time to change his mind. When he didn't, I spoke again. "Barbara seemed in a good mood. It's hard to believe she's a murderer."

"I can assure you she's no longer in such a good mood. Amazing how a little murder charge can ruin your whole day."

"And she confessed?"

"Yep, she cracked like a walnut after I told her we had the weapon."

"The gun? You have the gun?"

"Yep." He actually hooked his fingers around the belt loops of his pants as he said it. It reminded me of a Southern cop in some seventies movie who had just caught the good ol' boys making moonshine, rather than the sophisticated urban cop I had grown used to.

I took another sip and watched his irritating smile. He could barely contain his enjoyment of the whole situation. "So where was it?" I asked.

"The gun? Where I knew it would be. She tossed it in a Dumpster, in the back of an apartment building on the same street."

The image of Barbara in her sharp business suit and high heels driving around Susan Reed's neighborhood looking for a place to stash a gun struck me as ridiculous. But no more ridiculous than her killing Susan in the first place.

"But I knew it was her even before we found the weapon."

"How did you—"

"Susan's mother told us about Barbara Craigmore's intense hatred of her daughter." He sounded as smug as he looked. And I did have to give him points for gleaning that information. Marjorie Reed had never said anything like that to Kit and me. How *did* he do it? My shoulders sank, as if deflated in defeat, but I quickly reminded myself it was *his* job, not mine. So why did it bother me so much?

I'd never seen anyone look more self-satisfied than Dennis Culotta did as he continued his story. " . . . confirmed her employment with him and the fact that they were having an affair. Allen Craigmore's business went south, mainly due to his crooked work, but Susan was right there with him. If he hadn't killed himself, and if a full investigation had been done, Susan might have been brought up on fraud charges. As it was, Barbara Craigmore was left holding the bag. And an empty one at that. She was angry that Susan was able to walk away from the whole mess."

He stopped to take another sip of the wine, and for the first time since he'd arrived, his smile briefly faded. "This stuff sucks, by the way."

I nodded. "I know, but I wasn't exactly expecting company."

"So." He drained his glass, ready to return to the story of his heroics. "I also knew Barbara Craigmore had a gun registered in her name, a gun like the one used to kill Susan. When it was found and matched up with the casings left at the scene, she made a complete confession. Pretty good work, if I do say so myself, cracking the case in just over a week."

"Well, if it was so simple, I'm surprised it took you that long." I wasn't ready to congratulate him.

"Valerie, don't be bitter. Be glad we got a murderer off the street."

"Ah yeah, a real menace to society. If her husband was having an affair with society, that is."

"You don't think she should be punished, just because her husband was screwing the vic?"

I felt a warm glow, a good feeling for a change, as if Dennis were talking to me as a fellow detective. But it didn't last long.

As if he caught himself giving me unwarranted respect, he said, "Victim. A vic is a victim."

"I know. I watch *Law & Order*."

***

I waited until almost midnight to call Kit. I wanted to be sure the Parkinsons were gone. I was betting that by now Ellen would be passed out, hopefully in her own bed.

"Val!"

"Sorry to call so late. Have the Parkinsons left yet?"

"Yes. Finally. They left about twenty minutes ago. I was just telling Larry that he is never to invite them over again. I don't care if Brad scores the account for all of Saudi Arabia, I don't ever want—"

"Can you talk?"

"Val, what the hell do you call this?"

"I have news. Culotta was here."

"No wonder the man can't solve this murder, when he's always at your apartment—"

"He has solved it, Kit. He arrested Barbara Craigmore."

"What?"

"Yes, Barbara Craigmore. He says she confessed."

"Holy shit!"

"Holy shit, indeed. Do you believe it?"

"Certainly the smart money was on Fancy Fitzpatrick. Or maybe Mother Reed. I have to say I'm surprised; aren't you?"

"Yes. It seemed like she was working hard to keep her life together. Plus, she has a son. You'd think that since he lost one parent, she wouldn't do anything to—"

"Heat of the moment, Val. She probably did it without thinking about it."

"Maybe, but I don't see her as the passionate type. And why would she take a trip to Susan's house with a gun in her purse if she wasn't planning to kill her? In fact, why would she even be going to see her at all?"

"The skank ruined her life. She told us that herself. I think I can sort of understand it."

"But why now, after all this time?"

"Who knows? Maybe it's the economy."

"Huh?"

"Think about it. Because of Skanky, she's had to go back to work. How many houses can she be selling? Maybe it just got to be too much for her, and she was pissed."

"Yeah, she could have been pissed. But I can't understand why she would confess."

"Maybe we should ask her," Kit said.

"Huh?"

"Maybe we should pay a visit tomorrow. Ya know, go offer our friend some comfort," Kit said.

"Do you think we could? And what would we say to her?"

"We'll figure it out. We always do."

CHAPTER TWENTY-EIGHT

W hat's that?" I watched as Kit daintily got into my car carrying a yellow-and-pink gift bag with a froth of matching tissue spilling out of the top. She set it down between us and buckled her seat belt.

"A gift for Barbara." Her tone added *what else would it be?*

"Kit, really, you've outdone yourself. First of all, we don't even know that we'll be allowed to see her. Second, we probably can't take anything in with us. And third, what in the world do you get for someone in jail?" I couldn't wait to learn what gift was appropriate for a confessed murderess.

"Um, a fruitcake with a file? A gun?" She giggled, and even though it wasn't a mean laugh, it also showed little sympathy for Barbara Craigmore.

"Seriously, what's in there?" I nudged the gift bag with my elbow but kept both hands on the wheel. The morning traffic was snarled, with people making their way around local streets to jobs in suburbia or heading to the major arteries that would lead them to their work in downtown Chicago.

"Homemade brownies. No file, no gun. I'm keepin' my Glock for myself, thank you very much. Murder in the suburbs is getting a little too common."

"You are something else," I said.

"I know." I watched a tiny smile form on her lips as she fiddled with the tissue in the gift bag.

"You're in a good mood, considering," I said.

"Ya know, I am, Val. And why not? I know it's a tragedy for Barbara, but now we can get on with our lives, put this whole thing behind us."

"Yes, we can do that. But the thought of Barbara having to go to prison . . . it's horrible."

"She's got a good attorney, an expensive one. And if I were the judge, I'd let her off. As far as I'm concerned, she did us all a favor."

I swung my car into the parking lot of the jail, where we'd read Barbara Craigmore was being held. After we got out of my car, I followed Kit up the sidewalk to the double glass doors. Swinging the gift bag, she looked as if she were going to a wedding shower.

I made sure Kit stayed in the lead as we approached the front desk, happy to let her do the talking. I listened as she spoke in her most commanding voice to the officer sitting there. "We're here to see Barbara Craigmore."

"Oh, you are, are you?" The officer was writing something on a clipboard, and without his even looking up, I caught his smirk. I took it to mean *who the hell do you think you are, bitch?*

Kit was commanding, but she was also no dummy. She knew what she wanted, and she quickly changed her strategy to try to get it.

"Yes, sir. Do you think we possibly could?" She was all little girl, hoping against hope to get to see her best friend, Barbara Craigmore. "We're so worried about her, Officer

Schmidt." I hadn't even noticed his name tag before then, but Kit doesn't miss a thing.

I could see an immediate transformation in Officer Schmidt's face as he finally looked up, like someone removing a Halloween mask and revealing a sweet, childlike countenance underneath the scary monster. "Barbara Craigmore can't have visitors. Only a family member or her lawyer, and something tells me you aren't either." He sounded almost regretful.

"I could be her sister?" Kit actually batted her eyelashes, and I wasn't sure if I felt like groaning or giggling. I did neither. I didn't trust Officer Schmidt's mood not to change on a dime—or a groan or giggle.

"*Are* you her sister?" he asked.

"No." I was almost surprised—but greatly relieved—that Kit didn't lie to him.

"Then no dice. Sorry."

Kit held the gift bag up to Schmidt's face and gave it a little shake. "We are her best friends."

"Look, lady, I don't write the rules; I just enforce them."

I took hold of Kit's arm and moved her away from the counter, stepping in front of her.

"Is Detective Culotta here, by any chance?"

Schmidt turned his face to mine. "Let me guess. He's another one of your best friends?"

"Is he here?"

Schmidt sighed heavily, picked up the phone, and punched in a number. "Hey, Culotta, there are a couple of women out here wanting to know if you're available." After a lengthy pause, he put the phone down and looked up at me. "Take a seat. Detective Culotta will be right with you." He used his clipboard to indicate a long green vinyl bench on the far wall. I tugged at Kit's arm and led her to the bench.

"Good thinking, Valley Girl," Kit whispered into my ear, "asking for your boyfriend."

"Ha ha. But even though he's not my boyfriend, he might be useful. For once. By the way, tell me again exactly why we want to see Barbara?"

"Why not?" Kit looked surprised. "She's one of our peers, Val. And she's going down for murder. Aren't you at least curious?"

I didn't respond, but she was right. Part of me was curious. And at least a little part of me wanted to reach out in kindness to a fellow Realtor. I took a deep breath, preparing myself to face Culotta and, I hoped, Barbara Craigmore.

Culotta kept us waiting for twenty minutes. When he finally showed, he was holding a clipboard, just like his coworker Schmidt. He appeared to be studying it, and I wondered if it was just a prop the police use to make themselves look busy.

"Ladies," he said, finally tearing his eyes away from the clipboard, "what a pleasure to see you both. Are you here to congratulate me?"

"Can we see Barbara Craigmore?" I stood to meet his eyes.

He burst into a hearty laugh and turned toward Schmidt, who echoed his chortle.

"Well, can we?"

"Would you get a load of these two, Schmitty?" Culotta asked. When he looked at me again, his face turned to stone. "No, you most certainly cannot. I am sure Officer Schmidt has explained the rules. Family or attorney. You can leave any time."

I tugged at the shoulder strap on my purse and looked down at Kit. "Let's—"

"You really should be congratulated, Detective," Kit said. "You did an excellent job."

"Thank you, Mrs. James. But you still can't see Mrs. Craigmore."

"Oh, I understand." Kit stood up. "Rules are not meant to be broken, not even by you. As brilliant as you've been this past week, you don't run this police station. If the rules say we can't visit our friend, then not even you can break them."

"Exactly," Culotta said. "Glad you see it that way."

"Oh, I do. We wouldn't want to get you in trouble with your superiors."

"Precisely," I joined in Kit's game. "We'd hate to put you in a difficult position with your captain—"

"It's not as if you can do whatever you want around here—"

"Dammit!" Culotta slapped the clipboard against his thigh. "You have five minutes."

"Really, you are too kind," Kit said.

***

Since I'd never been in a jail before—unless you counted my too-numerous visits to Culotta (and one would have been too numerous)—I wasn't really sure what the room he put us in was supposed to be used for. There was no mirror for someone to watch us from another room. No windows, and only one door. In the center of the small space was an old wooden table, about six feet long, and three chrome chairs. Kit and I took seats across from each other and placed our hands in our laps, as if we were waiting to be served lunch. Culotta had taken our purses and the gift bag, but I noticed he hadn't patted us down for concealed weapons.

We waited in silence for fifteen minutes. Then the door opened, and Culotta led Barbara into the room. She looked surprised to see us, but not unhappily so.

Culotta indicated for her to take the vacant chair, and then he discreetly moved to the far wall, where he leaned with his arms folded across his chest. "Five minutes," he said.

"Valerie," Barbara spoke first. Upon closer inspection, I could see she was exhausted. Her lipstick had worn away, leaving only a slight pencil outline of her lips. She had dark smudges under her eyes, as if she'd rubbed all her mascara off her lashes. She was wearing orange scrubs, not unlike the kind you see on nurses except, of course, for the garish color.

"You remember my friend Kit James?" I asked.

"Yes, of course." She leaned forward, putting her elbows on the edge of the table and supporting her head in her hands.

"Thank you for seeing us," Kit said.

"I'm glad you came. Valerie, there's something I'd like you to do for me."

"Of course; anything," I said, but I felt a little leery of what I might be promising.

"I'd like you to sell my house. My attorney, Pete Chalmers, has the deed—"

"I thought your attorney was—"

"Pete is our family attorney. He's also a friend, and a good lawyer, but not up to handling a murder case. Anyway, I'd like the money from the house to be put in a trust for my son, Zach, and I'm just going to have Pete handle everything now," Barbara was saying. "If necessary, I've instructed him to dispose of the contents of the house and add the proceeds to my son's trust."

I hung on the words *if necessary*, and it hit me that Barbara could be gone for a long, long time. Out of the corner of my eye, I could see Culotta looking at his watch.

"Barbara, I am so sorry it came to this," I said.

She leaned back in her chair, and her hands fell onto her lap. "Me too. But the truth is, I'm glad it's over. I'm prepared for whatever happens next. I'm just so sorry that Zach might lose two parents. He doesn't deserve that."

"Is there anything else you need?" Kit asked.

A slight smile formed on Barbara's pale lips. "Everything is in order. Just sell the house, Val. I know you're a good Realtor."

I heard Culotta tap the face of his watch.

"I guess we better be going." I reached across the table, and Barbara raised one of her hands up to grab mine. Her grip was strong, but she released it immediately, as Culotta came forward.

"Okay, ladies, I think that's it."

We all stood at the same time, making the room close in. Culotta walked over to Barbara's side of the table and with a hand on her back, gently guided her to the door.

Just before they left the room, I remembered. "The key?" I asked.

Barbara looked at me with a little smile. "It's under a flowerpot on the back deck. You can't miss it. Stupid, I know. But I always think the suburbs are safe. Don't you?"

CHAPTER TWENTY-NINE

Sure enough, just as Barbara had said, the key to her house lay under a flowerpot on the back deck. What Barbara hadn't said, however, was that the terra-cotta pot stood about three feet tall and was almost as wide, and it was packed heavily with rich black soil and a cluster of crimson tulips. Luckily, Kit was with me. It took all our joint might to tilt the planter back, and then Kit swiped a hand underneath and grabbed the key before we let the pot drop back down.

"We're not putting it back there," Kit said. "I probably already have a hernia from lifting it once. Do women get hernias?" She didn't wait for me to answer, as she headed back around to the front of the house.

She opened the front door and then stooped to lift the doormat. After placing the key underneath it, she stood and smiled. "That's better."

"But Kit—"

"Val, it'll be fine. You can tell Barbara where it is."

I had reluctantly asked Kit if she wanted to come with me to Barbara's house. I'd told her I had a lot of work to do in preparation for putting it on the market.

Her response indicated that even if I intended to reshingle the roof, I better not even think about excluding her.

So here we were, both standing in the foyer, our eyes circling around Barbara's spacious abode. And again I was glad my pal was with me. I've been in dozens of homes without the owners present, but this was different. Even with Barbara's permission, I felt as if I were invading her privacy.

I followed Kit as she turned off the foyer and entered the familiar cream-colored living room with its dramatic cathedral ceiling. Orange and fuchsia throw pillows were scattered on the two matching sofas as well as the window seat, and the accent colors were repeated in an abstract oil painting hanging above the fireplace.

My eyes were drawn to the painting, and I approached the fireplace to get a closer look. How could I have not remembered this painting from our last visit?

"Look at these," Kit said. She was engrossed in examining the items on the shelves that were built in on one side of the fireplace. She held up two glass figurines, ballet dancers caught in impossible poses. "*Objets d'art*," she said. Her exaggerated French accent made me smile.

I took my camera out of my purse and backed up to the entrance of the room. "Kit, move out of the way. I need to take some pictures."

"Gee, Val, this is very exciting for me to see you in action. It's like watching Larry punch numbers into his computer."

"Well, Kitty Kat, watch and learn. This is how we working people roll." I shooed her away from the fireplace and took a shot. Next I turned my camera to the bay window. "Kit, make yourself useful. Fix that drape, will you?"

I took a dozen pictures of the room, and then we moved to the kitchen. It was a large room, dominated by a silvery granite island in the center. The only item on it was a large wire-mesh bowl holding a dozen bright-red apples. I wondered if Barbara had any idea when she purchased them that she might not get to eat them. As I got closer, however, I realized the apples were made of wax.

"Wow, some kitchen, huh?" I pointed the camera at the pristine stainless-steel appliances.

"Too big. A *real* cook would never be happy in a space this large."

I took a look around and realized the kitchen was nearly twice the size of Kit's. "Well, my entire apartment would fit into this room," I said, hoping to defuse any kitchen envy Kit might be feeling.

"Val, your apartment would fit into this *fridge*." She opened the door to the Sub-Zero appliance.

"No kidding." I took several more shots.

"Ya know, this room is spotless. Do you think Barbara cleaned it knowing she was going to the pokey?"

"I've no idea—"

"What the hell are you doing in my house?"

Kit and I whirled around to see Fancy Fitzpatrick's boy toy, the handsome young man we'd seen at Starbucks with her. I stared at him as he stood in the doorway. I didn't remember him being so tall and thin.

"Why are you following me?" He took a few steps toward us.

"Following you?" Kit asked. "We were here first. And what do you mean *your* house? Who are *you*?"

As I studied him, I was suddenly struck by his similarity to Barbara. The same clearly defined features, the same starched posture. I wondered why we hadn't connected him to his mother the first time we'd seen him. "You must be Zach Craigmore." I held out my hand to shake his. "I'm Valerie Pankowski. This is Kit James. We are friends of your mother's, Zach. I'm a Realtor, and Barbara—your mom—

asked me to sell this house." My hand remained in midair, waiting for him to extend his own. When it was clear he wasn't going to, I dropped it, feeling foolish.

"I know who Barbara is. And you're not selling my house. You ladies can leave now." He waved his left hand toward the front door.

"Look, kid," Kit said. "This is your mother's house." She turned to me for confirmation, and I nodded slightly.

Zach Craigmore looked as if he might burst into tears. I wanted to put my arms around him and tell him everything was going to be all right. But it would have been a lie. His father was long gone, and his mother was probably facing prison time.

Kit kept talking. "So you see—"

I put my hand on Kit's arm, signaling her to shut up. "Look, Zach, we don't have to do this right now. I can come back."

"No! Don't come back. The house is not for sale. My mother is . . ." I watched him wipe away a tear that was trickling down his unshaven cheek. "My mother is coming home. She's got to."

He began to cry in earnest, and suddenly I was hugging him. And he was letting me.

***

"Thank you," Zach said.

He and I were sitting at the round glass kitchen table on chairs richly upholstered in the same fabric as the blinds covering the French doors.

"Don't thank me until you've tasted it," Kit said. "I'm not used to cooking in another woman's kitchen."

I watched her in awe. Somehow she had managed to whip up an egg dish that would have made Julia Child exclaim *bon appétit*. She'd taken a dish towel and made an apron to cover her navy pants. Another dish towel was draped over her right shoulder. She set a plate before Zach, and somehow the eggs didn't smell like plain old eggs. In fact, they gave off a savory aroma more befitting a fancy eatery than a suburban kitchen.

Zach brought a forkful of food to his mouth. Then another. "Wow. This is the best omelet I've ever had."

"Technically, it's a frittata, without asparagus, unfortunately. But you can call it an omelet." Kit gave him a wink as she set down two steaming mugs of coffee in front of Zach and me and then returned to the island, where she picked up her own. She looked as if she cooked here every day.

"Have you seen my mom? Since she—"

"Yes," I said, hoping to save him from stating his mother's current residence. "We have. We saw her yesterday. She looked good, Zach." Geez. It sounded so lame. *Orange is definitely her color.*

"So, what were you doing with Fancy Fitzpatrick?" Kit took a seat at the table, and for once I was glad for her abruptness.

"I went to see Fancy to get some help. She and Liam are old family friends. I've known them all my life."

"What kind of help?"

"She knows everyone, doesn't she? I thought maybe she could find us a lawyer. You know, a really good one."

Kit and I exchanged glances. When we'd last seen Zach, at Starbucks, his mother had not been charged with the crime. Presumably, he had been thinking ahead and knew it was just a matter of time before the police caught up with her. I was filled with thoughts of my own child in that situation. If I had been charged with murder, who would Emily seek out? Tom? Larry?

"Your mom confessed, ya know. So it seems like you need a really good *judge*, not a lawyer," Kit said. "Does Fancy have any in her pocket?"

Zach put his fork down and hung his head. "I'm not sure. She said she'd talk to some people. But I don't know. What do you think will happen to my mom?" He turned to me, then to Kit, as if we held the answer, and I desperately wanted to give him a good one.

"We have to hope for leniency," I said, sounding lame again. *Why don't we join hands and sing "Kumbaya"?*

"Zach," Kit said. Luckily, she was ignoring my inane platitudes. She sat holding her mug with two hands, blowing on the steam that floated from the coffee's surface. "Why did your mom confess? Even after the police found the gun, with a good lawyer she could have—"

Zach shook his head vigorously. "I don't know. That wasn't the plan."

"You knew she murdered Susan?" I asked.

He shook his head again. "No! Yes!" His eyes grew suddenly wild as he turned from Kit to me. "Look, that Susan was an evil bitch, okay? Somehow she lured my dad into all kinds of shit. He lost his company because of her. She made things so bad he killed himself." His voice was rising as he ran his bony fingers through his hair. "After my dad . . . after he died, she moved on with her life like it was nothing to her. She left us in ruins, man. It finally got to my mom."

His emotions spent for the time being, he stopped talking and took a deep breath. He raised his arms and cradled the back of his head in his hands. I was struck by how thin his arms were. A black rope bracelet dangled on one wrist, a hexagon-shaped watch on the other.

"What will you do now?" Kit asked.

"I guess I'll stay here until . . . maybe even after things are settled. I don't think I'll go back to California."

"Do you have any other family living here?" my friend asked.

"No. My mom is my family. I need to be near her."

I wanted to look at Kit to signal her, but I couldn't pull my eyes away from Zach, away from that watch. I'd seen it before. A prism of the glass face caught the sun radiating through the French doors. It twinkled as if it were winking at me.

"Zach," I said. "Your watch . . . it's very unusual." I reached out to touch it, but he hastily pulled his thin arms down.

"It was a gift from my dad—he gave it to me when I graduated from high school."

"Then it must be very special to you."

"It is." He held up his wrist to examine the timepiece and gazed at it sadly. "I never take it off."

CHAPTER THIRTY

I played cards with your pal Culotta last night." Tom handed me his coat, presumably to hang up for him.

"Er, did your personal valet quit or something?"

"He's not very happy with you."

"We're talking about Culotta now, right?"

"Sit," he said.

I took the visitor's chair in front of his grandiose desk. I laid his coat neatly across my lap.

Tom placed his elbows on the desk and formed a steeple with his fingertips. He looked like a bank manager about to deliver bad news. "I heard they released Barbara Craigmore."

I nodded in confirmation.

"And they arrested her son, Mack?"

"Zach."

"Whatever. He did it?"

"Well, normally I would say that if the police arrested him, he must have done it. Since they arrested the wrong person initially, however, it doesn't necessarily hold true."

"She confessed; what did you expect them to do?"

Since Zach Craigmore had been taken into custody and his mother released, I was torn between joy and despair. Would I have confessed to a murder that I knew Emily had committed? Would I have borne the consequences of my kid's actions, especially if I felt they were justifiable?

When Kit and I had left Zach, he was still sitting at his mother's kitchen table. His anguish was obvious. But I was bothered by what was causing that anguish. His outburst about his mother didn't match the cool demeanor Barbara Craigmore had displayed whenever I saw her. Yes, she had appeared angry and bitter, all with good reason. But it was clear, on the surface at least, that Zach was much angrier than his mother.

And there was one other thing that really set off an alarm.

Leaving Zach alone in his mother's immaculate kitchen, Kit and I had raced back to her house, where she pulled up Susan Reed's Facebook page on the computer. We heaved a joint sigh of relief when we saw it was still available. Well, who would have taken it down? Her mom certainly didn't seem tech-savvy enough to close the account.

When we saw the unusual hexagon-shaped watch on Susan's wrist in eleven pictures she had posted of herself, I felt sure we had the answer for Zach's real torment. I'd also seen that watch on Susan's wrist in the picture of her and Larry in her apartment, when I'd been there with Culotta. So Zach's claim that his father had given it to him for graduation four years earlier and that he never took it off just couldn't be true.

"There could be two watches," Kit had suggested. "The one Zach was wearing wasn't necessarily the same one."

"Possibly, but don't you think it's worth Culotta checking out?"

The rest had come easily. Culotta had agreed to take a drive to Barbara's house and confront Zach. He reported back to us that Zach hadn't needed much prodding to admit that his father had not given the watch to him, but rather to Susan, Allen Craigmore's then-lover. When Culotta told Zach, truthfully or not, that that placed him in Susan's apartment before she had been killed and proved he removed it from her dead body, our favorite detective suddenly found himself with a *real* confession.

"See, this is why I never had kids." Tom took a cigar and rolled it between his thumb and forefinger.

"You never had kids so you wouldn't have to take a murder rap? Is that what you're telling me?"

"That kid is a piece of shit. He let his mother plead guilty, knowing all along he did it."

"Yes, but he's a sad young man, Tom. Maybe he thought he was doing his mother a favor when he killed Susan. In his eyes, she had destroyed their lives. He was avenging Barbara."

"You're defending him?"

"No, never. I just feel sorry for him, that's all."

"You should feel sorry for the mother, not the dumb-ass son."

"I do. I feel sorry for both of them. There are no winners here. Not even you, Tom, since we probably lost the commission on her house. If Barbara does decide to sell, she won't need the services of Haskins Realty. She can do it herself." Selling Barbara's house was the last thing on my mind, of course, but I knew Tom would soon be addressing the subject. May as well get it over with.

"Valerie, this is what happens when you underestimate your old Uncle Tom."

I sat up straight, faking eagerness. "Oh, fill me in, Boss."

"I spoke to Barbara Craigmore this morning. I'm taking her out to dinner tonight, at which time we will celebrate her freedom and discuss her real estate."

"You've gotta be kidding me." But I knew full well he wasn't.

"Don't be bitter, Val. It's a victory. Despite what you think, there *are* winners. In fact, we all win. She's a free woman. The murderer is in jail. And there's a nice little piece of real estate up for grabs."

"Ah, and this is *really* why you should never have had kids. There's no victory here, and trust me, no one wins."

Tom didn't nod in agreement, as I would have liked, or hang his head in shame, as I would have *really* liked, but he did put the cigar back in his pocket without lighting it, so I thought maybe I'd gotten through to him. A little.

When he spoke again, his words shocked me. "Culotta said you cracked the case."

"Really? He said that?"

"Not in so many words, Kiddo. What he actually said was you were a pain in the ass, and he should have arrested you for interfering. Crap like that. But it boiled down to the fact that you really solved the crime."

I debated whether to tell Tom that Kit was as responsible as I was for solving Susan's murder. But I didn't want to start him off on some rant that might spoil my moment of glory with him. It was all too rare.

"Oh, Culotta might have gotten there in the end," I said.

"Or maybe not. I was proud of you, Val."

We were both a little uncomfortable with the compliment. Tom immediately took the cigar out of his pocket again and began the long process of setting it alight.

"Aw, shucks, Boss," I said. "'Tweren't nothin'."

Death in Door County

I'm coming with you, Val," I heard, as soon as I put the phone to my ear. It was Kit, my friend for more than forty years. I looked across the small apartment at my daughter, who was stretched out on the couch in her pajamas, reading the back of a Honey Nut Cheerios box.

Emily caught the look on my face and mouthed, "What's wrong?"

I put my index finger to my lips, warning her to remain silent. "Are you sure you want to, Kit? We're staying two nights."

"Of course; it will be fun."

"But it's Mother's Day on Sunday," I reminded her. As if she would forget *that*.

"Don't they have cute shops and stuff up there in Door County?" She said it as if we were planning to visit Istanbul or someplace equally far away, instead of merely visiting the state that borders ours to the north. And she'd ignored the mention of Mother's Day.

I knew her son wouldn't be coming home from Texas for the occasion, and her husband, Larry, was in Florida for a golf tournament. I felt a stab of guilt that she would be alone for the weekend. But not enough guilt to actually invite her to accompany Emily and me on our visit to my mother's.

I grimaced into the phone. Sure, they have cute shops, cute restaurants, cute everything in Door County. None of which, by the way, Kit admires in the least.

As far as I'm concerned, Door County is a little stretch of paradise nestled neatly between the Bay of Green Bay and Lake Michigan. But the last time Kit dragged herself from Chicago to visit my mother, she was bored and tiresome. I think I made some secret promise to myself at the time to never take her there again.

"Okay, if you're sure," I said. But trying to hold on to my vanishing promise, I scrambled for the next reason why she absolutely should not accompany us. "Remember how tiny my mom's place is? You'd have to sleep on the couch, Kit."

"Fun, fun, fun," Kit said, as if I'd suggested she sleep in a tree house.

I felt certain she didn't mean it, but I produced a fake laugh in return, anyway.

I saw Emily roll her eyes and knew it was time to put the lid on Kit's plan. "And you really think you can spend two whole days with my mother?" I asked.

"Are you kidding? I'm looking forward to it. I haven't seen Jean for two years."

"It's been five."

"Two, five, what's the difference? I'm coming with you, Valley Girl. So break out the snakebite repellent. Wisconsin, here we come!"

Kit has been my best friend since we met as kids in our cozy Chicago suburb of Downers Grove. She's that one person everyone should have in life, the go-to friend, the one you share everything with, the one to call in case of emergency.

But even though we're so close, I can't bring myself to just *tell* her that my mother is no big Kitty Kat fan. Why doesn't she get it? She's the smartest woman I know, and my mother's certainly never made any secret of her feelings for my pal.

"So now what do we tell Grandma?" I asked Emily, after fiercely punching the disconnect button on my phone—the current equivalent of slamming down the receiver. Sometimes I miss the old technology.

Emily sat up, cradling the cereal box in her lap as if it were a sleeping baby. "Tough one, Mom. Not sure."

Okay, so Emily gets it. She knows how my mother feels about Kit. Heck, everyone knows except Kit.

"Why can't she see that Grandma doesn't like her?" I asked.

"And why *is* that? I never really understood it. Kit's so awesome."

"It probably stems from when we were young. Grandma always felt Kit was the instigator who led me into all kinds of trouble," I said, dismissing any collusion on my part. "Nothing too serious, just kid stuff," I added quickly,

3

lest my daughter think I lived a life of serious crime before she was born.

"I guess she can be a little headstrong," Emily said.

"Exactly." I joined her on the couch and snuck a Cheerio out of the box.

"Well, she's not gonna change at her age, so we should just roll with it and enjoy her." Emily continued rocking the cereal box a little.

"*Her* age? She's the same age as me."

"Mom, I'm talking about Grandma, not Kit."

We both laughed, as I reached across and ran a hand through her blond hair. I guessed we would get through it. Somehow.

"Have you ever noticed," Emily asked, shaking the sleeping baby/cereal box, "how Grandma and Kit are so much alike? They could be mother and daughter."

Wow. Why hadn't I ever noticed that?

Emily is my only child—an actress, although not a famous one (yet), and married to Luke, her adorable husband who does something clever with computers and thereby supports his wife. Her acting roles are few and far between, but her determination to succeed remains as strong as her talent (in her mother's opinion). Luke and Emily have an outrageously high-priced two-room apartment in Los Angeles (three rooms if you count the bathroom that is the size of those found on most planes). Her trips home to Chicago are rare and precious and very dear to me. Just like she is.

Her father and I are divorced, and I live in my own small apartment. The huge home she grew up in is solely occupied by David.

After the split, Emily acted as if I'd been unfairly forced to downsize, even though I tried to convince her I love my new little apartment and it was my choice to let her father keep the house—along with the enormous mortgage, high utility bills, and assorted costs that go with maintaining such a place.

***

"So I guess we should break the news to Grandma," I said. Emily and I were scrunched up on either end of the couch, both still in our pajamas, a pizza box between us. It was seven o'clock on a perfect Thursday evening.

I'd taken the week off work for Emily's visit. My boss, Tom Haskins—the owner of Haskins Realty—had readily agreed to the vacation. Not so much because I needed or had earned it, but because he loves Emily nearly as much as I do. He'd already taken us out to dinner twice that week, both times to pricey restaurants where he showed Emily off to his cronies as if she were his own daughter.

"Want me to do it?" Emily daintily wiped her mouth with a napkin.

"Of course." We both knew it was the logical solution.

"Wimp," she said.

"Show-off."

Emily did a superb job of preparing her grandmother for the additional visitor, but my mom wasn't pleased. After the initial blow had been struck, Emily and I remained huddled on the couch with my mother on speakerphone between us.

"Well, for heaven's sake, at least don't let that Katherine drive. I mean it, Valerie. Especially with Emily in the car."

Emily put her hand to her mouth to suppress a laugh. I immediately conjured up a vision of the grown Emily strapped into a baby's car seat in the back of my Lexus.

"I'll drive, Mom," I said. "Everything will be great. Emily will survive, and Kit is really looking forward to seeing you."

"Hmm. I don't know what all I'm going to tell William Stuckey."

Emily and I both smiled. William Stuckey is my mother's closest companion in Door County. Although she has known him for most of her life, she always refers to him by his full name. He was a good friend of both my parents' in Chicago and moved to Door County after his wife died.

A few years after my father passed away, my mother moved up there too, and I was so glad William lived nearby and seemed to like watching over her.

"Grandma, how is your boyfriend?" Emily winked at me.

"He's not my boyfriend, for Pete's sake."

"*Man* friend?" Emily tried again.

"I don't know what that is, Emily. Is it European?" My mother often assumes that if she doesn't understand something, it must be European.

"No, Grandma, it's just . . . well, I know William is your friend, and he's a man—"

"Good heavens, of course he's a man. What did you think he was, a cocker spaniel? I don't like that kind of talk, Emily. That's exactly the kind of thing that girl Katherine would say."

I thought it a little unfair that Kit was being blamed for Emily's choice of words. But on the other hand, I knew she would have loved being referred to as a girl.

And with the news broken to my mother, I was kind of glad she was going with us. Having just listened to my daughter tell one funny story after another about her crazy life in California, I recalled Kit had not seen her only child for a long time. I could share, couldn't I?

***

My mother's house, a two-bedroom one-story, is situated on the edge of Egg Harbor, a charming town that offers all the amenities anyone would ever need. And she has enough yard to satisfy the gardener in her that insists on growing tomatoes every year, a passion she took with her from her former life in Downers Grove. When my car pulled into her driveway shortly after noon on Friday, she was waiting for us outside.

At seventy-eight years old, the honey-blond woman with clear blue eyes and a small-but-curvy figure caught me off guard, and I was struck by how pretty she still is. She wore blue pencil pants and had a soft-pink wool cardigan casually wrapped around her shoulders over a short-sleeved cotton blouse. She could easily have been modeling for an L.L.Bean catalog.

She waved and smiled as Emily bounded out of the car to run toward her grandmother, the way Emily has done since she was old enough to bound anywhere. I took a moment to watch the two of them embrace.

"Jean looks fabulous," Kit said from the back seat. She had removed her Versace sunglasses and placed them on top of her head. The tortoiseshell frames blended perfectly with her shiny auburn hair, and I noticed her lipstick had not faded during the five-hour drive up from Downers Grove, even though we'd stopped at a Wendy's for hamburgers to eat in the car.

Emily had chosen the fast-food place, and Kit proclaimed the food surprisingly good, although I know she secretly hates fast food of any kind. As a gourmet cook, she often lectures me that the words *fast* and *food* are like oil and water. Never to be used in the same sentence, much less digested. But I was pleased that she was making an effort.

"She does look good, doesn't she?" I felt proud as I looked at my mother.

Then I made the mistake of pulling down the visor in front of me to take a look at myself. I hadn't worn any makeup for the drive and had pulled my short blond hair into a ponytail the size of a walnut. I looked as if we'd driven across the entire country without a stop. As I caught Kit's reflection over my shoulder, I realized she looked as if she'd been at a spa all day, getting the full treatment.

I started digging around in my purse for a lipstick, before my mother could ask why I wasn't at least making an effort, when her tapping on the window made me jump a little. "Open the door, Valerie," she said.

When I did as I was told, my mother leaned into the car. Her familiar scent of a gardenia-based perfume filled the space, wiping out the smell of French fries and pickles. She reached in to hug me and at the same time peered over my shoulder at the back seat.

"Hello, Jean," Kit said brightly.

"Hello, Katherine." My mother kept one arm wrapped around me, but reached out the other and took Kit's hand in hers. "I'm glad you girls all got here in one piece," she said, as if we'd beaten impossible odds by reaching Egg Harbor without falling into Lake Michigan.

"Of course, Mom." I released myself from her grip and stepped out of the car. "We had a fun drive, didn't we, Kit?"

"Yes," I heard my friend reply. "I counted more than a hundred cows."

"Well, you girls come inside and relax for a while. We'll go into town for lunch in a little bit, and then William Stuckey is taking us to dinner this evening."

"Fun." Kit clutched her brown Louis Vuitton overnight case as she stepped out of the car. "This will be fun."

What wouldn't be fun, I knew, would be telling my mom we already *had* lunch, from a fast-food restaurant, no less. She finds them even more distasteful than Kit does.

"Uh, how about we just go shopping this afternoon?" I asked. "Then we can save our appetites for dinner tonight."

"How *thoughtful* of you," my mother said, eyeing the two wadded-up Wendy's bags on the front seat. She flashed an accusatory look at Kit, as if she'd force-fed me a double cheeseburger. At least *I* was off the hook. And then she just had to add, "Valerie, you look like the dickens."

I followed my three favorite women into the house, carrying Emily's backpack and my overnight case. I've never really known what the dickens are, but it has been one of my mother's pet phrases all my life. Whatever they are, they aren't good.

***

William Stuckey had a home in the Lake View Coves Retirement Villas. After we stopped at the gated entrance and my mother greeted the guard on duty as if he were an old friend, I noticed there was no lake view. Nor any coves. And the one-story condos made of stone could hardly be classified as villas, although they looked luxurious. William greeted us at the front door. His home had a light, airy feel, with a lot of glass and chrome and a view of the swimming pool (apparently a substitute for the implied lake).

A tall man with a shock of white hair and a still-handsome face, William wore a gray suit and red bow tie. His eighty-two years were well concealed by his straight posture and broad shoulders.

He and my mother made a dashing couple, and seeing them together made me a little lonely for my father, who hadn't been as lucky. William bent down to kiss her on the cheek and then opened his arms to give Emily and me big hugs.

"You remember my friend Kit James," I said.

"Of course." William opened his arms and gave a third hug to Kit. "I never forget a beautiful redhead."

My mother was ahead of us, farther inside the "villa," and I wondered if she had heard William's flirty comment.

"You'd forget your own head if it wasn't attached to your neck," she said, without turning around. Okay, so she'd heard.

William's taking us out to dinner consisted of walking out through the sliding glass doors at one end of his living room and around the swimming pool to the restaurant on the other side, conveniently called the Lake View Coves Restaurant.

He'd made a reservation, which must have been mandatory, judging from all the full tables. Only the one reserved for us stood empty, a table by the window with a view of the pool (and William's home). Since it was only six o'clock, both were still visible.

"Ah, Edmundo," William addressed the waiter who appeared at our table as soon as we were seated. "I must be the luckiest man in America to have four such beautiful women at my table, don't you think?"

"Yes, sir, Mr. Stuckey." Edmundo whipped white linen napkins off our plates and landed them perfectly in our laps. "You are, indeed."

As soon as our drinks arrived, wine for four of us and a margarita for Emily, William led us in a toast. "To a wonderful weekend. May you find our little corner of the world as peaceful as Jean and I do."

If only William's toast had come true . . .

Patty and Roz
www.roz-patty.com

About the authors . . .

Now a proud and patriotic US citizen and Texan, Rosalind Burgess grew up in London and currently calls Houston home. She has also lived in Germany, Iowa, and Minnesota. Roz retired from the airline industry to devote all her working hours to writing (although it seems more like fun than work).

Patricia Obermeier Neuman spent her childhood and early adulthood moving around the Midwest (Minnesota, South Dakota, Nebraska, Iowa, Wisconsin, Illinois, and Indiana), as a trailing child and then as a trailing spouse (inspiring her first book, *Moving: The What, When, Where & How of It*). A former reporter and editor, Patty lives with her husband in Door County, Wisconsin. They have three children and twelve grandchildren.

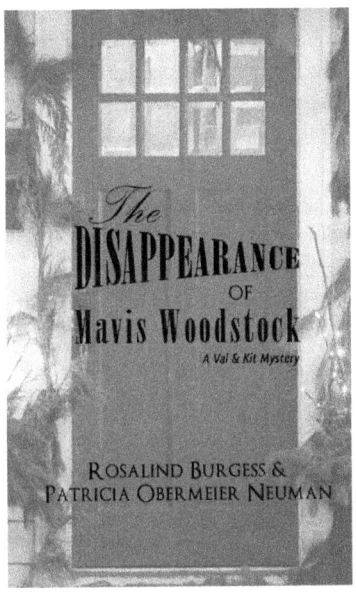

The Disappearance of Mavis Woodstock

Mavis Woodstock (a vaguely familiar name) calls Val and insists she has to sell her house as quickly as possible. Then she fails to keep her scheduled appointment. Kit remembers Mavis from their school days, an unattractive girl who was ignored when she was lucky, ridiculed when she was not. She also remembers Mavis being the only daughter in a large family that was as frugal as it was wealthy. When Val and Kit cannot locate Mavis, they begin an investigation, encountering along the way a little romance, a lot of deception, and more than one unsavory character.

What readers are saying about . . .
  The Disappearance of Mavis Woodstock

FIVE STARS! "Best book I've read in a long time; couldn't wait to go to bed at night so I could read this book and then couldn't put it down. TOTAL PAGE-TURNER . . . Cannot wait to read the next book in this series!!!"

FIVE STARS! " . . . well-written mystery . . . first of The Val & Kit Mystery Series. The two amateur sleuths, Val & Kit, are quirky, humorous, and dogged in their pursuit of righting what they felt was a wrongful death of someone they knew from the past. It's full of humorous, cagey, and a few dark personalities that keep you on your toes wondering what or who would turn up next . . . a fun, fast read that is engaging and will keep your interest . . . A tightly woven mystery with a great twist at the end."

FIVE STARS! "I thoroughly enjoyed this book, laughing out loud many times, often until I cried. I love the authors' style and could so relate to the things the characters were going through."

FIVE STARS! "This was a fun read! The story was well put together. Lots of suspense. Authors tied everything together well. Very satisfying."

FIVE STARS! "Enjoyed this tale of two friends immensely. Was shocked by the ending and sad to find I had finished the book so quickly. Anxious to read the next one . . . keep them coming!"

FIVE STARS! "Mysteries are sometimes too predictable for me—I can guess the ending before I'm halfway through the book. Not this one. The characters are well developed and fun, and the plot kept me guessing until the end."

FIVE STARS! "I highly recommend this novel and I'm looking forward to the next book in this series. I was kept guessing throughout the entire novel. The analogies throughout are priceless and often made me laugh. . . . I found myself on the edge of my seat . . . the ending to this very well-written novel is brilliant!"

FIVE STARS! "I recommend this book if you like characters such as Kinsey Millhone or Stone Barrington . . . or those types. Excellent story with fun characters. Can't wait to read more of these."

FIVE STARS! "A cliff-hanger with an I-did-not-see-that-coming ending."

FIVE STARS! " . . . well written, humorous . . . a good plot and a bit of a surprise ending. An easy read that is paced well, with enough twists and turns to keep you reading to the end."

FIVE STARS! "Very enjoyable book and hard to put down. Well-written mystery with a great surprise ending. A must-read."

FIVE STARS! "This is a well-written mystery that reads along at a bright and cheerful pace with a surprisingly dark twist at the end."

FIVE STARS! "I really enjoyed this book: the characters, the story line, everything. It is well written, humorous, engaging."

FIVE STARS! "The perfect combo of sophisticated humor, fun and intriguing twists and turns!"

Death in Door County

Val embarks on a Mother's Day visit to her mom in Door County, Wisconsin, a peninsula filled with artists, lighthouses, and natural beauty. Her daughter, Emily, has arrived from LA to accompany her, and at the last minute her best friend, Kit, invites herself along. Val and Kit have barely unpacked their suitcases when trouble and tension greet them, in the form of death and a disturbing secret they unwittingly brought with them. As they get to know the locals, things take a sinister turn. And when they suspect someone close to them might be involved in blackmail—or worse—Val and Kit do what they do best: they take matters into their own hands in their obsessive, often zany, quest to uncover the truth.

What readers are saying about . . .
Death in Door County

FIVE STARS! "When meeting an old friend for coffee and a chat, do you think to yourself 'Wow, I really miss them. Why do we wait so long to catch up?' That is exactly how I feel every time I read a Val & Kit Mystery. Like I just sat down for a hilarious chat over coffee and cake followed by wine and chocolate. These girls are a hilarious mix of Laurel and Hardy with a dash of Evanovich sprinkled with Cagney & Lacey. Comedy, love and mystery: a brilliant combination."

FIVE STARS! "I really enjoyed this book. Not only was I in Door County at the time that I was reading it and Door County has always been one of my favorite places, I am also a homeowner in Downers Grove, IL, which is where Val and Kit also live. I did read the first two books in The Val & Kit Mystery Series which I also thoroughly enjoyed. Being from Downers Grove, I got quite a kick out of the real names of most of the streets being used in the stories because I could just picture where the events were taking place. Even though all three books were mysteries, they were lighthearted enough to hold my interest."

FIVE STARS! "Whether you are a mother, daughter, grandmother, great-grandmother or best friend . . . This is a heartwarming and hilarious read that would be a perfect part of your Mother's Day celebration!!! I loved getting to know Val and Kit better. Their relationships with their loved ones had me laughing and weeping all at the same time!!! I loved ending my day with Val and Kit; it just made it hard to start my day as I could not stop reading *Death in Door County*!"

FIVE STARS! "Another page-turner in the Val & Kit Series! What a great story! I loved learning about Val's family."

FIVE STARS! "Really enjoy the Val and Kit characters. They are a yin and yang of personalities that actually fit like a hand and glove. This is the third in the series and is just as much a fun read as the first two. The right amount of intrigue coupled with laughter. I am looking forward to the next in the series."

FIVE STARS! "Just the right mix of a page-turner mystery and humor with a modern edge."

FIVE STARS! "The girls have done it again . . . and by girls, do I mean Val and Kit, or Roz and Patty? The amazingly talented authors, Roz and Patty, of course. Although Val and Kit have landed themselves right smack dab in the middle of yet another mystery. This is their third adventure, but don't feel as though you have to (albeit you SHOULD if you haven't done so already) read *The Disappearance of Mavis Woodstock* and *The Murder of Susan Reed* in order. This book and the other(s) are wonderful stand-alones, but read all . . . to enjoy all of the main and supporting characters' quirks . . . I can't seem to express how much I love these books . . . Speaking of characters . . . This is what sets the Val & Kit series apart from the others in this genre. The authors always give us a big cast of suspects, and each is described so incredibly . . . It's like playing a game of Clue, but way more fun . . . the authors make the characters so memorable that you don't waste time trying to 'think back' to whom they are referring. In fact, it's hard to believe that there are only two authors writing such vivid casts for these books. So come on, ladies, confess . . . no, wait, don't. I don't want to know how you do it, just please keep it up."

FIVE STARS! " . . . this series is a fun read. There's friendship, suspense, mystery, humor and a bit of romance for good measure. I can't wait to read what happens next."

Lethal Property

In this fourth book of The Val & Kit Mystery Series (a stand-alone, like the others), our ladies are back home in Downers Grove. Val is busy selling real estate, eager to take a potential buyer to visit the home of a widow living alone. He turns out not to be all that he claimed, and a string of grisly events follows, culminating in a perilous situation for Val. Her lifelong BFF Kit is ready to do whatever necessary to ensure Val's safety and clear her name of any wrongdoing. The dishy Detective Dennis Culotta also returns to help, and with the added assistance of Val's boss, Tom Haskins, and a *Downton Abbey*–loving Rottweiler named Roscoe, the ladies become embroiled in a murder investigation extraordinaire. As always, we are introduced to a new cast of shady characters as we welcome back the old circle of friends.

What readers are saying about . . .
Lethal Property

FIVE STARS! "Rosalind and Patricia have done it again and written a great sequel in The Val & Kit Mystery Series . . . full of intrigue and great wit and a different mystery each time. . . . *Lethal Property* is a great read, and I did not want to put the book down. I do hope that someone in the TV world reads these, as they'd make a great TV series. . . . I cannot wait for the next. Rosalind and Patricia, keep writing these great reads. Most worthy of FIVE STARS."

FIVE STARS! " . . . Val and Kit—forever friends. Smart, witty, determined, vulnerable, unintentional detectives. While this fourth installment can be read without having read the first three books (in the series), I'm certain you'll find that you want to read the first three. As has been the case with each book written by Rosalind Burgess and Patricia Obermeier Neuman, once I started reading, I really didn't want to stop. It was very much like catching up with old friends. Perhaps you know the feeling . . . Regardless of how long the separation, being together again just feels right."

FIVE STARS! "My girls are back in action! It's a hilarious ride when Val is implicated in a series of murders. We get a lot of the hotness that is Dennis Culotta this time around . . . Also, we get a good dose of Tom too. But the best part of *Lethal Property*? Val and Kit. Besties with attitude and killer comedy. The banter and down-to-earth humor between these two is pure enjoyment on the page. Five bright and shiny stars for this writing duo!"

FIVE STARS! "Enjoyed reading *Lethal Property* as well as all by Roz and Patty. Written in a way that I felt connected with the characters. Looking forward to the next one."

FIVE STARS! "OK . . . so I thought I knew whodunit early in the book, then after changing my mind at least 8-10 times, I was still wrong. (I want to say so much more, but I really don't want to give anything away.) Just one of the many, many things I love about the Val & Kit books. I love the characters/suspects, I love the believable dialogue between characters and also Valley Girl's inner dialogue (when thinking about Tina . . . hehe). I'd like to also add that (these books) are just good, clean fun. A series of books that you would/could/should recommend to anyone. (My boss is a nun, so that's a little something I worry about . . . lol) Thanks again, ladies. I agree with another reviewer . . . it IS like catching up with old friends, and I can't wait for the next one."

FIVE STARS! "As with the other books in this series, this can be read as a stand-alone. However, I've read all of them to date in order and that's probably the best way to do it. I'm to the point where I don't even read the cover blurb for these books . . . because I know that I'll enjoy them. This book certainly didn't disappoint. Plenty of Val and Kit and their crazy antics, a cast of new colorful characters and a mystery that wasn't predictable. And yes, more of Tom. As much as I like him and am hoping for a Val and Tom hookup, Dennis grew on me this installment."

FIVE STARS! "Reading *Lethal Property* was like catching up with old friends, and a few new characters, but another fun ride! I love these characters and I adore these writers. Would recommend to anyone who appreciates a good story and a sharp wit. Well done, ladies; you did it again!"

Palm Desert Killing

When one of them receives a mysterious letter, BFFs Val and Kit begin to unravel a sordid story that spans a continent and reaches back decades. It also takes them to Palm Desert, California, a paradise of palm trees, mountains, blue skies . . . and now murder. The men in their lives—Val's favorite detective, Dennis Culotta; her boss, Tom Haskins; and Kit's husband, Larry—play their (un)usual parts in this adventure that introduces a fresh batch of suspicious characters, including Kit's New York–attorney sister, Nora, and their mother. Val faces an additional challenge when her daughter, Emily, reveals her own startling news. Val and Kit bring to this story their (a)typical humor, banter, and unorthodox detective skills.

Foreign Relations

After sightseeing in London, Val and Kit move on to a rented cottage in the bucolic village of Little Dipping, where Val's actress daughter, Emily, and son-in-law are temporarily living and where Emily has become involved in community theater. Val and Kit revel in the English countryside, despite Val's ex-husband showing up and some troubling news from home. The harmony of the village is soon broken, however, by the vicious murder of one of their new friends. The shocking events that follow are only slightly more horrific than one from the past that continues to confound authorities. The crimes threaten to involve Emily, so Val and Kit return to their roles as amateur sleuths, employing their own inimitable ways.

And if you want to read about the mystery of marriage, here's a NON–Val & Kit book for you . . .

Rosalind Burgess & Patricia Obermeier Neuman

Dressing Myself

Meet Jessie Harleman in this contemporary women's novel about love, lust, friends, and family. Jessie and Kevin have been happily married for twenty-eight years. With their two grown kids now out of the house and living their own lives, Jessie and Kevin have reached the point they thought they longed for, yet slightly dreaded. But the house that used to burst at the seams now has too many empty rooms. Still, Jessie is a *glass-half-full* kind of woman, eager for this next period of her life to take hold. The problem is, nothing goes the way she planned. This novel explores growth and change and new beginnings.

FIVE STARS! "Love these writers!! So refreshing to have writers who really create such characters you truly understand and relate to. Looking forward to the next one. Definitely my favorites!"

FIVE STARS! "This book is about a woman's life torn apart . . . A lot of detail as to how she would feel . . . very well-written. I have to agree with the other readers, 5 stars."

FIVE STARS! "What a fun read *Dressing Myself* was! . . . I have to admit I didn't expect the ending . . . It was hard to put this book down."

FIVE STARS! "Great, easy, captivating read!! The characters seem so real! I don't read a lot, but I was really into this one! Read it for sure!"

FIVE STARS! "Loved it! Read this in one day. Enjoyed every page and had a real feeling for all of the characters. I was rooting for Jessie all the way. . . . Hope there's another story like this down the road."

FIVE STARS! "*Dressing Myself* deals with an all-too-common problem of today in a realistic manner that is sometimes sad, sometimes hopeful, as befits the subject. My expectation of the ending seesawed back and forth as the book progressed. I found it an interesting, engaging read with fully developed characters."

FIVE STARS! "Great book! It has been a long time since I have read a book cover to cover in one day . . . fantastic read . . . real page-turner that was hard to put down . . . Thanks, Ladies!"